Mercer

Butler Ranch

BOOK FOUR

HEATHER SLADE

Mercer

© 2018 Heather Slade

Second Edition

ISBN 13: 978-1-942200-41-3

MORE FROM HEATHER SLADE

TABLE OF CONTENTS

Prologue

New Year's Eve

This was definitely going down in the annals as the worst week of Quinn's life. And instead of going home, she was continuing the misery-fest by spending the best holiday of the year in New York City, where she lived—here, and alone, just like she'd spent Christmas.

The last time they'd spoken, her mother had told Quinn she was leaving town and would be unreachable until, at least, Thanksgiving. That holiday came and went without a word. She'd remained hopeful, and every day in December, she'd thought for sure her mother would call, or text, or something, but she hadn't. The countless messages, texts, and emails Quinn had sent went unanswered.

As morose as she felt, standing in the kitchen of the rental house, and staring out at the dark, dreary, and frigid-looking Pacific Ocean was only making things worse. Maybe if she went for a run, she'd feel better. And if not better, at least less pathetic.

Quinn changed her clothes, went outside, and stretched, only to go back in and put another sweatshirt over the one she was already wearing. She'd lived on the East Coast most of her life and was used to cold weather, but this felt different—this cold was bone-chilling.

Her start was slow, but as her muscles warmed up, she got into a rhythm. Instead of her usual two-mile run to the park and back, she kept going.

Once she got to the boardwalk, she took the wooden steps down to Moonstone Beach and continued her run. Surprisingly, there were quite a few people out walking, considering it was cold as hell.

When she got to the cliffs at the far end of the beach, she stopped and sat on a rock, checking her phone like she had every waking hour of every day for the last month and a half. Still nothing, not that she'd expected there to be.

She stood, stretched again, turned around to run in the opposite direction, and smacked right into the back of someone who had just come around one of the big rocks.

"Ow, shit. I'm so sorry. I wasn't watching where I was going," Quinn said to the woman she'd slammed into.

"It's okay, probably my fault. I wasn't looking either," the woman answered.

Something about her seemed familiar.

"You look familiar," the woman said to Quinn, which made her laugh.

"I was just thinking the same thing."

"Really? How funny. Do you live in Cambria?"

"Nope. Just visiting."

The woman studied her, and then pulled her hand out of her pocket, extending it. "I'm Ainsley Butler. It's nice to meet you…"

What were the odds that she'd run into a Butler today of all days?

"And you are…"

"Oh, um, sorry…I'm Quinn. Quinn Hess."

When she reached out to shake her hand, Ainsley didn't let go, and by the look on her face, she was feeling the same way Quinn had been a moment ago.

"Hey, Ains. What's up?" A very tall and insanely good-looking man jogged over to them. "Who's this?" he asked, looking at their still-clasped hands.

"Cris, this is…" Ainsley shook her head, like maybe she'd forgotten her name.

"I'm Quinn," she answered for her.

"Cris Avila, nice to meet you…wait a minute. Quinn?" He looked at Ainsley, who nodded.

"Quinn," she said, linking their arms, "this may sound crazy, but there's a family I want you to meet."

Grabbing the arm of a person she'd just met probably wasn't the most polite thing Quinn had ever done, but it had been a reflex. She'd grown so accustomed to being kept a secret, that someone knowing who she was, stunned her so much she felt light-headed.

"Sorry, I didn't mean to put fingernail marks on your arm." Quinn dropped her hand, shook her head, and looked out at the ocean. "How'd you know?"

"My brother Naughton told me you paid him a visit."

Quinn nodded. "Did he tell you anything else?"

It was Ainsley's turn to nod. "That you're my older brother Kade's daughter."

"Daughter—that's an interesting way to put it." Quinn regretted her words the moment she spoke them. There was no reason for her to be a bitch to Ainsley. The woman had been nothing but nice to her. "Sorry," she mumbled.

"It's okay. Tell me what you know about Kade."

"Other than that his name is on my birth certificate, not much."

1

Previous June

There were worse things than spending your twenty-first birthday in New York City with your four best friends, but there were better things, too. Quinn's only wish, this year, had been to hear from her mother. It didn't matter if she called, texted, emailed, sent a message via carrier pigeon, or showed up at her door—Quinn just wanted this to be the year her mom remembered her birthday.

The last time they'd spoken was almost a month ago when Quinn had graduated from Barnard. They'd gotten into an argument after a dinner celebration they had with those same friends, who'd also just graduated. Her mother had been rude throughout the meal, and Quinn had confronted her.

"You've known them for years; at least you could've been civil," she'd said.

It was obvious now that her provocation had been a waste of time. Her mother hadn't offered up as much as an explanation for her behavior, let alone an apology.

"I'd like to visit this summer," Quinn had said the next morning, hoping to smooth things over before her mother's flight back to California.

"It isn't a good time," her mother had answered.

"It never is," she'd mumbled, but her mother hadn't responded.

She'd been hurt, but really, she shouldn't have been; they'd certainly never been close. How could they have been? Her mother had shipped her off to the East Coast boarding school where Quinn had met her pals when she was seven.

Up until then, she'd attended Montecito's posh San Ysidro Day School. Quinn still wasn't sure why her mother had sent her away, but her assumption was that she didn't want her around then any more than she did now.

"You're so lucky that you don't have to put up with the same shit we do," she'd heard more than once from the friends she called her tribe.

Lucky? She guessed so. Quinn's father had died before she was born, so she hadn't had to deal with the never-ending drama her friends had with their parents' nasty divorces.

She'd also never wanted for much of anything. No expense had been spared when it came to her education or her standard of living. The only thing she'd wished for that no one had ever been able to deliver was a family.

Last night, her tribe had taken her out to celebrate turning twenty-one.

Quinn had stumbled in, sometime after four in the morning, and hadn't rolled out of bed until a little after one. She would've slept all day, but there was another party tonight, in Southampton, that was partially in her honor. If she didn't want to look like death, she had to get up, eat, and maybe even get some sun before it was time to leave.

She checked her phone, but there weren't any new messages since the last time she looked, and certainly nothing from her mother.

When she heard a rap at her apartment door, Quinn nearly spilled her hot cup of honey-chamomile tea down the front of her paper-thin camisole. She set the cup on the kitchen counter and waited, not anticipating a second knock. The building's doormen were steadfast in not granting admission to non-residents, and since she didn't know the only other occupant on this floor except to wave at on the rare occasion she saw him from a distance, whoever was knocking had to be on the wrong floor.

"Miss Sullivan?" she heard a vaguely familiar voice call out. "You have a delivery."

"Just a minute," she answered, looking down at the so-called pajamas she wore, ones that covered next to nothing on her thin frame.

"I'll just leave it," she heard the voice say.

"Thanks, but...um...hang on." Quinn looked through the peephole, but didn't see anyone.

She opened the door a crack and looked down to see a vase of white roses sitting on the other side of the threshold. She picked it up and set it on the console table just inside the door, where she usually left her mail and keys, and sometimes her sunglasses.

Three hours later, Quinn remembered the roses. In that time, she'd caught up with two of her friends, Aine and Ava, who were twins, about last night's adventures and what they were wearing to the party tonight. She'd showered, and then lay on her bed. The five minutes she'd planned to rest her eyes had turned into a two-hour nap.

In nothing but a light shift, she padded down the hallway and grabbed the card that came with her unexpected delivery.

"Happy 21st birthday, precious," it read.

A chill ran down her spine at the lack of a signature, particularly given her mother had never, ever, not once, called her "precious."

The idea of downing more alcohol-laden shots and dancing bayside with one hundred of her closest non-friends made Quinn nauseous. She was bored—out of her mind bored—so bored she was actually considering forking out the $500 fare it would cost to get back to Manhattan on her own.

Partying at the home of a has-been network morning show host sounded appealing, but the reality landed somewhere between awkward and disgusting.

For the last half hour, she'd occupied a bench close to the sand, staring at the moonlight on the water, and wondering who'd sent her twenty-one white roses.

If it had been Aine or Ava, neither would have been able to keep it a secret. The first thing one of them would've asked when she entered their apartment this afternoon was if she'd gotten anything interesting for her birthday. Penelope or Tara might've been more subtle, but again, she'd never heard any of her friends utter the word *precious*.

Quinn stretched her legs and stood, finally deciding to let her friends know she was heading home. When she turned away from the water, she caught a glimpse of someone who looked familiar, but she couldn't place him.

The gravel pathway she walked wasn't well-lit, so she could see the man standing with his shoulder up against the stone archway that separated the concrete surrounding the home's pool from its gardens, better than he'd be able to see her.

As she got closer, she was certain she recognized him from her apartment building, but what on earth was Mr. Bryant doing here? She knew she seemed like a snob for wondering.

She remembered feeling the same way the day he moved into the only other apartment on her floor. Initially, she thought he worked for the moving company but found out differently when she got on the elevator with the rest of the movers at the end of the day.

"I haven't met my new neighbor yet," she'd said. "I hope he didn't work you too hard today."

"No ma'am," one of the men had answered. "Mr. Bryant helped."

After seeing him that day, even from a distance, she'd been surprised the board had approved the sale. He looked like someone who should grace the cover of a SEAL romance novel, not that she read them, but still—he screamed military.

Creeping closer, she realized how much taller he was than she'd thought. Quinn fanned her face at the hard outline of his muscular back. Did the man really need to wear a shirt *that* tight?

It seemed as though he was looking for someone, but rather than making his way through the crowd, he stayed on the periphery.

Quinn hadn't decided whether or not to say hello, when he turned and looked straight at her.

"Hi," she murmured.

His eyes scrunched and then widened in recognition. "Hello," he answered.

In the light from the party, Quinn noticed that his hair, which she thought was brown, was more of a sandy color and, as she got closer, that his eyes were a light shade of hazel, like toffee.

"Mr. Bryant…" What could she say that wouldn't offend him? Her first inclination was to ask what he was doing there.

"It's Mercer."

Quinn's cheeks flushed. "I'm sorry, Mr. Mercer."

"Just Mercer."

Oh. *Mercer* was handsome. Very handsome, in fact, with a body that sped up her heart rate. His tight, black, v-neck shirt emphasized the muscles on the front of him as effectively as the back, and his arms were rock-solid.

Her first impression, that he was a military man, stuck. He kept his hair neatly trimmed, but his groomed, medium-stubble beard ruled him out as being active duty. Didn't it?

She shook her head at the memory she didn't realize she carried with her. It had been years since she'd spent time with her grandparents, not since she left for boarding school, but one memory remained of her grandfather talking about his days in the Marines.

She'd asked him what the word "jarhead" meant, and he'd told her it had nothing to do with the high and tight haircut he'd still sported, but had more to do with a Marine's willingness to follow orders without question.

"Our heads are hard, but sometimes empty," he'd joked.

They'd talked about beards that day too, because her grandmother had teased that his would hardly pass muster.

"What are you doing here?" The question slipped out, even though she'd decided, a minute ago, it would be rude to ask.

"Meeting friends," he answered almost too quickly, as if he'd anticipated the question. "You?" he added.

"With friends, although…" Quinn liked that he kept his gaze steady and didn't finish her sentence when she hesitated. "I was thinking about leaving."

"Me too," he murmured.

"I was about to call for car service, if you want to share a ride," she offered.

"I have a car."

Oh. Did that mean he was offering her a ride or declining her invitation to share one?

He turned to leave, but looked back when Quinn didn't follow. "Coming?" he asked.

"I should probably let my friends know…" Again, he didn't finish her sentence. "I guess I could just text them."

He nodded and motioned for her to follow.

"Here we are," he said, stopping next to a sleek convertible that reminded Quinn of a bullet.

"Nice car," she said after he'd opened her door, waited for her to be seated, and then closed it behind her.

"Thanks. It isn't mine."

"No?" *Interesting*. Maybe the apartment wasn't either, although Quinn hadn't seen anyone else come or go. "Whose is it?"

"Belongs to a friend."

"It's nice that your friend lets you use it." Quinn ran her hand over the supple, dark-colored leather. "What is it?"

"A Jaguar Series One E-Type. Uh...sixty-two."

He answered as though he expected her to know what that meant. Jaguar was the only part of it that sounded familiar. Having lived in and around New York City for the last fourteen years, cars hadn't been something she had reason to learn much about. She'd never even learned to drive.

Quinn relaxed in the comfortable seat of the Jaguar, shifting her focus from the man next to her to the warm summer breeze on her face.

"Cold?" he asked, once he picked up speed on the highway.

"It feels good. Although...maybe a little."

Mercer reached behind her seat and pulled out a blanket. "Mind if I leave the top down?"

Quinn snuggled under it. "No. It's fine. What about you? Do you have a jacket?"

"I don't get cold," he answered.

"Ever?"

"Not in the summer."

"Hmm."

Mercer turned and looked at her when she didn't continue. "Yeah?"

"Nothing."

He smiled. It was the first time she'd seen him do anything but frown. "You have a nice smile."

He looked away, as though he wasn't used to the compliment. "You do too," she heard him murmur.

She studied him longer than she should have. He probably felt her lingering gaze, but he didn't acknowledge it. Who was this man? And how did someone who looked as though he was under thirty, and had probably served in some branch of the military, afford a two-million-dollar apartment in the heart of Manhattan? Quinn supposed he could be a trust-fund kid, like she was, but he didn't appear to fit that bill either.

2

When Quinn dozed off, Mercer let out the breath it felt like he'd been holding since they got in the car.

His preoccupation with what he'd done earlier in the day made him sloppy. And tonight, instead of finding her without her knowing he was looking, she'd found him. He was glad she had, though. Otherwise, who knows how she would've gotten home. Southampton was a solid two hours from their building, with plenty of desolate areas along the way. He cringed, thinking about the danger she might've put herself in.

He looked over at her several times while she slept. The moonlight shone on her almost-white blonde hair and cast a glow on her flushed cheeks, likely so from too much time in the sun. Every day she grew more beautiful as he watched her change from a teenager to a young woman.

Mercer shook his head and silently cursed his former boss, the man responsible for the temptation he faced every day.

Mercer drove into the underground garage and parked in his reserved spot, but Quinn didn't budge.

"We're back," he said softly, so tempted to stroke his finger down her cheek.

She sat up with a start. "Oh. I'm so sorry. Did I really sleep all the way back? How inconsiderate of me," she babbled.

"You were tired."

She stretched her arms above her head, and her t-shirt rode up just a little, exposing the skin on her stomach. When Mercer looked up, her eyes were on him, knowing he'd stolen a peek.

Her gaze lingered long enough that he couldn't resist. He leaned forward, pulled her close to him, and brought his lips to hers. Quinn rested her palm on his thigh and opened her sweet mouth to his. He tightened his grip and deepened their kiss, until her groan brought him back to the reality of what he was doing. This wasn't a fantasy; his lips really were on hers, and the fruit he'd just tasted was forbidden.

He backed away, not allowing himself to look into her eyes. If he did, he'd lose what little resolve he possessed. Instead, he opened his door, walked around, and opened hers.

"Thank you," she whispered as she climbed out, touching her lips with her fingertips.

"You're welcome."

"You were my savior tonight, Mr. Mercer." She stepped away from the car so he could close the door.

"Just Mercer," he responded absentmindedly.

She had no idea how hard she'd just hit the nail on the head. Savior might not be the most accurate word. More like protector.

She waited for him to press the button when they got to the elevator, just like she'd waited for him to open her door. This was a woman who'd been taught that there was nothing wrong with letting a man take the lead. She understood it was about respect, not anyone believing she was incapable. Her manners were impeccable; he'd seen evidence of it often enough. As usual, he was filled with a sense of pride, even though he had nothing to do with her upbringing, no responsibility for her behavior.

When they reached the eleventh floor, Mercer didn't walk Quinn to her door. From the rounded corner he leaned against, he could see that she got safely inside her apartment without the possibility of her inviting him in.

She waved from just inside her door. "Sweet dreams, Mr. Mercer," she said and blew him a kiss.

"Just Mercer," he said to himself after Quinn's door had closed behind her.

He entered the keypad code and rested his thumb on the print reader until he heard the click unlocking his door. He stalked inside, slamming it behind him.

He turned around, rested his head against the wall, and closed his eyes. He took a deep breath as the promise he'd made repeated in his head. He'd vowed to watch over her, protect her, and keep her and the family safe. Talking to her, touching her, *kissing her*, or dreaming about her weren't part of that vow. Dreams were out of his control, but the rest of it—he knew better.

Mercer logged out of his email and shut his laptop computer. He was still too wound up from the drive home to sleep. Instead he paced, thinking about every self-imposed moral and ethical rule he'd broken tonight.

There'd be no going back to Quinn not knowing who he was now. He'd fought the whole idea of moving into this building, knowing it would be a slippery slope, and he'd been right. It was one thing for him to *coincidentally* be at the same party tonight. The next time he showed up where she was, it would be weird. And after that, it would be creepy.

He wasn't even scratching the surface of that kiss. It was everything he'd fantasized it would be. If she hadn't

made a sound, their lips might still be locked together—
in the front seat of a car inside a parking garage. *Jesus.*

He had to make some drastic changes, and soon.
Mercer checked the time. It was almost midnight on the
West Coast; his call would have to wait until morning.
Between now and then, he'd have time to decide how
much of what happened tonight he'd come clean about.

He picked up the tablet that sat next to his bed and
opened the book he'd started last night. Nothing like a
spy novel written by someone who knew nothing about
how things really worked to bore him to sleep.

Quinn breathed in the scent of her birthday roses
when she walked past them in the hall. She'd bet Mercer
was the kind of man who would send a gift like this to
a woman he was involved with.

She still couldn't believe she'd slept the entire way
home. He must think her so rude, although he hadn't
acted like he minded. *"You were tired,"* he'd said.

It wasn't like her to be so trusting of someone she
hardly knew, but she felt inexplicably safe with him, as
though he actually cared about her.

Quinn rolled her eyes as they filled with tears. She
was pathetic. She was so desperate for love and attention

that she was telling herself her neighbor, who she'd had exactly one conversation with, cared about her.

She managed not to check her phone until she crawled into bed. There wouldn't be a message from her mother, Quinn knew that, but she couldn't stop herself from hoping there would be.

Sleep came easily, once she closed her eyes, only because she allowed herself to fantasize about Mr. Mercer and the kiss they'd shared.

The dream she was having, that her phone was buzzing incessantly, seemed too real. Quinn bolted upright and grabbed it from the bedside table. *Aine* flashed on the screen.

"Hi," she answered.

"Where in the hell are you?" her friend yelled over the noise from the party in the background.

Shit. She'd forgotten to text that she was leaving. "I'm so sorry. I'm home."

"What? I can't hear you."

"I'm home," she shouted into the phone.

"You're where? It sounded like you said you're home."

"I am home," she shouted again.

"What the hell?" Quinn heard the phone rustling in the background and Aine say, "She's home." More rustling, and then, "Hang on."

Quinn waited while the noise from the party grew more distant.

"You just disappeared. What the hell, Quinn?"

Aine sounded drunk, which meant this conversation would continue to loop.

"Listen," Quinn began. "I ran into someone I knew who was heading back to the city, and I bummed a ride. I'm sorry I didn't let you know. Let's talk tomorrow, okay?"

"You just disappeared," Aine said again.

"Goodnight, sweetie. I'll talk to you tomorrow." Quinn disconnected the call and turned off her phone. Now that her friends knew she was home, there'd be no one else trying to reach her tonight.

—:—

Mercer entered the building's gym at six, like he did every morning, and hit his workout hard. He'd tossed and turned all night, rehashing the time he'd spent with Quinn, and everything he should've handled differently.

He was in the zone—that perfect equilibrium of speed and comfort—when he ran. His legs were loose, and his heart was pumping, so when the door to the gym opened, he only heard it somewhere deep in his subconscious. Most mornings he was the only one here, and never had he ever seen the woman whose eyes met his in the mirror. What the hell was Quinn up to?

She waved, the same little wave as last night before she'd blown him the kiss, and then approached one of the elliptical machines on the other side of the gym.

Mercer responded with a nod, and then focused his attention on the television he never watched, attempting to listen to the news he'd never cared about before. So much for his well-managed heart rate. Since the elliptical faced the opposite direction as his treadmill, he could see the mirror's reflection of her tight ass emphasized in her far-too-short running shorts. The tank top she wore barely covered her almost useless workout bra.

He wasn't the only one looking where he shouldn't. Quinn stared into the mirror in front of the elliptical until their eyes met for the second time. Mercer stopped the treadmill, got off, and scrubbed the sweat from his face with his workout towel. He pulled his phone out of his gym bag, feigned checking it, and then tossed it and his towel back inside.

"Have a good one," he said as he opened the door to leave.

"Wait," she said, stopping the machine. "You don't have to leave on my account."

"I'm finished," he grunted as he let the door close behind him. He felt like a shithead for talking to her that way, but he couldn't afford to let this thing with Quinn spiral.

The next time Mercer "ran into" her was on the elevator over a week later.

"Hi," she said, barely looking at him and making him feel like a huge asshole.

He nodded, again hesitant to encourage conversation.

"Nice to see you, Mr. Mercer," she said when the door opened to the lobby. She walked out, but not quickly enough to hide the hurt etched on her face.

He knew she was lonely; she had been most of her life. Other than the four girls she'd been close to since their boarding school days, Quinn didn't socialize much. There were the occasional dates, which sent his blood pressure skyrocketing, but second dates were rare for her.

The hardest thing, though, was that Quinn had never given up hope that, one day, she'd have a relationship with her mother—something Mercer knew could never be.

"Hey, Paps," Mercer answered the call that came in later that night from one of his partners.

"We need you here. Make the necessary arrangements, and fly out in the morning."

"What's going on?"

"Razor and I will fill you in when you get here."

Less than five minutes later, when another call came in, Mercer wasn't surprised to see "Barbie," Lena Hess's code name, show up on the caller ID.

"What can I do for you, Lena?"

"How's my daughter?"

What could he say that hadn't already been said? Having him say out loud what Lena already knew, wouldn't change anything. "She's as you would expect her to be."

"Did you speak with Paps earlier?"

"Yes, I did."

As much as he wanted to know what was going on, Lena was the last person he'd ask.

"Is there anything else?" he asked instead.

"No."

"We'll talk tomorrow, then," he said before disconnecting the call.

By the time he'd finished making "the necessary arrangements," it was one in the morning. He was about to call it a night, when he heard the elevator stop at their floor. He didn't hear footfalls in the hallway, so he called downstairs. He knew Vinnie was on duty; it had been one of the calls he'd made earlier.

"Mr. Bryant. I was just dialing your number. Miss Skipper is about to exit the building."

"Engage."

"Yes, sir."

Where in the hell did she think she was going in the middle of the night?

When he exited the elevator, Quinn's back was to him, and she was deep in conversation with Vinnie. Mercer first disarmed the emergency door, and then exited through it. He took the alley around to the front of the building, where he had two choices. He could wait and follow her, or he could walk through the building's entrance and engage *Miss Skipper* himself.

When he saw the signal from Vinnie, he knew his mind had been made up for him.

"Good evening, sir," Vinnie greeted him. "Pleasant night?"

Mercer nodded, his eyes landing on Quinn as though he was surprised to see her. "Can I walk you up?" He touched her elbow with his fingertips, and she weaved.

"I was just...headed out, actually," she stammered.

If her imbalance hadn't clued him in, her breath certainly would've. She'd been drinking, and not a little.

He intentionally raised his eyebrows, and she flushed.

"Early breakfast?" he asked.

She leaned into him. "Something like that. Are you hungry, Mr. Mercer?"

Not the slightest bit, but if he agreed to join her, he'd know where she was, and could get her back safely. "Starving."

Vinnie was a step ahead of them. "*Mmm, mmm.* I haven't had Sarge's chicken and waffles in months." He rubbed his belly. "Sounds mighty good, doesn't it?"

Sarge's Diner was a short walk, but they'd take the cab that had miraculously appeared at the front door anyway.

Mercer steadied her, putting his arm around her waist, and ushered her into the waiting vehicle. When he climbed in after her, Quinn rested her head against his shoulder. "I couldn't sleep..." she murmured.

Mercer nodded.

When she closed her eyes, he motioned with his index finger, and Tom, also part of his regular crew, knew not to bother stopping at the diner. Instead he drove around Manhattan, from Midtown to the Lower East Side and up again.

"We're back," he said softly when Tom pulled up to the entrance of their building, this time unable to resist running his finger down her cheek.

Like she had before, she woke with a start.

"Did I fall asleep again?"

He smiled. "Yes."

"I'm always sleeping with you." Quinn flushed. "That didn't sound right, did it?"

Mercer climbed out and offered her his hand. "Let's get you inside."

"We didn't eat. You were starving."

"I'll make a sandwich." Mercer guided her to the elevator, nodding at Vinnie's wink as they passed by.

When they reached the eleventh floor, he ushered her around the corner, to her door, and waited while she entered her code on the keypad.

"Do you want to…come in?"

Mercer pushed the door open and guided her inside.

"I could make you something to eat."

"I'm good," he murmured, guiding her through the foyer and down the hallway. "Let's get you to bed."

Quinn slipped off her shoes and waited while Mercer pulled back the sheets of her rumpled bed. Like a sleepy child, she crawled in, and he drew the sheet over her.

"Are you going to stay?" she whispered.

When her eyes closed, he leaned forward and kissed her forehead. "Not tonight, precious. Get some sleep."

"Mmm, you called me *precious*, Mr. Mercer," she said before she drifted back to sleep.

Shit. He had. Would she remember in the morning, or would this all be a hazy recollection that she'd assumed was a dream?

3

Mercer slid the note under Quinn's door before he could change his mind.

> *Going out of town for a few days. Breakfast when I get back? —Mercer*

In his head he added, *please don't pull another stunt like last night's while I'm gone.*

It was only four hours since he'd tucked her into bed. She'd sleep at least another five or six, if not more.

He wondered, again, how much she'd remember from the night before. Maybe mentioning breakfast in his note hadn't been such a good idea. It would serve as another prompt to convince her that she hadn't been dreaming. It was too late now, though. He kissed two fingertips and rested them momentarily on her door, hoping her life would be uneventful while he was away.

Last night, when he'd kissed her forehead, he felt the shift. It wasn't just a thought, it was a physical reaction acknowledging that things were changing. While Quinn had been a part of his life for quite some time, now he'd be part of hers too.

The ramifications of his actions over the course of the last couple of days hit him as hard as the plane landed. He'd crossed a line with Quinn. Several, in fact, and by doing so, a lot would have to change. He closed his eyes and wished, as he did so often, that he could run this situation by his former boss.

Doc Butler had been more than a boss to him. He'd been a teacher, mentor, and in some ways, a big brother.

They'd met when Mercer was a student in International Relations and Foreign Language at Stanford University. Doc's youngest sister, who was Mercer's age, was also a student at the prestigious institution.

Given he was also cross-enrolled as a Marine-option Navy ROTC student, he'd landed on Doc's recruitment radar.

Once he'd graduated with his bachelor's degree, Mercer's life went in a direction he never could've imagined. Instead of becoming a second lieutenant with a four-year service commitment, he went straight to Camp Lejeune, in North Carolina, to complete nine months of special forces training.

At twenty-two years old, Mercer became the youngest member of an elite team comprised of active duty service members and CIA agents, called the Special Activities Division of the agency's National Clandestine Service, or NCS.

Four years later, Mercer accepted a job with a private-intelligence organization called K19 Security Solutions, which Doc had founded with Paps and Razor, two other guys from the team. The job turned into more when he was offered a stake in the company. Now, two years later, Mercer was wealthier than he'd ever dreamed, doing a job that included asset protection as well as covert influence and rigorous interrogation—or worse—when necessary.

Mercer powered up his phone and sent a text to Paps. *Landed.*

The space where Mercer's vehicle was usually parked was empty. It should've been his first indication that something was up. He pulled out his phone and sent another text. *Missing transport.*

Situation. L4P23.

Mercer took the stairs to the fourth level and walked to the twenty-third spot, where instead of a vehicle, he found a bike waiting. "Hell, yeah," he murmured, smiling as he picked up the helmet sitting on the Ducati Monster 1200.

This wasn't situational. This was Paps and Razor giving him a gift.

Thanks, guys.

Mercer brought the bike to life, trying to decide which of the many backroads he could take from the private airfield near San Luis Obispo, through the hills to Harmony, a small town on the Central Coast of California, where K19 owned a house. It wasn't the only property they owned. There were many, including Mercer's apartment in Quinn's building.

They'd chosen to buy in Harmony because of its relatively remote location, lack of a business district, and close proximity to Paso Robles.

Mercer rolled his shoulders as he left the parking structure. This is what he'd needed. Even fifteen minutes out on the open road, away from the oppressing heat and noise of New York City, would help him face whatever shit was about to hurl his way.

"Appreciate the ride, boys," Mercer said to Razor and Paps when he walked into the house from the garage where he'd parked the Ducati.

Paps scrubbed his face with his hand. "Hey, Eighty-eight." The man looked as though he hadn't slept in several days.

"What's going on?"

"We need to tighten Skipper's detail," answered Razor.

"Why?"

"What does the name Rory Calder mean to you?"

Four years ago

"*Jesus Christ.*" His boss slammed his phone on the table, hard enough to have broken it.

"What's up, Doc?" Mercer asked.

"That shit never gets old," Doc snapped.

"Sorry, sir," Mercer mumbled.

"Close the damn door."

Less than fifteen minutes later, Mercer had been briefed on a case that went back eighteen years, involving a Marine-turned-Russian-spy named Rory Calder, a rape, a secret marriage, and a baby.

The baby's NCS-supplied birth certificate listed her name as Quinn Analise Sullivan.

The cover story was that Quinn's father, Angus Sullivan, an officer in the Marines, had been killed in action before she was born. Her mother, Lena Hess, who came from a prominent family in California, never took Quinn's father's last name.

In actuality, the Sullivan identity had been created to ensure that no one knew the baby's connection to either her mother or father.

The reason Doc had slammed the phone down, and brought Mercer in, was that Quinn, code named

Skipper, had started proceedings to legally change her last name from Sullivan to Hess. The call had come from Lena, asking Doc to put a stop to it. That job landed in Mercer's lap.

The next time he'd heard Calder's name was right after a K19 morning meeting, when Doc asked Mercer to come into his office.

"I've accepted an assignment, and it's the most dangerous of my career," Doc told him.

The mission, he explained, was to find a former agent who'd gone rogue. Without him saying, Mercer knew the agent Doc was referring to was John "Leech" Hess, Lena Hess' father, and Quinn's grandfather.

The information had been compartmentalized and slow to come in, but according to Doc, the long-retired agent was on a suicide mission. His intention was to infiltrate Russian intelligence and assassinate the spy who had not only betrayed his country, but Leech himself, along with dozens of other agents who had been assassinated when their covers were blown. That spy was Rory Calder.

"I need a promise from you, Eighty-eight," Doc said.

"Anything, boss."

"Quinn."

One word—one name—and Mercer knew what Doc expected of him; he vowed to protect her until the day his boss returned.

Less than a month later, they'd received the news that Doc had been killed in action.

Even Mercer wasn't sure if he was truly dead or in so deep, no one was certain.

Doc, Paps, Razor, and Mercer, the four men who owned K19 Security Solutions equally, each had a safe-deposit box that was to be opened by the other three in the event of one's death.

Since that day, Mercer had continued to honor his original promise, as well as meticulously carry out the other instructions Doc had left for him in the safe box.

In the four years since he'd first heard her name, Quinn had gone from a teenager who only required peripheral monitoring, to a young woman who would find herself in grave danger if the man they were talking about discovered her true identity.

"Give me the rundown," Mercer said to Paps.

"He's resurfaced, and the timing couldn't be more concerning."

"This means Leech didn't get to him," added Razor. "Neither did Doc."

Given both men were missing, presumed or reported dead, the natural assumption was that Calder had gotten to them first.

"What's he doing here?" Mercer asked.

"Right now, playing prodigal son returned from the dead, and elbows deep in his family's wine business."

"How long has he been back?"

"No one knows," Razor answered.

Even more concerning given that meant he had been operating under the radar, doing God knows what or for how long.

"Where's Lena?" Mercer asked Paps. He knew she was there; her pearl-white Mercedes CLS400 Coupe was parked in the same garage where Mercer had left the Ducati.

Paps groaned and shook his head.

Yeah, there was no love lost between Paps and his asset. They'd pretty much hated each other since the day he was assigned as lead on her detail. Mercer had to admit, if he'd been her lead, he might've killed her himself by now.

"She's sleeping," Razor grunted.

It was well after noon, but Mercer wasn't surprised to hear she hadn't been up yet this morning. The news of Calder surfacing had to have spooked her since she'd lived the last twenty-one years of her life, expecting him to. The woman lived under constant protection, seven days a week, twenty-four hours a day. There was no semblance of privacy, no sneaking off for a vacation on her own, and no real time spent with her daughter.

Razor spun back around in his chair. "So, Skipper…"

Mercer rolled his shoulders.

"Hello," came a voice from the hallway.

Both Razor and Paps stood when Lena walked in, but she didn't take either of their seats. Instead, she stood with her arms folded.

If he'd never met Quinn, Mercer wouldn't have been able to guess her mother's natural hair color. Like her daughter's, her shoulder-length hair was almost white, although he wondered if she realized it looked more gray than blonde. Also like her daughter, Lena was tall and thin, but her body had lost the natural athleticism Quinn possessed. The tan hue of her skin didn't look any more natural than her hair, and her bright-orange lipstick and matching fingernails made her look cartoonish.

"What are you going to do?" she asked.

"We have a plan, Barbie, and as I've said numerous times, it isn't for you to worry over, just for you to carry out."

Lena's eyes shot daggers at Paps, and then she turned to Mercer.

"Can we talk in private?"

He nodded, and then led her into another room that they'd set up as a typical common area, with sofas, chairs, and a media center.

"I'm the one who discovered he was back."

"How?"

"He came to view the property."

Lena had recently put half of the Hess Estate on the market, and from what he'd heard from Paps, interest had been far greater than they'd anticipated.

"Who signed the non-disclosure?"

"There has been so much interest in this land that it's been impossible to keep up with every showing."

He was ready to throttle her. "*Who* signed the non-disclosure, Lena?"

"Someone named Trey Deveux, which is why it didn't register."

The name meant nothing to him either, but there was no doubt Paps and Razor had passed it on to their team to investigate the connection.

"Tell me how you discovered Calder," Mercer coaxed.

"Yesterday, when I was taking a walk in the vineyard, I saw someone come out of the wine caves. I *knew* it was him, but I convinced myself my eyes were playing tricks on me. And then he approached me." Lena shuddered. "He could've killed me if he'd wanted to."

Mercer doubted that; she was never without protection. "He couldn't have. Paps was there."

"There's something else you should know."

Mercer nodded, indicating she should continue.

"Enzo Avila has been storing wine in our caves."

"Why?" And what the hell did that have to do with anything?

"There's a bond issue. They overproduced and didn't bring their tax bond up to the appropriate level."

"So he's hiding it."

Lena nodded.

Which meant the Alcohol Tax Bureau was involved, or would be if they found out about it. When his conversation with Lena ended, Mercer would ask Paps what he knew, because obviously, he would know more than she did.

"How does this relate to Calder?"

"I'm not sure."

Mercer sighed. "What else do I need to know right now, Lena?"

"What about Quinn?"

"She's safe."

"How can you be sure if you're here?"

Mercer felt his shoulders tightening, the way they did whenever she questioned him. "That isn't your concern."

"She's my *daughter*."

Mercer knew the argument Lena wanted to have with him would go nowhere. Other than reassuring her that her daughter was safe, as he had countless times before, there was nothing more for them to talk about.

"Have there been any offers on the property?" he asked.

"Not yet, but I expect there will be soon."

Mercer was glad to hear nothing had come in yet. Something about Calder being in the wine caves nagged at him. What reason would he have for snooping around down there?

When he walked away, he was relieved that she didn't follow.

"Is it possible to cancel the contract on the Old Creek Road property listing?" he asked his two partners.

"Why?" Razor wanted to know.

"Because there's got to be a reason Calder was in those caves," answered Paps.

"I agree," Mercer added.

"Easy enough," said Razor, picking up the phone.

A few minutes later, he ended the call. "Done. Wendt will take care of it."

Peter Wendt had been Doc and Lena's attorney for years, but more importantly, he was a former operative with close ties to K19 Security Solutions.

"Who's gonna tell Barbie?" Razor asked next.

"I will," sighed Mercer.

Paps had to deal with her every single day in one way or another, even when someone else was on her detail. The least Mercer could do was give him a break today. As he walked away to find out where she'd gone, he didn't hear Paps protest.

Lena's reaction was much as he'd expected.

"I need to sell that property," she argued. "I need the money."

"No, you don't," countered Mercer.

"The three of you seem to have forgotten the man who raped and left me for dead twenty years ago is back. If you think I'm going to sit around and wait for him to finish the job, you're wrong. I'm outta here, just as soon as I can make arrangements."

Mercer wanted to roll his eyes, but didn't. Even if Lena was capable of making arrangements to disappear, there would be no way she'd get away with it. Whatever she did next, wherever she went, would be planned and orchestrated down to the last detail by K19.

"I agree you shouldn't be here, and when it's appropriate, we'll make the necessary arrangements. You *know* this. You also know there is more than enough money available to allow you to live comfortably wherever you go, for as long as you're there."

Mercer had no idea what had possessed Lena to want to sell the balance of the Hess Estate in the first place, but when she decided to, he, Paps, and Razor had seen no reason to stop her. However, things had changed, and now they had to get to the bottom of why Calder was snooping around in the caves.

"But—"

Mercer didn't interrupt her with words, he just shook his head.

"I've never liked you."

That had been obvious four years ago, when, instead of Doc, he'd been the one to quash Quinn's attempted name change. While her concern had been warranted, Mercer wondered, at the time, if she'd also hoped to use it as an excuse to spend time with her former husband.

By then, Doc had been involved with another woman, and even if he hadn't been, Mercer doubted he would've shared Lena's interest.

"I still don't understand why he put you in charge of my daughter. I guess you're better than Tweedledum and Tweedledee in there." She motioned toward the other room.

He refused to have this conversation with her. She had no idea of the lengths the two men she'd just disparaged had gone to in order protect her family, and she never would. Although Mercer, too, had wondered why Doc had chosen him when he called him into his office, a year and a half ago, and made him lead on Quinn's detail.

"*What the f—*" they heard from the other room.

Lena raced in ahead of Mercer who saw that, by the time they entered the room, the screens were dark.

"I don't like any of you," she muttered as she spun on her heel to walk out.

Mercer followed.

"I'm having dinner with Maddox on Friday," she said before slamming the bedroom door closed.

Good. By then he'd know about the land Doc had left him. Mercer went back in to find out what Paps had been swearing about.

"Let's flip a coin and see who gets to go beat the shit out of him," he heard Razor say.

"Who?" Mercer asked.

"Lang Becker. Peyton's ex is trying to get custody of her boys."

In the end they decided Paps should be the one to go into the bar and talk to Lang since he looked more like Doc than Razor did. Given Lang was typically half in the bag by this time of day, it wouldn't be hard to convince him that he was being visited by Kade Butler's ghost, or the man himself. Either way, the plan was to scare him shitless enough that he'd agree to drop the custody petition.

Paps was rubbing his chest when he walked out of the bar and back to the truck. "It would be funny if it didn't hurt so fucking bad."

Mercer knew exactly what Paps meant. Whether they were all equal partners or not, Doc had been their leader, and his loss hit all of them damn hard.

4

Precious. Mr. Mercer had called her precious. While everything else from last night was a blur, that word, spoken in his voice, was crystal clear. It hadn't been a dream; he'd been here, in her apartment.

Quinn meandered to the kitchen, practically walking on air, but stopped when she saw a piece of paper on the floor, just inside her door.

"Mr. Mercer," she whispered.

As she ran her fingers over the words he'd written, something occurred to her. She carried the note into the kitchen and over to the dining table where she'd moved the vase of roses. They'd wilted, but she hadn't been able to bring herself to throw them away.

She pulled the card from between the thorny stems and held it next to the note. The handwriting was a perfect match. Quinn wondered how he'd known it was her birthday, her twenty-first at that?

It didn't matter. A handsome man had given her flowers, kissed her, and called her "precious." He'd left her a note and invited her to breakfast. He wasn't someone she'd met at a party, or in a bar. He wasn't a player; he lived in her building.

As excited as Quinn had initially been to tell her tribe about Mercer, something made her hold back. Even when they went on and on about the guys they'd met, she found herself wanting to keep *her guy* to herself.

She replayed every minute she'd been with him over and over in her head, until even that got boring. Then, she imagined what it would be like when he came back. After all, he had invited her to breakfast.

A few days. That's what his note had said. He'd be out of town a few days. What did that mean? More than two, right? But less than five. Five would be several. Wouldn't it?

She thought about asking one of the doormen if they knew when he'd return, but he would hear about it, and then he'd know exactly how immature his just-turned-twenty-one neighbor really was.

Instead, she'd begged off going out, because she'd much rather stay at home, close her eyes, and think about him, than hang out at a crowded, noisy party, where she couldn't hear her own thoughts.

"What is going on with you?" Aine asked over the breakfast she'd forced Quinn to go out for.

Of her four friends, Quinn was closest to her and her twin, Ava.

"Is it your mom?" she asked.

That was the second best thing about Mercer, after how heart-poundingly hot he was—when she thought about him, she didn't think about her mother, at least not as much.

"I don't know," she lied. "I'm just not feeling it."

"Feeling what?"

"Life."

That part was true. She'd graduated from college in May, and since, hadn't done a single productive thing. While she didn't need to, financially, mentally she did.

She told herself the reason for her inactivity was because she didn't know where her mother was, but if she had known, would it have made any difference? Likely not.

Looking forward to seeing Mercer when he returned was all she'd been thinking about. But what if he blew her off again like he had when she came into the gym? What would she have to look forward to then?

"I think I need a job," she finally answered.

"*A job?*"

"God, Aine. Don't look so horrified." Yes, a job. Something meaningful to do with her life, so it wasn't such a vast wasteland of nothingness.

"I'm not horrified."

Quinn laughed. "Yeah, you are."

Aine laughed too. "What do you want to do?"

With a degree in Urban Studies, Quinn had options. She'd interned her senior year with a privately-funded historical preservation group; they'd even offered her a job. She should call them. The position wasn't supposed to be open until the fall anyway, so maybe they hadn't filled it yet.

"Quinn?"

"Sorry, Aine. I'm thinking."

"I know, but I'm worried about you. I mean, really worried."

"Don't be. I'll be okay."

"We're hitting Amity Hall tonight."

"I don't know..."

"I'll pick you up at nine. I'll drag you there if I have to."

Maybe going out would be good for her. Better than sitting around here, doing nothing on a Wednesday night.

—:—

Mercer had a full day ahead of him. Once he delivered the necessary paperwork to the attorney, there was a great deal of money that needed to be moved. He, Paps, and Razor had discussed it the night before, and the plan was for Lena to ghost within the next few days. To do that, she'd require cash.

Someone rapped on the door of the bedroom, which served as Mercer's office when he was on the West Coast. Instead of getting up, he rolled the desk chair over and swung the door open. Both Paps and Razor stood in the doorway.

"Anything we can do to help?" Paps asked.

"We need Lena gone as soon as possible."

"Agreed," said Razor. "Been workin' on it."

Mercer decided now was as good a time as any to tell them about him and *Skipper*. "There's something I need to tell you about Quinn and me—"

"We got your six, Eighty-eight," said Paps.

Mercer shook his head. Of course they already knew.

"Looky, looky," said Razor, holding his laptop. "Skipper's decided it's time to grow up."

"Let me see." Mercer took the laptop when Razor passed it over to him.

Sure enough, Quinn had followed up on a job offer at the same place where they'd arranged for her to intern before she'd graduated.

"I'm up." Razor took the laptop when Mercer handed it back, shut it, and put it into a bag he then slung over his shoulder. "Tabon Sharp has an interview to conduct." He looked at his fingernails. "Maybe a series of them. I wouldn't mind getting to know 'Quinn' a little better myself."

Paps rested his hand on Razor's shoulder. "Knock it off, *Tabon*."

Mercer didn't remember ever hearing him address Razor by his given name, or in that tone of voice.

While he and Razor were around the same age, it had been Paps who'd stepped into the lead, or father figure, role after they'd received news of Doc's death. That wasn't where he got his code name though.

When Doc first met him, Gunner Gadot had a habit of raising his hands in the air like guns and shouting "pap-pap," as he mimicked firing.

"It was so damn annoying," Doc had said when he told Mercer the story shortly after he'd joined the team. "Calling him 'Paps' cured him of that habit."

What had started out, back then, as a four-man operation, now had at least fifty contractors on pay-roll at any given time. He missed those days, when things were so much simpler. Now, it seemed their sole purpose was to tie up loose ends of things that had happened years before—more like loose pins on a bunch of grenades, and all were potential land mines. Case in point: Rory Calder.

Doc's mission hadn't ended when he was reported killed; it had changed, and was now *their* mission—him, Paps, and Razor. Instead of looking for one missing operative, they were now looking for two. Whether they found them dead or alive remained to be seen, but no matter what, they needed to be found.

Calder's sudden reappearance intensified the urgency of the search. If there was any possibility whatsoever that either man were still alive, the team had to find out why he was here, what he was after, and who else came with him.

Lena came out from wherever she'd holed herself up, holding her phone for them to see. "He's made contact." The phone ended up on the floor where she'd thrown it, and seconds later, they heard a door slam.

Mercer picked up the phone and looked at the screen. "Calder is asking her to meet him."

"*Jesus Christ,*" Paps hissed. "He has her number."

"Hold up a minute," said Razor. "Let me see that."

Mercer handed the phone over.

"Typical Barbie overreaction. This isn't her burner phone; it's her regular number."

"I should've seen that," mumbled Mercer, as irritated with himself for overreacting as he was with Lena.

"My bad, too," added Paps. "We're all on edge, and it has to stop now."

Mercer and Razor both nodded.

"Let's get our heads out of our asses and refocus." Paps pointed at Razor. "You need to be gone."

"Yes, sir." He picked up his bag and slung it over his shoulder. "Do either of you have time to locate a bunk for me in New York?"

"I'm on it," answered Mercer.

When they'd arranged for the purchase of the apartment in Quinn's building, they'd originally intended to use it as an East Coast base, much like the house in Harmony was when they were on the West Coast. However, with Mercer's new relationship with Quinn, and her upcoming interview with *Tabon,* Razor would have to stay elsewhere.

"I need a break," Paps said once Razor was gone. "I'm getting too old for this kind of shit."

Mercer was over ten years younger than Paps, but he agreed. The last year and a half had been hell for all of them, and Calder's reappearance made it exponentially worse.

"Let's regroup," Paps said the next afternoon, pulling a beer out of the refrigerator. "Want one?"

Mercer nodded and took a drink out of the bottle Paps handed to him.

"Lena's meeting with Maddox Butler tomorrow. What should we do about Calder's request?"

"It only makes sense that she'd ignore him. She'd have zero reason to agree to talk to him."

"Right. So we do nothing but wait."

"Pretty much," Paps muttered. He stood, looked out of the kitchen window, and scratched his chin. "Head out," he said.

"Meaning?"

"Back to the city."

Mercer had no idea what to say, so he waited. It was unlike Paps to call shots, particularly with him and Razor.

"When things heat up, we'll get you back here. In the meantime, your time is being wasted."

He'd argue, but Paps wasn't wrong. There was nothing that he wanted more than to get back to Quinn.

"I saw that."

"What?" Mercer asked.

"You smiled."

"Nah. You're seeing things."

If New York weren't on the opposite side of the country, Mercer would ride the Ducati all the way there. Instead, he'd buy one when he got back. Driving around Manhattan would be a colossal pain in the ass, but once he got out of the city, there'd be plenty of back roads he could tear up.

He couldn't sleep on the flight, which was unusual. Threats, while still there, were contained in the sky, so he typically took advantage of the downtime.

Today, though, anxiety kept him awake. Quinn's life had been quiet while he was gone, with the exception of her thankfully uneventful time out last night.

"She's distracted," Tom told him when he checked in to report she was secure in her apartment.

That was his fault, but he didn't need to say it. Tom knew it as well as he did. He'd been gone three days, but it felt like twice that long.

He lost three hours of his day traveling from one time zone across three others, but he was back in Manhattan and almost to his apartment. He didn't have a plan, but somehow, he'd see Quinn tonight, even if it meant he had to camp out in the hallway to feign running into her. Mercer always felt better when he could lay his own eyes on her instead of relying on someone else to give him a report.

—:—

Day four. God, this was agony. Quinn had gone from breathlessly awaiting Mercer's return, to certain that, once he did, he'd have forgotten the note, maybe even forgotten about her.

She still hadn't mentioned him to her friends. If he ended up being less interested in her than she'd let her imagination run away with, she'd be humiliated and embarrassed.

The other thing was…how did she describe him? Of course Aine, Ava, Penelope, and Tara would first ask what he looked like, followed by what he did for a living, who he knew, and who knew him—most of which she didn't know.

He'd moved in over two months ago, and the little digging she'd tried to do with the co-op board led nowhere.

"We respect the privacy of our residents, Miss Sullivan. You know this," Mrs. Markham, the most likely member to gossip, had told her yesterday.

She'd pushed harder. "Yes, I understand, but given he lives on my floor, I would appreciate knowing more about his background. I'm sure you understand my concern."

Mrs. Markham had literally patted her hand, and then fanned her face. "He's a handsome fellow, isn't he? And that *physique*. My, oh, my."

"I hadn't noticed."

"You hadn't noticed, and I celebrated my thirtieth birthday last week. Come now, there's no shame in admiring a good-looking man, my dear. Try getting to know him, and then perhaps your questions will be answered."

Mrs. Markham had to be eighty, or close, and Quinn supposed she was right. The best way to find out everything she wanted to know about the man was to ask him herself. She only hoped she'd get the chance.

Mercer looked around the corner, like he did every time he exited the elevator on the eleventh floor, and there she was, leaning up against the door jamb.

He didn't give himself time to think, he just acted. He dropped his bag on the floor of the hallway and stalked over to where she waited.

"Hi," she murmured the moment before he put his arms around her and held her against him, his lips finding hers while he wove his fingers in her hair.

"Hi," he answered, pulling back long enough to look into her eyes before he returned to ravishing her mouth with his.

He rested his forehead against hers, struggling to find a way to explain his impetuous actions. "Quinn…"

She put her fingertips on his lips. "I missed you, Mr. Mercer."

He smiled. "I missed you too, Miss Quinn."

"Just Quinn."

That made him laugh as he ran his finger from her hairline, down her cheek, to her mouth. He gripped the side of her face, and his mouth descended on hers once again. How many times had he woken to a dream that he was kissing her, each time feeling like a traitor for doing so? He couldn't stop now, though. Quinn wasn't his ward, or his charge, or his asset. In the last eighteen months, she'd crawled inside his heart, where he planned to keep her forever, even if it meant leaving K19.

Quinn took his hand and led him inside her apartment. "Wait," she said, "your bag."

He'd just as soon leave it out in the hallway than bring it into her apartment, but either would be irresponsible.

"Give me a minute." Before she could protest, he kissed her again. "I'll be right back."

Mercer left Quinn standing in the foyer of her apartment, picked up his bag, and rounded the corner to the door of his. He entered his code, scanned his thumbprint, and pushed inside when it clicked. He was about to set his bag on the floor when an eerie feeling came over him. Nothing was amiss; there was no sign of forced entry or otherwise, but something felt off.

If Razor had been in the apartment while he was away, he would've known it. A war waged inside him.

Every instinct told him to check the surveillance footage, yet a beautiful woman was waiting for him; one who was insecure and treading as lightly as he was, albeit for entirely different reasons.

This was the perfect example of how dangerous and careless his actions over the course of the last week had been, and illustrative of the consequences of his heedlessness.

"Mercer?" He heard her voice from outside his door.

He dropped the bag he was still holding, turned around, and walked out, closing the door behind him.

"Is everything okay?"

"Yes," he answered, leading Quinn away from his apartment.

"Would you tell me if it wasn't?"

He smiled, something even he acknowledged he did rarely, but so easily with her. "No."

"What are you up to, Mr. Mercer?"

"Right now, I plan to take a beautiful woman to dinner."

She studied him, looking first into his eyes, and then from head to toe.

"Tell me what you're thinking, Quinn."

"I'm starving."

"How's Indian sound?" he asked.

"Ajento?"

Mercer nodded and followed her into her apartment.

"In that case, it sounds fabulous. Let me...um... change."

He motioned for her to go ahead, and then closed the door behind him. "Go," he told her when she stood in the foyer as though she were waiting for permission.

She took a step forward. "Kiss me again, first."

Instead of her lips, Mercer kissed her forehead and turned her around so she was facing the direction of her bedroom. He smiled when she folded her arms and huffed. "Go, little one, I'm starving."

She walked away, but looked back over her shoulder. "I prefer 'precious' over 'little one.'"

Mercer shook his head, and walked in the opposite direction, to her kitchen, where he found both his note from a couple of days ago and the card that he'd included with her roses. There it was, all the evidence she needed to confirm he'd been the bearer of the birthday flowers. He wondered how she felt about that, whether it made her uncomfortable, what kind of questions she'd level at him during dinner.

While she changed, Mercer sent a text to Razor, asking him to check the surveillance footage for the building, the eleventh floor, and the apartment. He didn't need to explain why, or ask him to sweep each and every room, nor did he need to ask him to check out Quinn's apartment while he was at it.

"Are we taking your friend's fancy car?" she asked once they were in the elevator.

"Let's walk," he answered.

The elevator came to a stop in the lobby, and Mercer stepped forward, putting his back against the open door, and motioning for her to go ahead of him.

"Everything okay?" she asked again once they'd exited the building.

He nodded. "Yes, why?"

"You don't miss a thing, do you?"

"What do you mean?"

"Are you avoiding someone, Mr. Mercer? An ex-girlfriend lives in the neighborhood perhaps?"

"Don't be silly," he answered, taking her hand in his and squeezing it lightly.

"It's either that or you're a spy on some sort of secret mission."

"Even sillier," he said, stopping at the crosswalk and pulling her into him. He wrapped his arms around her shoulders and brought his mouth close to her ear. "You have an active imagination, Miss Quinn."

She reached up and kissed his cheek. "Light's green," she said, pulling him toward the street.

Mercer held back, though, waiting until the other pedestrians left the curb, and then looked left and right for cars.

Quinn shuddered.

"What was that?" he asked.

"You were very paternal there for a minute." She laughed as they stepped up on the opposite curb.

"Yeah? Well, this isn't." Mercer backed her away from the crowded sidewalk, inside the narrow enclosure of a walk-up, and kissed her hard.

"That did the trick," she said, taking a deep breath. "I'll never think of you in that way again."

He brought his mouth near her ear. "Damn, woman. What you do to me."

"The feeling is mutual."

He ushered her back out onto the sidewalk. Fortunately, the restaurant was less than half a block away, and the aroma was making his stomach growl. Otherwise, he'd take her home instead.

"Have you ever been to India?" she asked once they were seated near the back of the restaurant where Mercer could see anyone coming or going.

"I have."

"I haven't. Although I've always wanted to go," she said as she studied the menu.

"Do you mind?" he asked when the waiter came to the table.

Quinn set her menu down and folded her hands on top of it. "Not at all."

"Two Kingfishers." He looked over at her, and she nodded.

He proceeded to order what he knew were her favorites, with a few of his mixed in, and added a request to keep the heat level to medium.

"Why do I think you would've requested extra heat if I wasn't with you?"

Extra heat. Did she have to use those words? Mercer's body was already warm just from their short, kiss-ladened walk from the building to the restaurant. Instead of answering, he reached across the table and took her hand in his.

"Tell me about your week."

"Well," she began. "I solved the mystery of who sent me flowers on my birthday."

Mercer nodded. "What else?"

"I tried to figure out how you knew."

"And?"

"No theories. Although, I pretty much decided to leave that one alone."

"Why's that?" God, he was enjoying this.

"With so many Mercer mysteries, I figured that wasn't as important as some of the others."

He grazed the back of her hand with his fingers, and then turned it over, slowly caressing her palm. He knew better than to throw this out there, but he did it anyway. "If you had one question, what would it be?"

"Here's the thing, Mr. Mercer. How is it that, without knowing you at all, I know you have no intention of answering any question I ask?"

"I'll give you one."

"Hmm...I like this. One question and you'll answer honestly?"

"To the best of my ability."

"I expected the caveat."

Mercer felt the flames surrounding him. Soon he'd be engulfed in a fire of his own making. He'd tossed the match when he gave her flowers, threw kindling on the smoldering embers when he kissed her, and now he was dousing their lives with lighter fluid. He leaned forward, pulling her closer to him, and looked deep into her eyes. "Make it a good one, Quinn."

"You were away for a couple days. Where did you go?"

"To the West Coast. On business."

The waiter delivered their beer, as well as papadums with mint and coriander chutney, vegetable samosas with imli chutney, and crispy onion bhajis.

"My favorites," Quinn commented. "I won't have any room for dinner, not to mention naan; it's always been my weakness." She paused. "When I asked where you were, that wasn't my question, by the way."

"I knew that," he answered, holding each dish for her to take from.

"Of course you did, Mr. Mercer. Is there anything you don't know about me?" She smiled. "Don't answer that."

Once she had a little of each appetizer, Mercer served himself.

"Tell me more about your week," he said, waiting for her to begin eating before he did.

She dipped the papadum into the imli chutney. "I have a job interview on Monday."

Mercer brought a small piece of the bhaji to his mouth and closed his eyes as he chewed it.

"It's the best, isn't it?"

"This place? Yes. One of my favorite places to eat outside of India itself."

Quinn studied him. "What would you say if, someday, I asked you to take me to India?"

"Yes."

"Simple as that?"

Mercer took a drink of his beer and leveled his gaze at her. Her eyes were fixed on his, and she hadn't taken a breath.

"I'll take you everywhere, Quinn."

She smiled and her cheeks flushed, maybe because of the spiciness of their food, but more likely because of the intensity of the conversation they were having.

"Who are you?" she murmured.

"Who do you think I am?"

She thought for a minute. "I have no idea."

"Does that frighten you?"

"Should it?"

"Answer the question, Quinn."

She set her fork on the edge of her plate, moved it to the side, rested her forearms on the edge of the table, and folded her hands. "No, Mercer. Nothing about you frightens me. So, I'll ask you again. Should it?"

"Trust your instincts."

She unfolded her hands and held them open on the table, and he rested his palms on hers. "I'm not hungry anymore," she told him.

"I am."

Quinn tried to move her hands out from under his, but he held them tight.

"Not for food."

"No?"

He shook his head and signaled the waiter. "We'll take the rest of our order to go, please."

"Mercer?"

"Don't worry, Quinn. We're going to take our time and see where this thing between us goes."

She flushed and looked away from him.

"Okay?"

"Yes," she answered, and then stood. "Excuse me."

"Of course," he said, standing too.

Mercer had gotten the all-clear twenty minutes ago. If Razor had any concerns whatsoever, he would've said so. No additional alert meant he hadn't found anything, although that didn't ease Mercer's mind. Trusting his instincts, like he'd told Quinn to, kept him alive.

"Ready?" he asked when she returned to the table.

When she nodded, he put his free hand on her waist and led her to the front door.

"Need any help?" she asked, peering at the over-loaded bag he held in his opposite hand.

He smiled. "I got it."

Mercer didn't rush, and neither did Quinn. He asked again about her scheduled interview, and she told him everything he already knew about the historical preservation group. He loved her enthusiasm and seeing her so animated. There'd be no question she'd get the job, but knowing she'd bring such passion to it, filled him with pride.

He had no idea what would happen between them when they got to her apartment, but whatever did wouldn't be because he planned it.

Right now, he wasn't watching over her or orchestrating the safety of her life without her knowledge. Instead, he was a man who was so drawn to a woman that he couldn't think about anything other than having her in his arms.

When the elevator reached their floor, Quinn hesitated. He rested his hand on the small of her back and guided her toward her apartment.

She stopped and leaned up against the wall outside her door. "Please tell me you're coming in, Mr. Mercer."

"I am."

She sighed. "And will you stay?"

He set the bag of Indian food on the floor next to her feet and leaned in, trapping her between his body and the wall. He kissed her forehead, each of her eyes, each cheek, and then the tip of her nose. "Slow, precious. That's how this is going to go."

His lips settled on hers, and she gasped, opening her mouth to his. He cupped her face with his hands, which had been flat against the wall, and deepened their kiss.

He kept it slow and gentle, savoring the feel of her tongue caressing his.

Mercer felt Quinn reach over and punch her code into the door's keypad, and then heard it click open. He turned her inside and trapped her once again, this time between the wall in her foyer and his body.

"I could kiss you for hours," he murmured, pulling back to look into her glazed eyes.

"I wish you would," she whispered.

"Invite me in."

She smiled. "You are in."

"Further in."

Quinn ducked under his arm and held out hers. "Please come in, Mr. Mercer."

"I'd love to."

He followed her into the kitchen, where he unpacked the Indian food onto the counter.

"The best part is how good it will be later," she said, taking a whiff of the tandoori chicken he'd ordered.

"Are you sure you're not hungry now?" he asked.

"Not for food," she repeated what he'd said earlier. She took his hand and led him out of the kitchen into the living room that looked much like his own.

Walls of windows afforded a view of the vibrant lights of the city, breathtaking right after the sunset. Off to the side sat a piano, which he knew she played well, and beautiful artwork adorned her walls. The only thing he didn't see, were photos. Even though he knew there weren't any, it still took him by surprise. There wasn't even a picture of her tribe of five.

Mercer didn't have photos in his apartment either, but that was different. It wasn't his home, and even if it had been, it wouldn't have been his thing. He had digital photos of people who mattered, like Quinn, that he could look at when he felt like it.

His lack of photographic memories didn't bother him, but hers did.

"What are you thinking about?" she asked, pulling him over to the sofa that faced the city view.

When she sat, Mercer sat as close to her as he could get, putting his arm around her shoulders so she could rest her head against him. "You."

"Do you think about me a lot?" she asked.

"I do." More than she could dream.

"I think about you, too."

They sat in the still quiet, touching but not talking, caressing but not kissing. Quinn ran her hand over his chest, and then to his arm. Her fingers trailed down to his forearm, to his hand. When she moved to his thigh, he trapped her hand with his.

"Careful, precious," he warned.

She blushed and tried to pull her hand away, but he held tight.

Mercer couldn't pinpoint the exact day or time when he'd looked at Quinn as a woman rather than a teen-ager. He hadn't felt the earth turn on its axis, or ever felt the need to analyze the change. It had happened slowly, naturally, just like things would proceed between them.

The enormity of the responsibility he felt for every aspect of this woman's life was ever-present, yet not suf-focating. It just was. No one could know her the way he did, and as disturbing as some might find that to be, Quinn said he didn't frighten her. Not that she knew the extent of it.

"Mercer?"

"Yes?"

"This is okay, right? You're feeling it too, aren't you?"

"It isn't okay, precious. It's perfect. Don't go in search of something negative that isn't there."

She rested her head back against his shoulder and sighed. "That's what people do, don't they? If some-thing feels too right, they doubt its authenticity."

He nodded. "Whatever is supposed to happen between us, will. Trust your instincts." It was the second time, or maybe even the third, he'd said those words to her, but there wasn't anything more important he could tell her. He wanted her to trust him, and since she hardly knew him, she only had her instincts to rely on.

"I'm worried about something, but it isn't this," she began.

When she didn't continue, he turned her body so she was facing him. "Tell me what's bothering you, precious."

"I don't know where my mother is."

If there were anything that could be awkward between them, it was this subject. He could listen, but he couldn't comment. If she trusted her instincts, like he kept insisting she should, she'd sense his discomfort.

"I haven't talked to her since May, when she was here for my graduation."

Mercer looked into her eyes, focusing solely on how she felt about her mother's absence, rather than what he knew about it.

"We've never been close…"

"No photos," he looked around, commenting on what he already knew.

"No."

"Why not?"

She thought a long time before she answered, and he waited, not in any hurry.

"I'm not sure how to say this…"

He tilted his head.

"You already know my answer, don't you?"

He shook his head. "I don't."

She took a deep breath. "I've always been alone. Seeing photos where I'm not, seems like…a lie."

She'd never been alone, and maybe someday he'd be able to tell her so. Mercer pulled out his phone and did something so out of character for him that he chuckled. He pulled her close and took a photo of them together.

"Let me see," she said, pulling at his arm.

Without looking, he held the phone for her to see.

"Wow. I think it's the best photo I've ever seen of myself." She giggled. "It's a good photo of you too."

He turned the phone so he could see as well. She was right; it was a fantastic photo of her. She was photogenic anyway, but this—she looked happy, and unfortunately, that was a rare thing.

"Will you send it to me."

Mercer shook his head.

She moved away from him, but not far enough that their bodies weren't still touching. "Why not?"

"Soon you'll have proof that this isn't a lie, precious."

"I pray it isn't," she whispered, resting her head against him.

It was close to midnight when Mercer's stomach rumbled again. He'd hardly eaten anything at dinner, and before that, he had no idea when he'd last had food. He took a deep breath, not wanting to disturb her.

"You're leaving, aren't you?"

He shook his head, stood, and held his hand out to her, but she crossed her arms and pouted.

"Okay, if that's the way you want to play it," he teased. He crossed his arms too and walked toward the kitchen. "I can't promise I'll leave much for you."

Quinn flew off the sofa, ran into the hallway, and around to the kitchen from the other entrance. "Oh, no, you don't. That Chicken Makhani is *mine*."

Mercer shook his head and laughed.

"What?"

He pulled her into him. "I like seeing you happy, Quinn."

The smile left her face. "How do you know the difference?"

"Because I do." His hand gripped the side of her face, and he covered her mouth with his.

She ran her tongue over his lower lip. "Mmm, peppery," she murmured, tasting the papadum he'd just eaten.

He pulled her body closer, pressed his hardness against her, and then reminded himself that he'd told Quinn they'd take things slow.

When he moved away, she sighed, and he tweaked her nose.

"I'm hungry," he grumbled.

"For food," she said, and he nodded. "Me too."

They heated their leftovers and sat at the table in her kitchen, talking easily about unimportant things. Quinn did more talking than Mercer did, but he doubted that would ever change.

He didn't want to walk down the hallway and around the corner, to his apartment, but he had to. It was close to two in the morning, and if he didn't leave now, he knew he'd end up in her bed, buried deep inside her.

"I know this sounds silly…"

"Go on," he said when she bit her bottom lip.

"This has been one of the best nights of my life."

"Mine, too, precious."

When Mercer crossed the threshold of his apartment, his unease returned. He watched the same surveillance recordings Razor watched, and like his partner, he saw nothing. No one had been in the apartment, no one on the floor, and no one in Quinn's apartment. The only logical explanation was that his foreboding feeling had nothing to do with the walls that surrounded him, but from something inside him instead.

He scrubbed his face with his hand and rolled his shoulders, wishing he could shake the chill that kept up the hair on the back of his neck.

Before he'd kissed her goodnight, Mercer put his cell number in her phone and asked her to call him in the morning when she was ready for their breakfast date. She'd rubbed her belly and told him she couldn't imagine being hungry again for days.

"Coffee, then," he'd said, and she'd smiled.

"I'll let you take me anywhere, Mr. Mercer, or was it everywhere? Breakfast, coffee, India."

He closed his eyes, remembering how good her body felt next to his. She was everything he'd dreamed she'd be. There had been an outside chance the Quinn he'd thought he knew wasn't the real version of her— that the reality of her couldn't possibly compete with his fantasy. If anything, she was funnier, smarter, sweeter, even more beautiful than he'd imagined.

It would've been easy to stay with her tonight, and she would've let him. But that wasn't what he wanted. Not with Quinn.

His phone buzzed with a message from Paps letting him know there was no significant news from California, and telling him to enjoy his weekend.

If he could shake his dread, he would do just that. As it was, he was on edge, and even getting a decent night's sleep probably wasn't going to change that.

5

Quinn was walking on air. For years she'd listened to her friends, Tara especially, talk about how they'd "fallen in love," with some guy they'd just met. But now she got it.

Mercer was all she could think about. She wanted to be with him all the time, and hated that he'd left last night, although she understood why he had.

What she didn't understand was why she had such faith in him. It was as though, somewhere deep in her heart, she knew she could trust him with not just her dreams, but with her nightmares too.

She sent him a text telling him she was awake and ready for breakfast whenever he was. She watched to see if the three moving dots would appear, indicating that he was responding, but none did. A few minutes later, she heard a knock.

She opened the door and leaned against the jamb. "I thought maybe you'd changed your mind."

"Invite me in," he said.

She moved to the side and motioned for him to enter.

"You first," he said, putting his hand on the small of her back. He directed her through the foyer and into the living room, where they stood, looking out at the morning's view of the city.

He put his hands on her waist and turned her to look at him. "I know it's difficult for you to trust me," he began, but paused. "This may sound...hard to believe, but I'm not going to desert you, Quinn. I may have to travel—it's part of my job—but when I do, I'll try to let you know as far in advance as I can."

"Why are you telling me this?" she whispered, tears welling in her eyes.

"Because I don't want you to waste time or energy worrying about this. I'm here, and I'm not going anywhere. As I said, if I do, I'll tell you."

"You must think..."

Mercer put his fingertips on her lips. It was the first time he hadn't waited for her to finish her sentence, and it jarred her.

"Don't decide what I think. Focus on what you think, what you feel."

She nodded and raised her hands so they rested on his rock-hard chest, and then moved to his shoulders, and then to his face. "I like it when you kiss me this way, Mercer."

She held his face, and then reached up to kiss him. When his hand cupped the side of her face too and he deepened their kiss, Quinn felt her knees giving way.

Her body was plastered against his, but she wanted to be closer still.

She let him back her away from the window and up against the wall that divided the room from the kitchen. When she instinctively tilted her pelvis, she felt his hardness push against her, and she moaned.

Mercer slid his hand under her shirt and inside the cup of her bra, circling the hard bud of her nipple with his fingertips.

At the same time, his lips trailed from hers down her neck. With both hands, he pulled her shirt up and over her head, tossing it to the side. Looking into her eyes, he unfastened her pink, lacy bra, slid it off her shoulders, and threw it where the shirt had landed.

He covered her left nipple with his mouth while his fingers toyed with the right. Quinn weaved her fingers in his hair, pulling it as he lapped her sensitive flesh. She was lost in him, and every part of her body pulsated with need. He switched to her other nipple, dragging his tongue across her skin.

She tensed, suddenly aware that she had no idea what came next. Mercer stood and looked into her eyes.

"Why did you stop?" she whimpered, covering her breasts with her palms.

Mercer held her wrists in his hands and moved them away. "Let me look at you."

Her cheeks flamed. She closed her eyes and slouched as far as his body would allow her.

"Open your eyes, Quinn."

With them half-opened, she looked up at him. "I'm embarrassed. I've never...you'd think...but..."

"You are so beautiful," he murmured, running his gaze from her eyes, down to her exposed breasts, lingering before he returned to her lips. "Last night, I told you I could kiss you for hours. I could spend hours just looking at you too, precious."

"You don't understand..."

Again he waited, and when she couldn't continue, he took a deep breath.

"Here's what I understand. I love that no one else has seen you this way. I love that no other lips have been where mine just were. I told you that we're going to take this slow, which means I'm going to pay attention to everything you tell me, whether it's with your eyes..." He stopped to kiss each eyelid. "Or your mouth." He softly kissed her lips. "Or any other part of your body." He trailed his tongue down to lave each nipple, and then knelt in front of her, resting his cheek against her tummy. He put his hands on her bottom and held her close to him. "Feel no shame or embarrassment with me, Quinn."

"Who are you?" she whispered. "How do you know me so well? God, is this even real?"

"Does this feel real?" He circled her belly button with his tongue.

"Yes," she moaned.

When he stood again, bringing his lips back the way they came, she somehow sensed he was going to stop. He held her face in his hands and kissed her hard. It wasn't quick, he lingered, lavishing her with his tongue, exploring her mouth in the same way he'd explore her body.

"I'm craving chicken and waffles," he whispered into her ear.

She opened her eyes wide. *What did you say?*

"Breakfast, precious." He stepped back and picked up her bra, sliding the straps up her arms, and then reaching behind her to fasten it once the cups covered her breasts. "Stay still," he said when she reached for her shirt. "Let me do it."

He lowered it over her head. When she put each arm through a sleeve, he pulled the cotton fabric over her tummy.

"Mercer?"

"Yes?"

"Did I do something wrong?"

"Never. Just let yourself feel, Quinn. You'll know what feels right."

She let Mercer lead her out of the apartment, to the elevator, down to the lobby, and out into the oppressive heat of the city.

His touch never left her, whether it was his fingers on the small of her back, or his hand holding hers. Each time they stopped at an intersection, Mercer put his arm around her shoulders and pulled her close to him, kissing her forehead or her lips.

He never left the curb first, instead waiting for the throng of people to move past them, and then he'd look before leading her across the street.

As they walked, every once in a while, she'd catch their reflection in the windows they passed. The shirt he wore today was another v-neck, but white instead of black. His shorts were light blue and white striped, and he wore slip-on shoes without socks. His legs were ridiculously powerful, like the rest of his body.

He was safe and yet, so dangerous. He looked out for her, soothed her, loved on her, and it all felt too good to be true.

How could they possibly have this strong of a connection? It didn't make sense, but then he'd told her not to go looking for something negative; let herself feel, and she'd know what felt right. He felt so right.

There was a wait when they got to Sarge's Diner, but only a short one. They stood near the entrance, out of the way of the crowded sidewalk, and didn't speak. He rested his back against the cool brick of the building and pulled her close, his arm circling her shoulders again. She put her hands just above the waist of his shorts and sneaked her fingers under the fabric of his shirt. She heard and felt his gasp, loving that the effect she had on him was so evident.

Quinn leaned forward and kissed his skin, right above the v of his shirt. She could see the edges of a tattoo on his chest, but not enough to know what it was. His arms and legs were free of ink, which fueled her curiosity about what he kept hidden.

"Careful, precious," he warned like he had last night when she rested her hand on his thigh.

The buzzer in his pocket went off, alerting them that their table was ready. She couldn't decide if she was happy, because she was so hungry, or disappointed that she could no longer lean against him, feeling his body touching so much of hers.

They were seated near the back of the restaurant. Mercer took her hand and guided her to the side of the booth that faced the entrance, and then sat next to her.

She smiled. "Cozy."

"I like the feel of you next to me."

Quinn studied the menu even though she already knew what she wanted. She looked up at the same time the front door opened. "Shit," she said under her breath.

Mercer looked up too, but didn't say anything.

Penelope was in the front of the group, just inside the front door. Tara, Aine, and Ava were behind her. None of them had noticed her yet, but it wouldn't be long before they did, she was in their direct line of sight. Now she wished she'd sat with her back to the door.

It wasn't that she was ashamed of being with Mercer—look at him, he was practically a deity. She just wasn't ready to share him yet.

Mercer's gaze went to the front door and back to her again, but he still didn't speak.

"My friends..." Quinn didn't know what to say. This thing he did, where he didn't finish her sentences was nice at times, but at others, like now, she wished he would.

She'd never realized how often the four women she spent most of her time with, did. How often had Quinn been at a loss for words about something until one of them finished her sentence for her?

Tara noticed her first, waving around Penelope who was deep in conversation with the hostess. Quinn saw her turn to speak to the twins, and then ease her way past the crowd at the entrance to walk back to their table, Aine and Ava in tow.

"Hello, there," Tara said, looking between Quinn and Mercer.

"Hey," Quinn answered.

"This is why we couldn't reach you this morning." Ava grinned. "I told you she was up to something," she said to her sister.

Tara reached across the table and introduced herself and the other three, since Penelope had just joined them.

"I'm Mercer," he said, shaking each of their hands as one stepped aside for another to get a good look at him.

Quinn knew their eyes were on her, but she couldn't bear to look at any of them.

Aine pushed past the other three and sat across from them. "So. Holding out on us, huh?"

Quinn looked up, afraid of what she'd see on Aine's face, and was immediately relieved when she saw her friend's smile.

"I'd hold out on you too," she added, winking at Mercer.

"How'd you two meet?" Ava asked.

Now the interrogation would begin, thought Quinn. The endless questions about who he was, what he did.

"He lives in her building. On her floor, if I'm not mistaken," Aine answered for her.

Quinn nodded, looking into her friend's smiling eyes. She didn't see judgment, just love.

"Well, then," said Aine, standing. "We'll leave you two to breakfast and catch up later. Okay?"

Quinn nodded, as stunned as her other three friends by Aine's atypical bossiness as she shuffled them away from the table.

"Those were...well, I guess you know who they were since they introduced themselves to you. They're my four best friends, who are probably going outside to talk about us."

"Because they don't know anything about me."

It wasn't a question, but she answered it like it was. "I wasn't ready to share you yet. I hope you're not... you know, that I didn't hurt your feelings."

"By not sharing me? Never, precious."

She looked into Mercer's eyes, marveling at the way he just accepted her as she was, taking things the best possible way instead of the worst.

While she'd never been in a real relationship before, all four of her friends had been, and none of the guys they'd been with were anything like Mercer.

"I'm not ashamed of you," she said, and then wished she hadn't. "That didn't come out right. I'm sorry."

"Never thought you were." Mercer motioned with his head to the approaching waitress. "What are you in the mood for this morning."

"Chicken and waffles. Oh, and tea."

"May I?" he asked, and she nodded.

"Two orders of chicken and waffles, extra crispy, one tea, one coffee, and some water, please."

"Crispy waffles? Crispy chicken?" the waitress asked.

"Both, please," he answered.

It probably wasn't that unusual for someone to like their chicken or their waffles crispy, right? Or did he, once again, hone into the way she preferred things?

"Extra butter and the syrup warm," he added.

The waitress smiled at him, but then who wouldn't, with his warm eyes and almost baby-face beneath the scruffy beard that made him look as tough as his body was, rather than unkempt.

"Who are you?" Quinn mumbled again.

When the waitress walked away, Mercer leaned closer and whispered in her ear, "Trust this, precious. Trust me."

She felt her eyes glazing over and her breath catching at the pure heat of his words. "I do," she heard herself say, although she hadn't meant to.

"Would you like to spend time with your friends this afternoon?

"Um, no. I mean, if you have other things to do. Of course you have other things to do. So, yes, sure. I can just stay when we're done with breakfast if you need to go," she rambled.

"No, thanks."

"Wait. What?"

"I said, no, thank you. I don't want you to stay while I leave."

"Why not?" Again, it sounded so much worse out loud than she meant it to.

"Because it'll be easier for them to get to know me if we spend time with them."

"Oh. Okay." Quinn's head was spinning. Who *was* this guy, and how could he be *this* perfect?

"Trust," he murmured, almost too quietly for her to hear.

6

Seeing Quinn around her friends wasn't new to him, but watching her react to their reaction to him was fascinating. Mercer saw her nervousness, and then watched as it began to fade away. Her friends were polite, not asking him direct questions, but conversing about the city and their lives, to see what he'd add.

They went to the Union Square farmers' market, and then stopped at an Italian deli to pick up food for later. Every so often, he'd step away, giving them time to talk without him hearing. After a few minutes, she'd come looking for him, and he'd smile.

As much as he wished it were different, Quinn's insecurity was expected, given the way she grew up. There was nothing Mercer could do to go back and change the circumstances of her life to this point, but he certainly could help her build the confidence a woman as bright and beautiful as she was, should have.

He excused himself when they walked by his favorite wine shop, happy when they offered to wait outside. As he perused the shelves of rare wines, from the corner of his eye, he could see where the five women stood. Their conversation was animated, and every once in a while, one would shield her eyes from the glare and peer in the window, although he knew they couldn't see him.

No doubt her friends were grilling Quinn, but after spending so much time with them today, he was confident she could handle their interrogation. He certainly knew plenty about the four of them—everything really, but the most important detail was that they were all ferociously protective of one another.

They'd met at boarding school, and then went on to Barnard together. Some of their childhoods had been more difficult than Quinn's, but that was because, without her knowing it, she'd been protected from the people who might destroy her.

She'd grown up believing she was alone in this world, with the exception of her grandparents and mother, who were missing from her life far more than they'd been in it. Her perceived reclusion wasn't what she believed it to be, but she couldn't be made aware of that yet, if ever.

"We're having a small gathering at my dad's place on Fire Island this weekend," Penelope said when he came back outside. "We'd love for you and Quinn to join us. There's plenty of room and a guest house in the back of the main house."

He didn't need to look at her to know Quinn was hopeful. "Sounds wonderful," he responded.

"Oh, good," Penelope breathed, evidently expecting him to decline.

"You can drive out tonight or in the morning, whichever you prefer," she told him.

"Tomorrow would be better, I think," Quinn answered when he looked to her.

Mercer picked up the shopping bags he'd left on the sidewalk, and waited.

"Ready?" she asked, and he nodded, unsure what they were doing next, but it didn't matter, he was happy to do whatever she wanted to do.

Soon the girls said their goodbyes, and he set the bags back down as, one by one, they hugged him and told him how great it was to meet "Quinn's new boyfriend." She blushed at their words, and he winked, which made her drop her eyes and smile.

"Wait, where's your wine?" Ava asked. "You didn't find anything?"

He told her it was being delivered, and glanced at the shopping bags as explanation.

"Well, have a *fantabulous* dinner or *whatever*," Aine said, kissing his cheek. "You're good for her," she whispered.

"How are you?" Quinn asked once they were more than a block away from her friends.

"I'm fine. How are you?"

She shook her hands as though she were trying to get something off of them. "A nervous wreck."

He smiled. "They like me."

"No, they don't. They *love* you."

He smiled again and pulled her close to him with his free arm.

"So...when we get back..."

"What would you like to do, precious?"

"Me? I mean, I don't care, but I'm sure you have things...uh, you know...to do."

He stopped a half block from their building. "If there is something I need to do, I'll tell you." He hoped it didn't sound as though he was scolding her, but it was time he was more direct.

"Okay. I'm sorry," she mumbled, "I've just never—"

Mercer stopped her words with his lips. "Don't you have any idea how much I want to be with you?" he asked after he'd thoroughly kissed her. "*Trust,* Quinn."

"But..."

He waited. He'd already interrupted her once, this time he'd wait to see what she would say.

"I don't have a lot going on in my life right now, and I'm feeling a little...boring. I mean, you've been to India,

right? Who knows where else? I haven't traveled anywhere. I went to school, I have friends, but that's it.
What you see is what you get."

Mercer looked her up and down and smiled. "I love
what I see, precious. You're fascinating. You're smart,
and funny, and beautiful, and you make me happy."
She also made him talk more in one day than he had in
the last week.

"Really?" she asked, smiling too.

He pulled her close again and kissed her forehead.
"Yes, really. Now let's get back to your apartment and
decide what we want to do tonight."

—:—

They talked about seeing a Shakespeare play in the
park, but decided to stay in and make dinner together.
They had a lot of food to eat, between what they'd gotten at the deli and the farmers' market, especially since
they were leaving for Fire Island in the morning.

Quinn had wanted to ask him at least ten times if he
was sure he wanted to go, but stopped herself, knowing
he'd tell her again to trust him.

"Turn your phone on," he said while he made a plate
of antipasto.

She picked it up, not having realized it was off.
"Why?"

"Because they're going to call you when the wine arrives."

"Oh." He must've known then, when he bought the wine, that they'd be coming back to her place. When she looked up, he was watching her. "Yes. I know," she said. "*Trust.*"

After the wine arrived and they'd eaten, they sat in the living room and fell asleep cuddled together on the sofa. Quinn woke before Mercer did, and studied him while he slept.

His features looked as though he'd been chiseled from stone. And his body? *God,* she didn't know where to start. She wanted to run her hands under his t-shirt and take a peek at the tattoo she knew ran across the whole of his chest. She let her mind wander to what he'd look like with no clothes on at all. She closed her eyes and shuddered with the thought of it.

"I feel the same way about you," he said, startling her.

Quinn grasped her chest. "You scared me."

He moved her so she stood, and then scooted down so he was flat on the sofa.

"What?" she asked when he pulled her back toward him.

"Come here, and lie on top of me."

She wasn't exactly sure how to do what he was asking of her.

"Give me your hands," he said. When she did, he supported her arms. "Now, put your right knee there." He motioned with his head for her to put it in the open space near his hip. "Okay, now put your left knee on the other side of me."

Quinn did as he asked, keeping her body off of his by supporting herself on his hands. When he dropped them, she fell onto him, first with a gasp, but then she giggled. "You did that on purpose."

"Sure did." He wrapped his arms around her waist, so their bodies were flush together, and she could feel his hardness.

"This doesn't feel slow, Mr. Mercer."

He moved his hands from her waist to her cheeks. "Look at me." Their faces were so close their noses almost touched. "If there is anything that makes you uncomfortable, all you need to do is say so."

"I know that." She tried to look away, but he wouldn't let her.

"I won't rush, but I won't stop moving this thing between us forward either. We'll take our time, and that isn't measured. It's based on how we're both feeling."

She felt her cheeks flush. "Okay."

He smiled. "How *are* you feeling, Quinn?"

"Honestly?"

"Always."

"I wish there weren't any clothes between us."

Mercer groaned and grasped her bottom with both of his hands. He moved one and stroked her hair. She rested her head on his chest and sighed.

"This isn't hormones, precious. This is real, and it's right, so long as both of us want it."

"It isn't just that I've never felt this way. I've never gotten this close to anyone, but you already know that."

Mercer ran his tongue over her lower lip, and then nibbled at it. "Kiss me," he said.

She looked into his eyes.

"Go ahead, precious. Kiss me. Any way you want to."

Quinn gave in and kissed him the way she'd thought about while she'd watched him sleep. She ran her tongue over his lips, and then inside when he opened his mouth to her. She pressed hard into him, and then backed off and was slow and gentle.

She trailed her tongue down his neck and over the top of where she knew his tattoo started. "I want your shirt off," she breathed, and he groaned.

"Am I hurting you?" she asked.

"Oh, yeah."

"Do you want me to stop?"

"Never."

Quinn kept scooting her body down his. "I don't want to wait," she whispered.

When she put her hands under it, he pulled his shirt over his head and threw it on the floor.

Quinn ran her eyes over the ink on his chest, studying the detail of the two wings that flowed out from his sternum. Using her tongue, she traced the outline of the left one from the bottom, where the ends of each feather were jagged, to the smooth, flowing top. When she finished, she started at the top of the right wing, until she'd outlined both.

"Mercer?"

"Yes, precious?" he groaned again, as though he couldn't allow himself to breathe.

"What does your tattoo mean? Are these angel wings?"

Her tongue went back to tracing each line, this time on the intricate pattern inside the wing, but Mercer didn't answer. She stopped and looked up to see he was grimacing. "Are you okay?"

He took three or four deep breaths and brought his hands down to her sides, pushing her further into him. "Do you know what you're doing to me?"

She did. She could feel him so rock hard it almost hurt where her body pressed against him.

Quinn turned and rested her body between his and the back of the sofa. Her fingers traced over the ink on his chest in the same way her lips had. "Tell me what it means, Mercer."

—:—

Mercer took a deep breath. This question could be the one he'd promised to answer honestly; that's how deep it was.

He'd gotten the tattoo shortly after Doc had been reported killed, and he knew that, for the rest of his life, he would be Quinn's protector. That's what the wings meant to him; he was a protector of others, but most importantly, of her.

It wasn't something he could be glib about, or could give her any answer but an honest one. Not knowing what else to do, he sat up, rested his feet on the floor, and put his head in his hands.

"If it's too personal, I understand," she said from behind him.

"It isn't that."

Quinn scooted around him and went into the kitchen.

"Come here," he said, following her, but she pulled away from him when he tried to put his hand on her arm.

"It's hard to remember sometimes that we really don't know each other," she said. "I feel like you know me so well, and I want to get to know you, too. I'm sorry I was intrusive. I won't be again."

"Quinn..." Every time he tried to get close, she moved farther away.

"I think we should call it a night," she said, turning to look out the window.

"You sure about that?"

She nodded.

He knew he'd hurt her feelings, but he wasn't ready to tell her the story behind his tattoo, which meant he had no way to soothe her uneasiness.

"What time would you like to leave in the morning?" he asked.

"It was nice of Penelope to extend the invitation, but..."

"You'd rather not go...correction, you'd rather I didn't go."

She shrugged and he nodded. Quinn was putting the bricks back in her wall and retreating to a place where she wasn't as vulnerable, with her four best friends. He had no choice but to let her.

"Goodnight, Mercer," she said, holding the door open for him.

"I didn't mean to hurt you." He tried to stroke his finger down her cheek, but she backed away.

"No one ever does," he heard her say before she closed the door after him.

Back in his apartment, Mercer thought long and hard about what he was doing.

His first move, giving her flowers on her birthday, had opened a door he never should have. Kissing her was number two, and leaving her a note saying he was going out of town was his third mistake.

For the last several months, since receiving the news of Doc's death, he'd done his best to ignore his deep attraction to the woman he was responsible for protecting. At first he tried to tell himself she was too young for him, but she wasn't. She was a twenty-one-year-old woman, not a child or a teenager. It wasn't possible to turn such powerful feelings off, and her visceral response had only encouraged him.

Quinn wasn't a puppet he could manipulate, though, and sometimes that's what he felt like he was doing. He was keeping secrets from her, and there'd be no getting around that fact. Once she found out how their "relationship" began, she'd feel betrayed. Coming clean with her now wasn't an option either.

If she did go to Fire Island, Mercer would excuse himself from her detail and bring in someone else from the K19 team. It was the only way they could continue. For the time being, he couldn't be the lead on her surveillance.

"I need backup," Mercer said when he called Razor.

He laughed. "Yeah? Skipper gettin' under your skin?"

This wasn't a joke to him.

"Hey, I get it, okay?" Razor said, reading his silence. "It's not the same as fallin' for the source, and it definitely isn't the same as fallin' for the target, but fallin' for the asset can sometimes feel just as wrong."

Razor was right. He'd failed the mission, the team, the asset, Doc, and himself. He'd broken every rule, except sleeping with her, and he'd come damn close earlier tonight. If an employee had done what he had, they'd be terminated.

Mercer took a deep breath. "I get it. I fucked up. The only solution, now, is putting someone else in charge of her detail. Permanently."

"You're being way too hard on yourself, Eighty-eight."

"Doc picked me, Razor. He trusted me to keep her safe, not to fall in love with her."

"Don't be so sure."

"What does that mean?"

"History has an interesting way of repeating itself."

He wasn't in the mood for riddles—not now, or ever. He was the kind of person who said what the hell he meant, unless he couldn't say anything at all.

Razor spoke again before he did. "Meet me at Paddy Murphy's in fifteen."

Mercer couldn't decline. They were brothers more than partners. He, Paps, Razor, and Doc had gone through hell and back together. If one asked another to meet, saying no wasn't an option.

They were almost through their second round of beer and Razor was about to tell him what he'd meant earlier, about history repeating itself. Instead, he laughed.

"Who's on whose detail?"

"Shit," Mercer said, following Razor's line of sight in time to see Quinn coming in the revolving door.

"At least you were here first. *Wait. Shit.*"

Their only option was for one of them to try to duck out before she saw them. There'd be no way to explain why Mercer was having a beer with the CEO of the historical preservation group she'd be working for.

"You or me?" Razor asked.

"You."

"That's what I figured." Razor turned his ball cap around and managed to get out the door without Quinn noticing him, mainly because her eyes were glued to Mercer's as she walked up to the bar.

—:—

Quinn heard Mercer's door close, and then the elevator—things she'd never noticed before.

She'd been hoping he'd knock on her door and refuse to let her back away from him. But he'd done the adult thing instead. He'd left when she asked him to, and he didn't come back.

Where are you? Headed to the island? she texted Aine.

Nope. Tomorrow. Going to Paddy Murphy's now for a couple with the tribe.

I'll meet you.

What about your hot date?

Cooled off early.

Sorry, honey. See ya soon.

Paddy Murphy's was one of the tribe's favorite hangouts, especially hers. Unlike other bars, there seemed to be an unspoken rule that if a woman didn't express interest first, guys left her alone. If a man didn't follow that rule, they were quickly shown the door. Given the mood she was in, she'd appreciate not having to worry about someone hitting on her.

When she walked in the door, her eyes went straight to the man sitting at the bar. "I'd ask what you're doing here, but I guess this place is more your style than mine."

Mercer raised his glass. "Buy you a beer?"

"Sure." Quinn sat on the stool next to him and noticed the empty glass Mercer pushed away. "Am I interrupting?"

"Nope. Had a beer with a buddy, and then he left. What would you like?"

"A Harp, please."

The bartender asked to see Quinn's ID when Mercer ordered, so she pulled it out of her purse and handed it to him. He looked at it and then turned around and rang a bell that sat behind him.

"Sorry," she apologized. "It's an Irish thing. The last name Sullivan gets the bell rung every time."

Mercer nodded and watched the bartender smile and set a frosty mug in front of her.

"Thanks for the beer." Quinn motioned to an empty table. "I'm meeting friends. See you, Mr. Mercer."

He put his hand on her arm. "I'm sorry about earlier, Quinn. I wasn't ready to talk about my ink. It wasn't personal. I just handled it badly."

"I'm the one who's sorry."

"What's this? I didn't expect to find you two here together," said Aine, standing between them.

"Coincidence," Quinn answered and nodded her head toward the open table. "I'll be right over."

"Gotcha. Nice to see you again, Mercer," Aine said before walking away.

"So, like I said, I'm sorry. I shouldn't have pried."

When he reached up and tucked her hair behind her ear, she leaned into his hand and closed her eyes. His lips brushed hers, and it felt like heaven.

She sighed when he pulled away. "And then I made it worse."

He shook his head and smiled. "You were reacting to me, precious. I'm the one who hurt your feelings."

"I'm sorry, but I should go...I told Aine I'd meet her here."

"Understood."

"Are you leaving?"

Mercer raised his almost empty glass.

"Bartender?" she said before he could answer. "I'd like to buy this man another round."

Mercer smiled. "Guess not, and thank you."

"Give me a little while?"

When she turned around to look again, Mercer's bar stool was empty, but there was a coaster over his beer, so he must've just stepped away. Quinn hated the momentary panic she felt when she looked up and he wasn't there.

She didn't feel like herself when it came to him, and it pissed her off. She was a damn grown-ass woman, a Barnard graduate, and member of the tribe of five, who never *sniveled*. And that's what she'd been doing. Mercer made every one of her nerve endings stand up and take notice, and because of it, she responded to him like the innocent she was. *Not anymore, though.* She'd never apologize for her lack of experience, not that he was asking her to. She was the one who'd put herself in the slot left open by insecurity, and now she'd take herself out. She turned her back to the bar, squared her shoulders, and looked up at Aine, who was studying her.

"I don't even want to ask," she said.

"I don't want to be that girl."

Aine nodded and waited for Quinn to continue.

"I'm like a clingy puppy, and I hate it. I hang on his every word. I don't want to be away from him for a minute, because I'm so afraid he'll never come back."

"Speaking of coming back, he's headed this way."

Quinn turned around in her chair and waited for him to approach their table.

"Can I speak with you for a minute?" he asked.

Quinn was about to say he could tell her whatever it was in front of Aine, but her friend had left the table and was headed to the ladies' room. She pulled out the chair next to her, and he sat down.

"I have to go out of town. I didn't expect to leave again so soon."

"Not a problem. See you when you get back, Mercer." It took a tremendous amount of restraint to stop herself from asking when that would be.

"I don't have to leave until tomorrow morning."

She was at a crossroads. Would she do as she'd resolved and stop her sniveling, or would she invite him back to her place? She took a deep breath and bit her lip before she spoke. Mercer, of course, waited.

"I made other plans, thinking we'd cut our night short."

He nodded, and she could swear she saw the flicker of a grin.

"Good girl," he said, leaning forward to kiss her forehead before he stood.

She was about to blast him for his condescension, but stopped herself from doing that, too. No need to swing from one side of the pendulum to the other.

"Walk me to the door?"

How could she say no without coming off like a total bitch? "Sure," she sighed.

He took her hand when she stood, and led her outside.

"I'll be in touch as soon as I can," he said, and she nodded. "Quinn?"

She refused to meet his gaze, until he put his fingers on her chin.

"I don't know what you want me to say, Mercer."

Instead of answering, he leaned forward and covered her mouth with his. Every ounce of resolve she'd thought she had, melted away when his tongue caressed hers. She put her arms around his neck as his encircled her waist.

"I can't," she said, pulling back.

"Can't what?"

"Change my plans with Aine and go back to the apartment with you."

"I don't expect you to."

"Oh." She wanted to kick herself, and knew her face was flaming with embarrassment.

He cupped her cheek with his palm. "I very much want you to, Quinn, but I don't expect it. You know the difference."

She tried to pull away, but he held her close.

"I don't want to feel this way."

He smiled. "Which way?"

"Don't be obtuse." Quinn tried again to wriggle from his grasp, but he wouldn't let her. "You suddenly don't know how I feel, but you always have before."

He kissed her forehead again, released his arms, and then caught her before she could stumble backwards. "I'll be in touch," he said before he turned and walked away, leaving Quinn ready to scream and run after him. Instead she went back inside the bar.

"This is such bullshit," she said, slumping into her chair and wanting to pull her hair out. "Hey, Pen," she said, not realizing her friend had arrived.

"How long have you been seeing him?" Penelope asked.

"I'm not seeing him." She laughed at the look on both Pen and Aine's faces. "I don't know. A couple of days."

"Uh huh."

"What?"

"No offense, Quinn," said Aine, "but it's kind of nice seeing you like this."

"Are you kidding me? *Nice?* There is absolutely nothing nice about the way I'm feeling."

"Falling in love is always nice," said Pen.

"I'm *not* falling in love."

Aine patted her hand. "You're right. You've already fallen. Now you're just in it."

Quinn glared at the two of them, wanting to wipe the grins off their faces with the back of her hand. "This isn't funny."

"What isn't?" asked Ava, approaching the table.

"Quinn is in love," Aine answered.

Ava clapped her hands. "Oh, *goody.*"

"And Ava's not," Aine added.

"Can we please have one night without talking about men?" Ava implored.

First Penelope laughed, and then Aine joined in. Soon Quinn and Ava were laughing too. That was the way Tara found them—bent over, laughing so hard tears ran down their faces.

"What's so funny?" she asked.

"We're not going to talk about men tonight," Pen said between guffaws. She was laughing so hard, she snorted.

Tara looked at Quinn and rolled her eyes. "You're usually the sensible one."

"Those days are over," said Aine. "She's in love with Mercer."

"I wish you'd quit saying that," said Quinn, wiping her tears away. "I'm not in love with him."

"Yeah, right," said Tara. "Who's ready for some shots?"

When all four raised their hands, she went to the bar to order for them.

7

"Take as long as you'd like. I'm not going anywhere," he'd said when she left him alone at the bar, trying hard to ignore the phone vibrating in his jacket pocket.

Mercer had put the bar coaster over the top of his beer and had gone to the men's room. Once inside he'd checked his phone, expecting to see a message regarding Quinn's whereabouts. Instead, there'd been one from Paps.

Need you back.

Tonight?

Tomorrow. Sorry.

Paps knew better than to apologize, and Mercer had known better than to acknowledge it. It was the life they'd chosen, and when they were needed, they came. It was that simple.

Mercer hadn't anticipated Quinn's earlier behavior, but he'd been glad to see it. She'd never been anyone's doormat, and he didn't want her to be his. He liked her feisty. He'd even thought she might belt him when he'd called her a good girl. He shook his head and smiled. There were times she reminded him of Doc. They had a similar sense of humor—when she let it show. Quinn may look like her mother, but in Mercer's opinion, she wasn't anything like Lena.

"Hey, Eighty-eight," Paps answered when he called.

"What's happened?"

"Calder showed up at the restaurant where Barbie was having dinner with Maddox."

"And?"

"Nothing else to report, although Butler invited him to stay at the ranch tonight."

"*What?* Are you shitting me?"

"Fortunately, something happened between Maddox and Alex, and Calder left on his own."

"Why would he have made that offer?"

"Calder played it off like he had nowhere to stay. I don't know what his motivation was. At one point, I thought it was to see if Alex would invite him to her place."

"That would've solved our problem," said Mercer.

"How so?"

"Maddox Butler would've killed him."

Paps laughed, but he knew as well as Mercer did that there was nothing funny about that bastard being back in the States.

They'd known Calder was staying on the Tablas Creek Winery in one of their guest houses. The property had gone under contract, and soon Calder Wines would own it, so they assumed the current owners had permitted him to stay there in the meantime.

"Barbie is all spun up."

Not a surprise, but her being so, only made things harder for Paps. He couldn't rein her in without blowing his cover of protection if she spiraled out of control.

Having someone who had beaten the shit out of her to the point where she came close to dying be so close had to terrify her. He understood that, as well as the need to get her out of there as soon as they could.

On the other hand, if she suddenly disappeared, as was the plan, how would Calder react?

Mercer would rather see something significant enough happen between them that the piece of shit would take credit for forcing her to leave.

"Did he say anything else to her about wanting to meet?" Mercer asked.

"Didn't have a chance, although it appeared he was angling to get her alone."

"He wants that land."

Paps agreed. "I'm sure that's it. The first time he contacted her was shortly after Wendt arranged for it to be taken off the market."

"Why does he want it so badly? Gotta be something there."

"I don't know, but my gut is telling me that whatever it is, is something we should attempt to find before he does."

Mercer didn't agree and said so. Maybe once he found whatever he was looking for, he'd either return to Russia or, at least, establish a contact that they could monitor.

"You're right. That might be a more useful outcome," Paps said. "See you tomorrow, Eighty-eight."

Mercer ended the call, went into the kitchen, and opened the bottle of wine that sat on the counter. It was one of his favorites, a 2015 Butler Ranch Vin 22 Syrah. He'd had the wine often enough that he knew a lot about it. The soil of Vineyard 22 was rich in limestone, and thus, produced grapes that maintained good acidity throughout the growing season.

Through Doc, Mercer had learned that Maddox began experimenting with this particular vineyard several years ago, destemming and crushing the fruit directly into new French oak barrels, using the bound wooden staves to both ferment and age the juice.

As a result, the wine was full-bodied with a vibrant hue and aromas of ripe plums and brambly fruits. Its richness on the palate and flavors of black fruit, along with its firm structure and silky tannins, provided a long and luscious finish.

He thought about Quinn, wishing he could share it with her, but it was far too soon for that. Like so many other things, this was something he couldn't talk to her about yet.

Given he had little wine in the apartment that wasn't from the Butler Ranch winery, it had necessitated his stop earlier to stock up on different labels.

Paps and Razor were craft beer connoisseurs, but he and Doc had always preferred wine. Mercer had learned a lot about the intricacies of wine tasting as they'd traveled the world together. Sitting on the edge of a Tuscan vineyard with the breeze on their faces as a *signorina* brought them taste after taste, had given them a brief respite from the horrors they faced almost daily in their line of work.

Doc once told him that his family thought he had little interest in the ranch or the winery. They'd been wrong. It wasn't that he wasn't interested; it was that he'd known he had a different calling.

"One day, Maddox will be considered one of the greatest winemakers of all time," Doc had told him. "And Naughton, it's like the vine's juice flows through his veins instead of blood."

What Naughton didn't know yet was that Doc had come to an agreement with his parents which made him heir to Butler Ranch.

Their father, Laird, had been an only child, so when his parents passed away, the ranch became his. With seven siblings, Doc had feared that when their parents died, there'd be turmoil over its ownership. To him, the possibility of Naughton being the one to walk away, represented what was paramount to tragic. He'd told Mercer that he'd do anything to prevent that from happening.

So, he'd left money in a trust to be paid out to each of his siblings on the day Naughton married, equivalent to their share of the ranch.

As far as the winery went, there was also sufficient money left in a trust to buy out any of his brothers or sisters who wanted to sell their stake in the family business. Otherwise, they'd be considered silent partners, each earning a share of the income generated, like they did now.

What Doc had done ensured Naughton and his future wife, whoever that may one day be, would live in the ranch's main house and raise their family on the land passed down from their grandparents.

Naughton had also been given two-hundred acres of the land Doc owned that had once belonged to Lena's parents. He'd deeded the land, half to Maddox, half to Naughton, before he'd left on his last mission.

He'd told Naughton about the property, even walked the vineyards with him, and made him aware of the stipulation under which Maddox would learn of his inheritance. Mercer was aware of it too, and while he didn't understand Doc's logic, it wasn't for him to question his motives, but simply to carry out his former boss's wishes.

Mercer finished the wine in his glass and poured what was left of the bottle.

Maddox was the third of the siblings to receive a message from Doc. Coincidentally, the youngest brother, Brodie, had received his and had gotten engaged to Peyton Wolf the same day Quinn turned twenty-one.

Mercer only knew that because he'd been the one to arrange for Paps to have the letter and box, which had been inadvertently left in Argentina, delivered to Brodie.

A little over a month ago, they'd feared Brodie had been killed in a small-engine plane crash in Argentina. Maddox and Naughton, both helicopter pilots, volunteered to help the search team. Little did they know they were aided by two of their older brother's business partners. Paps had been the one to locate the crash site, but he and Razor took a step back when the search had turned into a recovery mission.

Now, not only was Brodie engaged, Peyton was pregnant with their child.

One of Doc's sisters, Skye, had received a letter shortly after Doc died, however, what her brother had done for her happened well before that final mission when, a few years prior, Doc had arranged for Skye to meet the man who was now her husband, Mac Campbell.

As with the rest of the letters that had been delivered or were waiting to be, Mercer didn't know what Doc wrote to Skye.

Mercer rubbed his chest, wondering if angels really did exist. If Doc was really dead, was he watching over them all? If so, what would he think about Mercer's budding relationship with Quinn?

He shuddered at the thought. Few people had ever intimidated him, but Doc certainly had, and he'd hate to think that he wouldn't have approved of Mercer falling in love with her.

His phone vibrated, and he looked at the screen. The message said Quinn had entered the building with her four friends. Vinnie also added that it appeared they'd consumed more than their share of alcohol, but hadn't left Paddy Murphy's until a few minutes ago, when Tom picked them up in his cab and brought them here.

The man had balked at driving around a big, yellow minivan, but soon realized the reason K19 had insisted on it rather than a sedan. Tom had shuttled the tribe of five home more nights than he could count.

Mercer listened for the elevator, but couldn't make out much of the conversation they were having in the hallway. He heard Quinn's door open, and waited for the sound of it closing. Instead, he heard a knock at his own door at the same time a text from Quinn appeared on his phone.

Are you awake?

Yes, he answered.

He was already to the door when her next text came through. *Can we talk?*

"Hi," she said when he opened it.

"Hi."

"Did you get my text?"

Mercer nodded. "I did."

"And?"

Mercer hesitated momentarily, doing a quick run through in his head of the state of his apartment. He stepped aside and motioned for her to come in.

"I didn't want you to leave without saying good-bye." Her eyes filled with tears, and he put his arms around her.

"I'll be back as soon as I can," he whispered, and he felt her nod.

She shifted and kissed him, far more passionately than he'd expected. Her hands slid under his shirt, and she plastered her body against his.

"Whoa, there," he said, taking a step back.

As soon as he saw the look on Quinn's face, he kissed her again, slower, softer, and gentler than she'd kissed him.

"Don't make me leave, Mercer," she whispered against his lips. "Let me stay with you tonight."

A war waged inside of him. He was tempted to tell her that if he did, she'd have to sleep in the guest room. At the very least, he'd tell her upfront they wouldn't be having sex. That wasn't why she was here, though, as much as she thought it was. Quinn needed reassurance from him that he'd be back, and when he was, they'd be together.

"Please," she begged.

Mercer took her arms from around his neck and stepped back far enough that he could look into her eyes. "Listen to me," he said. "Are you listening?"

She nodded.

"There isn't anything I'd like more than to feel your body against mine, but, precious, it can't be like this."

"Why not?"

He pulled her into the living room that looked so much like hers, and over to the sofa. He sat down and cuddled her next to him.

"I want you, Mercer," she said, trying to get her hands back under his shirt. "Don't you want me?"

"Not like this."

She tried to stand, but he pulled her back down next to him.

"Let me go," she said, but her head settled on his shoulder. "Just let me go."

"Never."

"Do you promise?"

"I swear on my own life." If she hadn't had so much to drink, he'd tell her now what his ink meant. He almost wished he had earlier, just so she'd believe him.

"Come on. Let's get some sleep."

She tried to pout, but her eyes were drifting closed. "Is it bad that I always fall asleep when I'm with you? I mean, not always, but I *can* sleep." She looked up at him. "I'm not making any sense, am I?"

"You're making perfect sense. Now, come on, let's go."

She crossed her arms, and the pout was back. "I don't want to."

"Okay, but I can't promise you any blankets if you don't climb into bed first."

Her eyes opened wide, and she looked up at him. "Really?"

Mercer laughed. "Yes, really, but if you don't move in the next ten seconds, I'll carry you into the bedroom."

"I kind of like the sound of that."

Quinn squealed when Mercer scooped her up and tossed her over his shoulder. She giggled all the way down the hallway, past the office door that he needed to remember to come back and lock, and into his bedroom. He set her down on his perfectly made bed, took her shoes off one at a time, and then tried to figure out what of his she could sleep in. Her jeans had to go, and when they did, the shirt she wore wouldn't cover anything below her waist.

He walked over to his dresser, pulled out the first t-shirt he laid his hands on and tossed it to her. "Put this on, precious, and I'll be right back. Bathroom's in the same place as yours, by the way."

He went back down the hall to grab his laptop, put it in his bag, and lock his office door. He had to be up and out of here early tomorrow, far earlier than Quinn would want to wake up, and he wasn't quite sure how he'd handle that. There was no way he could leave her in here on her own, even with his office locked up tight.

When he walked back into the bedroom, her clothes were neatly folded on his dresser. Jeans, shirt, and bra in a nice little pile. *Jesus*—he should have his head examined. He was about to crawl into bed with the woman who occupied every single one of his fantasies, who, by his own decree, he wouldn't lay a hand on tonight. He didn't see panties in her pile of clothes. He was about to thank God, but decided instead to pray she was still wearing them.

"What's K19 Security Solutions?" she asked, stretched out on his bed, wearing the last t-shirt he should've given her.

"A security firm," he answered honestly.

"Is that who you work for?"

"No." Also the truth. He didn't work for K19. He, Paps, and Razor owned it.

"Why do I think there's more to the story?"

"Because you have a very active imagination."

Mercer went into his bathroom and saw a discarded package that had once contained the extra toothbrush that was neatly placed on the edge of the sink he obviously rarely used. When he walked back into the bedroom, she'd crawled under the covers, and her eyes were drooping. She was going to hate him at zero six hundred hours when he made her get up.

He got into bed and was about to turn off the light when Quinn put her hand on his arm.

"Yes, precious?"

"Do you always wear so many clothes to bed?"

No, he didn't, but tonight he'd considered full tactical gear. Even that wouldn't prevent his body from reacting to having her almost naked next to him.

"Please take your shirt off, Mercer."

He looked into her eyes, wondering what she was up to.

"Please," she said again.

He pulled the shirt off with one hand behind his back, and tossed it on the floor.

"Thank you," she whispered, and when he rested his head on the pillow, she scooted over and put her head on his chest.

"I've always wanted to sleep on the wings of an angel," she murmured. "Thank you, Mr. Mercer, for being my guardian angel."

Out of the mouths of babes. Someday she'd know how much she could trust her instincts, when she realized everything they were telling her was so dead on.

Mercer had never been more sure and, at the same time, more conflicted about anything in his life. This

thing with Quinn was the best, yet most fucked-up relationship he'd ever been in, not that there had been
many. In his line of work, being involved could only
ever be superficial. But really, was this any different?
Was it any less superficial? Maybe for him, but certainly
not for Quinn. He'd shown her so little of himself. He
was a face and a body who she felt safe with. Otherwise,
she knew nothing about him.

As he lay next to her, Mercer came to a decision.
When he got to California, he would have a talk with
Paps. He needed his guidance, and if asked, he knew
the man would give it to him.

Mercer woke before the alarm went off, like he
always did. He slid Quinn's arm from around his waist
and went into the kitchen to make a cup of coffee and
heat water for tea, if she wanted some. He didn't have
much to eat in the house, but Quinn probably wouldn't
be hungry anyway. More than likely, once he woke her,
she'd pad over to her apartment, fall into her own bed,
and go back to sleep.

He checked the time; he had forty-five minutes before
Tom would be downstairs, waiting. Just long enough
that he could shower and spend a few minutes watching
her while she slept.

He'd just put shampoo in his hair when he heard the bathroom door open. Like hers, his shower was more than big enough for two people, and was enclosed by clear glass. This wasn't a mistake on her part. Quinn knew full well what she was doing by coming in here.

His K19 t-shirt was the first to go, followed by her panties. Quinn, with sleep-laden eyes, stood before Mercer, naked, waiting for him to invite her into the shower with him.

There was no way for him to hide his body's instinctual reaction to her, no way for him to deny he wanted her. When he reached out his hand, and she put hers in it, he drew her under the water with him.

—:—

The breath Quinn had held from the time she walked into the bathroom came out in a gasp when Mercer put his arms around her and brought her naked body flush with his.

He palmed her bottom with his strong hands, holding her pelvis against his hardness. He brought one hand to her breast and toyed with her nipple as he had the other day. Quinn moaned and felt her knees weaken as her desire for him pooled between her legs.

Mercer gently pushed her up against the wall and rained the body wash that represented his scent to her over her shoulders and down the valley between her breasts. He ran both hands down her arms, over her torso, and then knelt before her.

"Open your legs, precious," he whispered, tapping on the inside of her thighs. With deft fingers, he brought the lather through her folds, and her body shuddered.

He looked up, into her eyes. "Put your hands on my shoulders," he told her, and rather than gently resting on them, her fingers dug into his hard muscles.

When his hands moved to the back of her legs, where she was ticklish, she giggled, but when her eyes met the smolder of his, she stopped laughing.

Mercer stood and turned her body so her back was to him. Once again he dribbled the body wash over her shoulders and down her back.

"Put your hands here," he said, guiding them to the cold tile.

When she did, his hands resumed their exploration of her body. Once he'd touched every part of her, he put his arms around her waist and drew her against him. She could feel him, harder than he'd been before, pressed against her bottom, and she moaned.

He reached in front of her and turned the water off, then stretched to grab a towel from the warmer that sat right outside the shower door. He used it to dry her hair, and then ran the plush Egyptian cotton over her arms and legs. He wrapped it around his back and pulled her into his embrace, encircling them in the towel big enough to cover them both.

They still stood within the confines of the shower, looking into each other's eyes.

He brought his forehead to hers. "I'm leaving town, precious. As much as I want to stay right here with you, I can't."

"I know," she sighed.

"Do you know how much I want you?"

Quinn shifted her weight from one foot to the other. "I can feel it."

Mercer took her right hand and rested it near his heart. "This is where I want you to feel it."

"I do," she murmured before he covered her lips with his.

His fingers wove into her hair, and the towel that had been around them fell to the shower floor.

It wasn't just his lips that kissed her, his whole body did. Every place they touched felt like a kiss.

Quinn heard a ping from the bedroom, and while he stopped kissing her, his fingers were still in her hair.

"I've never wanted to leave less than I do now, Quinn."

When she tried to step back, he held her tight. "I'll be back as soon as I can be."

"I'll be waiting."

8

Quinn crept into her apartment, hoping not to wake her four friends who were sleeping God knows where. Hopefully, her bed would be empty, but if not, she'd stretch out on any open sleeping space, close her eyes, and will herself to dream of Mercer's hands on her body.

He hadn't let her ride the elevator down with him, but had kissed her soundly at her door.

Regardless of what insecurities she allowed to creep in while he was away, his promise of keeping in contact with her while he was gone would reassure her.

Aine was sitting up in Quinn's bed when she came in.

"Sorry. Did I wake you?"

"Yes and no. I was half awake when I heard the door open."

"Where is everyone else?" Quinn hadn't bothered to look in either of the spare bedrooms on the way to hers.

"I have no idea. Crashed somewhere around here. I called dibs on your bed, knowing you wouldn't be back until morning. Although I didn't expect you before ten, or not at all."

"He had an early flight."

"Right. It's coming back to me now. He was leaving town. For work?"

Quinn nodded.

"What's he do?"

"Um...I'm not really sure."

"Is that who he works for?" Aine asked, pointing to the shirt Quinn was still wearing, the one Mercer had agreed to let her keep when she told him it would be almost like having him wrapped around her.

"He said it wasn't."

"But you don't believe him?"

"I don't know. It seemed as though there was something he didn't want to say."

"Let's look 'em up." Aine was out of bed, heading for the kitchen. "Want tea?"

So much for going back to sleep and dreaming of Mercer. "Uh, sure...if we're officially awake now."

"Hell, yeah, we are," Aine shouted behind her. "I want to hear everything."

Quinn looked up at the ceiling. She'd wanted to keep Mercer to herself for what felt like so long; now though, she felt ready to share him.

The first time Mercer texted her, Quinn was telling Aine about their morning over a cup of tea.

Thinking about how to make this morning up to you, he texted.

She flushed and showed her phone to Aine.

"It's like he knew what we were talking about. Is this apartment bugged?" she said to the ceiling. "If it is, Mercer, this is Aine, and I just read your text, so please don't send Quinn any racy photos."

Quinn giggled, but a weird feeling momentarily settled over her. She shook it away as quickly as it came.

"Come on, let's Google him," she heard Aine say as she walked down the hallway back to the bedroom, where she knew Quinn left her laptop.

"Him, or K19?" she asked.

"Both."

Twenty minutes later, they didn't know anything more than they had when they'd started. There was no record anywhere of a company called K19 Security Solutions and worse, Mercer Bryant had no internet footprint whatsoever.

It was obvious that Aine didn't know what to say any more than Quinn did.

"I'm sure there's a logical explanation," she offered.

Quinn shrugged. "I can't imagine…"

"I wouldn't worry about it. I mean, he lives in your building. They don't let just anyone in. Plus, don't these apartments go for a *bjillion* dollars?"

She laughed. "Not quite a bjillion, but you're right, he would've had to pass an extensive background check to even be considered by the board."

"I'm ready for the beach. How about you?" asked Aine, changing the subject and heading to the guest rooms to wake up Penelope, Tara, and Ava.

A couple of hours later, they were on the ferry headed to Fire Island.

Last night, Quinn had decided not to snivel or obsess about Mercer. Once they were on the island and had said hello to Pen's dad, she'd put on her bikini and take a nap on the beach. In the meantime, she'd do her best not to think about the man she woke up with this morning—the one whose air of mystery was beginning to trouble her.

—:—

For the first five minutes of his flight, Mercer waited for Quinn-related guilt to creep in, but it didn't.

Maybe it was his resolve to talk the situation over with Paps that was setting his mind at ease, or it was his own acceptance that what had once been a forbidden fantasy, had become his reality.

When he closed his eyes, he could see the way she'd looked this morning, naked, and so open to him.

Leaving her was as painful now as it had been when they both had to dress and exit his apartment.

He adjusted his jeans, repositioned himself in his seat, and opened his eyes when he heard Delaney, the flight attendant for the private aircraft, ask if she could bring him anything.

"I'm good, thanks," he answered, but neither she nor her gaze left his body. Not his eyes, *his body*—the part of his body that had just come to life with thoughts of the naked woman he'd been with that morning.

"Are you sure you wouldn't—"

"Positive, Del." He closed his eyes again, willing her away. This wasn't the first time she'd made an offer for more than food and beverage service, and not the first time Mercer had turned her down. There may have been a time he would've considered having dinner with her, and maybe even more, but now it was inconceivable. Another reason he couldn't wallow in self-hate over his feelings for Quinn; she was the only woman on earth he was attracted to.

There was a message from Paps, asking Mercer to meet him in San Luis Obispo instead of the house in Harmony. He found the Ducati where he'd left it what seemed like far longer than two days ago, and texted confirmation.

The airfield was only a short distance from the restaurant where they were meeting, and being on the bike made parking easier, so Mercer arrived before Paps did. Instead of waiting inside, he went into the store next door, which touted local artists.

"Those are mine," said a woman behind the counter.

"Very nice," he murmured.

The handmade frames were just what he was looking for. Each had a message etched into the wooden frame, but none were quite right.

"Are you looking for anything in particular?"

"I'm not sure."

Ten minutes later, he left the shop empty-handed, but the artist promised his order would be ready for pickup by the next afternoon.

"Saw the bike," said Paps when Mercer joined him at the table.

"I was next door, buying a gift for Quinn."

"I see," he answered.

"We need to talk."

"You need to talk."

He got that right. "Razor said something cryptic last night."

"Razor? *Nah.*"

Razor rarely said anything that wasn't.

"He said history repeats itself."

Paps raised his eyebrows. "Did he say anything else?"

"We were interrupted before he could elaborate. If it relates to Doc and Lena, it's easy enough to figure out."

Paps nodded.

"What would Doc think?"

He looked past Mercer. "I can't answer that."

"I'm in love with her," he blurted.

His partner nodded for the second time.

"What Razor said surprised you, but not my confession?"

"It wasn't unexpected."

"You're not going to tell me what Razor meant, are you?"

"I'm not. And neither is he."

"If it's something I should be read in on—"

"Doc would've done it four years ago."

Mercer had to concede that point.

"Maddox Butler was in Harmony this morning," said Paps, changing subjects. "He saw me."

"Where?"

"He was parked in front of the diner. I was coming back from the warehouse."

"Are you concerned about it?"

Paps shrugged. "Not really, but I wouldn't be surprised if he showed up again."

"Did he recognize you?" Mercer didn't think Paps and Razor had spent much time with Maddox and Naughton while they were in Argentina searching for Brodie's crash site, but maybe it was more than he'd originally thought.

"Seemed more like he saw a ghost."

Paps resembled Doc, but certainly not enough that his own brother wouldn't have known the difference. From that distance, though, Mercer could understand Maddox's reaction.

"I can handle things here for the next few days if you want to take a break."

Paps sighed. "I'll go home once responsibility for Barbie is with her next set of handlers."

Paps' family lived outside of Washington DC, in Annapolis, Maryland, not far from where Mercer grew up in Cape Charles, Virginia. Both had spent their summers sailing at either end of Chesapeake Bay.

Paps owned a Hinckley Bermuda 40, he'd named *Whiskey Tango Foxtrot*, and Mercer's family still owned *Aurora*, the Hallberg-Rassy 42 that his father had commissioned by German Frers in the early nineties. There'd been plenty of smack talk back and forth over the years, but both were considered among the best sailing yachts ever built.

"I could stand a trip home."

"I hear ya, Eighty-eight."

"What would you think of establishing contact?" Paps asked a few minutes later.

"With Maddox?"

"Naughton."

"Sure." Mercer nodded. That made more sense.

"They're walking the property today."

"Maddox and Naughton?"

Paps nodded. "It won't be long before they discover the caves and Enzo Avila's hidden barrels."

"Yep."

"They could assume it's Hess wine," suggested Paps, but Mercer shook his head.

"Maddox will taste it, and once he does, he'll know it's too young to have been made on the estate."

He knew Paps was skeptical, but any of the winemakers in this region would know the difference. Hell, even Mercer knew enough to study the hue and color transitions to determine a wine's age. He'd probably know by taste too, although that would be more difficult.

Paps' phone pinged, and he read the message on it. "They're in the caves now."

The message had to have come from Sonny Lista, code name *Max*, a member of the K19 team who'd gotten himself hired as one of Naughton Butler's vineyard workers at the Old Creek Road property.

"Enzo Avila is there too. The Butler boys haven't seen him, and none of them have seen Max," laughed Paps.

"What a Charlie Foxtrot."

"You were right," Paps said a few minutes later. "Max reported that Maddox knew right away that the wine couldn't have come from the estate vineyards. Their initial theory was that someone who had a bond issue was hiding the barrels there. He also mentioned that Avila practically shit himself when he heard their conversation."

The phone pinged again, and Paps studied it. "Well, whattaya know. Guess who else is there?"

"Calder?"

"Bingo."

"Max says he looks happy as a pig in shit, or a piece of shit in shit." Paps laughed to himself. "My guess is because he heard the part about someone having a potential bond issue."

"It'll be interesting to see if he makes use of the information."

"This confirms our suspicions, Eighty-eight. Don't ya think?"

He agreed. There was a reason Calder was in those caves, and it didn't have anything to do with the wine stored in them, because until today, he had no idea of their significance. That he came back at all was the more important piece of intelligence. "What the hell could be in there?" Mercer said as much to himself as to Paps.

"Let's hope whatever it is, leads us to Doc and Leech."

Neither of them needed to say it, but Mercer knew Paps hoped it led them to where they'd find them alive, however slim the chance might be.

"Interesting."

"What?"

"Calder is on his way to see Barbie," Paps said, still studying the phone's screen.

"Shit." They were at least a half hour away. Mercer didn't know much about Max, but he sure as hell hoped the guy had it in him to protect her.

"He has backup," Paps said, resting his phone on the table.

"Who else do we have on the ground?"

He rattled off the names of three other contractors Mercer knew nothing about. Later, when he was back at the Harmony house, he'd get up to speed.

"I'd never leave him on his own," Paps added.

"Why not?" He wasn't questioning his partner's decision-making capabilities, he just wanted to know more about why he didn't trust him.

"You never did ask where 'Maxwell' got his code name."

Mercer shook his head.

"Lista translates to smart."

Maxwell Smart. Yeah, that didn't fill Mercer with confidence either. "Not the sharpest tool in the shed?"

"That, or smart enough to make us think he isn't. Ready to roll?"

Mercer pulled up across the road from the ranch gates, where it was easy to keep the bike and himself under cover, while he waited for word that Paps had arrived, and had some idea what they were walking into.

The message came a few minutes later. *All clear.*

Mercer pulled through the gate and parked the bike in the woods not far from the house where Lena had been living for the past few years. When he walked inside, she and Paps were sitting at a table in the kitchen, but neither said anything.

"There he is," said Paps, motioning for Mercer to join them. "Tell him what you told me, Barbie."

"He's *blackmailing* me," she hissed.

That took him by surprise. "With and what for?"

Lena looked at Paps who nodded for her to continue. Mercer got the feeling she wasn't asking for permission as much as she wanted Paps to tell him so she didn't have to.

"He says he has something on my father, 'bad enough that the ramifications of it getting out would be significant.' Those were his words, by the way, not mine."

"Go on," Mercer encouraged.

"The first thing he asked was what I knew about the wine being stored in the caves. I told him I didn't know anything, but I doubt he believed me."

No, he wouldn't have; he'd been trained to know when someone was lying, just like he, Paps, Razor, Doc, and any other operative or agent had been.

"Tell him what he wants, Barbie," said Paps, not even attempting to disguise his impatience.

"Tell him yourself," she muttered, but then cleared her throat when Paps glared at her. "First, he wants me to sell him the rest of the estate. Second, I get the impression he's going to use his knowledge of Los Cab's wine in some way."

"Any theories?" Mercer asked, looking at Paps.

"He saw Enzo," Lena said before Paps could respond.

That, he already knew. "So, he knows who the wine belongs to and, based on what he overheard, that they have a bond issue."

Lena nodded.

"Time to get the ATB involved," said Paps. "I'll handle it," he added.

"Why are you still here?" Lena asked when Mercer stayed after Paps left.

"To help you pack, although it appears you've gotten a good start." There wasn't much left in the house that he could see.

"I'm serious about leaving, whether you help me or not."

"It's already been arranged, Lena."

"When?"

"Soon."

She huffed, and he walked over to what looked like a pile of photos.

"I still want to go through those. I'd like to take a few with me."

"Not a problem."

"Everything will be kept in the warehouse, right?"

Mercer nodded. The warehouse they'd purchased near the house in Harmony had once been used by

Randolph Hearst. He'd stored the artifacts he'd collected from around the world while *La Cuesta Encantada,* his castle above San Simeon, was being built. Given it had sat empty for over seventy years, K19 had gotten it for next to nothing.

Mercer heard Lena's breath catch, but didn't look at her. He'd learned, in the time he'd known her, that she was a proud woman who would hate it if he knew she was crying.

Mercer looked out at the vineyards through the wall of windows. This wasn't the main house on the property, but he preferred it over the one up on the hill. "This will be over soon," he said. It was both uncharacteristically reassuring and optimistic of him to say so.

"Why are you being so nice to me?" she asked, joining him at the window.

"This isn't easy for you."

She shook her head. "I have to leave my home; I can't talk to my daughter, and I have no idea where my father or Kade are, what kind of danger they're in, or if they're even still alive. So, yeah, you're right. This isn't *easy on me.*"

Everything she said was true; there was no way for him to assuage her.

"Before you say anything else, I know this is all my fault. I can't go back twenty years and change it."

"Nothing's your fault, Lena. No one has ever said that."

"Right. No one has said it, but I've lived with the guilt every single day. I wouldn't trade my daughter for anything in the world, including my own life, but my refusing to terminate my pregnancy changed the lives of a lot of people. Ultimately, I fear Kade and my father paid the highest price."

Her unguarded admissions were rare and unexpected. Mercer was shocked to the point that it took him a minute to respond.

"You can leave," she said before Mercer had come up with anything else to say about Doc and her father. "I know there are goons watching me."

"Protecting you," he corrected.

"Whatever. It feels the same."

"What about Maddox Butler? How did you leave things with him."

"I wasn't able to say much at dinner. You know why not."

He nodded and walked toward the door. Lena followed.

"Mercer?"

He turned around and waited for her to continue.

"I need to talk to my daughter before I leave."

"Yes, you should."

"Thank you," she said as he walked out.

They were two words Mercer didn't remember hearing her ever say before.

Mercer was getting on the bike when a text came through from Paps.

Razor's on Skipper detail this weekend.

It made sense, since he was in New York already. *Lena's making contact now.*

Why?

Lena had never made it easy for them, but that didn't mean they couldn't treat her with compassion. Today was the first time that he could remember that she hadn't been combative, and he'd found himself feeling sorry for her. The least they could do was let her talk to her daughter before she left.

9

The man sitting at the bar looked familiar, but Quinn couldn't figure out from where.

"Do you know him?" she asked Aine, pointing in his direction.

"Doesn't look familiar to me."

There was something about him that reminded her of Mercer, although he looked nothing like him and appeared older. She was studying him when she realized he was waving at her, and then motioned her over.

"Quinn," he said when she approached. "Nice to see you."

"Mr. Sharp?"

"Please, call me Tabon."

"I have an interview with you in a couple of days."

He nodded. "I'd offer to buy you a drink, but that might not be…appropriate."

Quinn laughed. "It's okay. I should join my friends anyway. Nice to see you Mr. Sharp…um…Tabon." She shook his hand before walking away.

"Who is that?" Ava asked.

"Tabon Sharp. I have an interview with him on Monday," she explained.

"Damn. He's *hot,* Quinn."

"He is?" She was about to turn around to take another look, but Ava grabbed her arm.

"Don't look."

"Why not?"

"Because he's staring at us."

Before Quinn could say anything else, Ava walked in Mr. Sharp's direction.

"So you knew him after all," said Aine.

"He's my future boss. At least I hope so."

"That's right...*the job.* Although if he were my boss, I might consider working too."

Quinn looked over her shoulder and saw that Mr. Sharp hadn't hesitated to buy Ava a drink.

"I wonder how he feels about twins."

"What? *Ew.* Didn't you hear me? He's going to be my *boss.*"

Aine laughed and hip-bumped her. "I'm kidding. You're a mess, girlfriend."

"I am?"

"I'll say. Go call him for God's sake. Just ask him. 'Hey, Mercer, how come you don't exist?'"

"He exists..."

"You know what I mean. Now, go call him."

Quinn nodded. "You're right."

She walked out to the restaurant's patio and down the steps that led to the beach. She waited until she got close to the water before she pulled out her phone and found the number Mercer had added to her contacts the other day. She held her breath while she waited for him to answer.

"Hi, there," he said.

"Hi."

"How are you?"

Now that she was talking to him, she had no idea what to say.

"Quinn? Are you there?"

"Why isn't Mercer Bryant anywhere on the internet. I mean, there's nothing. No social media accounts, no mentions in articles, no photos, no professional affiliations. Nothing. Why?"

"What's this about?"

"Answer the question."

"Is this your question?"

"*Jesus.* Should it be?" This was turning out so much worse than she'd thought it would be.

"No."

"Are you going to answer me anyway?"

"My line of work necessitates a certain amount of anonymity."

"What is your line of work?"

"Are you sure you want to have this conversation over the phone?"

"Where are you?"

"On the West Coast."

"Where?"

"Near San Luis Obispo."

"Why?"

"We'll talk about the work I do when I get back."

She listened to the sound of him breathing, and took her time, trying to decide what to say next.

"Why do you call me 'precious'?"

"Because you are."

"How can someone you don't know be precious to you?"

"Because you are," he repeated.

"You aren't being honest with me."

"We'll talk when I get back."

"Will we, really?"

"Yes."

"And will you tell me the truth?" She waited, but when he didn't respond, she ended the call. "Goodbye, Mercer."

"Where's Quinn?" she heard Tara ask.

"Right here." The last place she wanted to be.

"We're going back to my dad's," said Pen.

"Sounds good. Where are Ava and Aine?"

"Here, unfortunately," she heard Ava say.

Thankfully, she thought but didn't say out loud. If Ava had left with Mr. Sharp, Quinn wasn't sure she'd be able to show up for her interview on Monday.

Ava handed her a card. "Tabon said you should call him about your interview."

"Is he canceling?" she gasped, taking the card out of her friend's hand.

Ava laughed. "No, he isn't canceling. God, Quinn. Paranoid much?"

"Why does he want me to call him?"

"I told him we were leaving late Sunday because of your interview. He asked if we'd stay on longer if you could reschedule."

"Ava, I don't want to reschedule. This is a *job*, not something I'm volunteering for."

"Settle down." Ava looked at Aine. "What the hell is her problem?" she asked, and then looked back at Quinn. "He wants to set up an interview *here* so we don't have to go back into the city."

"Oh."

Ava shook her head and walked away.

"Am I really that annoying?" she asked Aine.

"No. You're not. She's just on edge."

"Why?"

"She heard Dash is engaged."

Quinn nodded. Dashiell Finnegan had been Ava's first love and had broken her heart two years ago when he suggested they take a break. That wasn't what he meant though. It wasn't temporary; it couldn't be fixed, or put back together. News of his engagement just cemented its permanence.

"I talked to Mercer."

"And?"

"I don't know anything more now than we did before we decided to internet-stalk him."

"We weren't stalking him, just doing research."

"That's because there was nothing to stalk."

"What did he say?"

"His line of work necessitates a certain level of anonymity."

Aine raised her eyebrows, but nodded her head. "That makes sense. What else did he say?"

"That we'd talk when he gets back."

"See? That isn't so bad."

Quinn wished she could agree. More, she wished that they hadn't looked him up in the first place and she was still in blissful ignorance, imagining him as her knight in shining armor, her guardian angel, her protector. Instead, she was fretting over who he was and why he called her precious.

They'd just gotten back to the guest house where she and Aine were sleeping, when Quinn's phone buzzed. She pulled it out of her pocket, hoping it was Mercer, instead it was the last person she'd expected to hear from.

"Hello, Mother," Quinn said when she accepted the call.

"Hello, Quinn."

"I've been calling—"

"I called to tell you that I have to go out of town for a few months, and you won't be able to reach me."

"What do you mean by 'a few months'?"

"I'm not certain. I'm hoping to be back before Thanksgiving. Goodbye, Quinn."

"Wait—"

Quinn heard the three chimes indicating the call had ended. "Unbelievable," she said to herself.

"Who was that?" Aine asked when Quinn walked inside the guest house.

"My mother."

"*Seriously?* What did she say?"

"She's leaving town, and I won't be able to reach her while she's away."

"How's that different? Wait, that was a shitty thing to say. I'm sorry."

Quinn shrugged and walked into the bedroom. *No different.* It wasn't any different now than it had been any other time of her life. Her mother had been unreachable for the last twenty-one years.

—:—

"Do you think Calder really has anything on Leech?" Mercer asked Paps late Sunday morning.

"I don't know. As it stands, even if he does, he has no reason to use it. Wendt contacted him directly and told him that the seller has been forced to withdraw the estate from the market because, legally, it wasn't hers to sell. What could he say then, that he knew Leech wasn't alive, because he or his Russian cronies killed him? Otherwise, Barbie's keeping her mouth shut about the wine."

Mercer still wondered. He doubted someone like Calder would be placated so easily.

"Has Max briefed you?" Paps asked.

"Not yet." He was planning to get with him later, though. "Who vetted him?"

"Razor."

That made him feel better. Razor didn't mess around when it came to people they'd work closely with. While

Max didn't seem like the smartest guy they'd ever hired, Mercer's guess was the man had other strengths.

"Mad and Al are up to their same old tricks, but it appears to be just another one of their speed bumps. Shame she wasn't pregnant," he heard Paps say.

This part of the job made him uncomfortable. In his opinion, it wasn't necessary to talk about the personal lives of their assets if they didn't directly relate to the mission. Not that Maddox Butler and Alex Avila were assets. If anything, they were ancillary, only important to him as they related to Mercer's commitment to Doc.

"Maddox has been sniffing around," added Paps.

"Meaning what?"

"We should anticipate he'll continue to stick his nose where it doesn't belong."

The last thing they needed was for Maddox and Calder to engage any further than they already had. If things between them went south, they might be forced to turn Doc's brother into an asset, and that was definitely not something he, Paps, or Razor would want to do.

Last night, Lena had told him she intended to inform Maddox of her departure. Mercer wasn't sure yet when that might be, but told her she needed to be ready to go when they made the decision it was time.

She also asked what she should do about Calder wanting her to sell him the property, and he told her that had been handled.

"Also, everything is set with the ATB," Paps told him. They were aware that the Avilas were hiding wine, and if the time came when they were alerted to that fact, they'd bring Paps and Mercer in as part of the team. Otherwise, a hundred barrels of wine hidden in someone else's caves to avoid paying an insurance bond didn't amount to shit to them.

"Give me the rundown," Mercer said to Max when they met a couple of hours later.

"As I told Paps, Enzo Avila was in the caves when Maddox and Naughton found the wine, and so was Calder."

Mercer nodded. "What else?"

"Earlier today, Maddox asked Lena if she knew who it belonged to. She said she didn't, but he suspects she's lying."

Dammit. Paps had been right; Maddox was sniffing where he shouldn't be. "What else have they found?"

Max shook his head. "Nothing yet. By the way, what's the backstory on Calder?"

That wasn't information he needed to know, and that he asked, bothered Mercer. He walked away without answering, and Max didn't follow. He wasn't sure what Max was up to, but the more questions he asked, the less Mercer trusted him, and the less he'd read him in on.

Calder's on the property, said Max's text.

One of the other contractors had already informed Mercer, who was headed back from the west side of the estate. He'd been looking for two structures that were rumored to be on the property, but he hadn't found either yet.

Where are you?

Front gate perimeter.

By the time he got there, Max reported Calder was gone.

"Barbie asked Maddox to meet her at Il Conti for dinner," he told Mercer, who nodded.

He was familiar with the place.

"Calder overheard," he added. "I think he's planning to be there."

Mercer nodded again. Calder was about to act; he could feel it in his bones. He only hoped that, when he did, he left Lena out of it.

"We'll meet there prior to their expected arrival," Mercer told Max. "I'll brief Paps."

"Incoming," Paps said, motioning toward the front door of Il Conti later that evening. Mercer turned around in time to see Alex Avila walking into the bar area, where he was seated. When he turned back, Paps was gone.

She sat at the bar, a few stools over from him, and chatted with the bartender. A few minutes later, Calder joined her but showed no signs of having recognized Mercer.

Instead, he leaned in and kissed Alex's cheek, before she leaned away from him. They talked briefly about the wine she'd ordered, and then she suggested they move to a table.

Mercer sent a message to Paps, confirming that he was still at the bar and that Max was at a table in the dining room. He also let him know that Calder had joined Alex, and it appeared that he'd invited her to meet him there.

Several minutes later, Maddox walked in with Lena. Mercer wished he'd been the one sitting at the table in the dining room rather than Max, only so he could see everyone's reaction. Calder was likely the only of the four who had prior knowledge of who would be there, since he'd obviously been the one to invite Alex Avila.

It wasn't long after Maddox and Lena had stopped by Calder and Alex's table, and then took their seat at a table not far from them, that Alex stormed out. Maddox wasn't far behind her.

Mercer stayed where he was, but alerted Paps. When he saw Calder approach Lena, he decided to move into the dining room and join Max.

"You're looking very *mature* this evening," Mercer heard him say.

"Fuck you," Lena hissed through clenched teeth.

"Now, now. Is that any way for you to talk to the former love of your life?"

It didn't appear he rattled her, in fact, Lena looked bored. "What do you want?"

"The list has grown somewhat since the last time we talked, sweetheart."

"I can't help you. Find someone else to blackmail."

"I disagree. I think you're in the perfect position to help me get everything I'm after."

Mercer realized he was holding his breath, willing Lena not to react, and she didn't. She wore the mask of disinterest well, and he was proud of her.

"Stay the hell away from me," were the only words she said to him before Maddox returned to the table a few moments later.

In the conversation that followed, Maddox shut Calder down when he tried to discuss the rumor that the Avila family's Los Caballeros Winery had a bond issue.

When Maddox stood to leave and offered to walk Lena out, her eyes met Mercer's for the first time since he'd entered the dining room.

He shook his head and turned to Max. "Let's get her out of here."

Max stood and walked toward the restrooms. Mercer motioned with his head for Lena to follow, and then heard her decline Maddox's offer and excuse herself.

Mercer sent a message to Paps that Max was transporting Lena, and to be on standby. It was only a few minutes later that Mercer watched as it dawned on Calder that Lena wasn't coming back, and left himself.

Paps followed Calder to the Tablas Creek Winery and stayed until another of their team could take over his surveillance.

Mercer had been back at the house in Harmony a little over an hour when Paps walked in with Lena behind him.

"I want her gone," he said after she'd gone into the bedroom and slammed the door behind her. He scrubbed his hand over his face. "Does she really need to do that?"

"I hear you. Although I felt sorry for her last night. Earlier tonight too."

Paps pretended he was falling off his chair.

"She was contrite."

"It's an act."

Mercer didn't like Lena anymore than the rest of them did, but every once in a while, he thought they could be a little more understanding of the hellish life she'd been forced to live.

"Heard from Razor?" Paps asked.

"No. Should I have?"

Paps shook his head. "Not a bad assignment."

"Seriously? You're gonna go there?"

"Nah, just givin' you some shit."

He had plenty of it swirling around him; he didn't need more from Paps. He got up and walked away.

"Callin' it a night?" he asked.

Mercer nodded before he shut the bedroom door behind him.

It was one in the morning on the East Coast, and since Razor was the lead on Quinn's detail for the time being, Mercer didn't expect to hear from him or anyone else, and he hated it.

For the last almost year and a half, there'd been very few days he hadn't known what she'd eaten for breakfast, lunch, and dinner, where she'd gone, and who she'd talked to. Not knowing those things was making him crazy.

It was worse than that, though. She wasn't speaking to him, and it was his own fault.

Mercer got up and went back to the kitchen where he found Paps still sitting at the table.

"I'm going to tell her the truth."

Paps shook his head. "No, Eighty-eight, you're not."

"I'll lose her."

"Tell her now, and you will for sure. There won't be any coming back if she's dead. Let her be mad at you. Hell, let her hate you if it's gonna keep her safe." Paps paused. "You *know* this."

10

Quinn found Mr. Sharp's business card sitting on the kitchen counter. After the call from her mother, she'd forgotten she was supposed to call him.

"Mr. Sharp? This is Quinn Sullivan. You asked me to call," she said when he answered.

"Call me Tabon, and yes, I did."

"Something about the interview?"

"Right. My guess is you're not any more anxious to get back to the city than I am. Why don't we meet tomorrow at ten? How about at Michael's?"

Quinn agreed, thanked him, and ended the call, but didn't set her phone down. Instead, she stared at it, wishing she'd hear from Mercer.

She hadn't heard from him after she'd ended their call—although she shouldn't have expected to, since she'd essentially hung up on him.

She thought maybe he'd send her a text, but there'd been nothing. Maybe she shouldn't have been such a bitch about his reticence to talk about himself and what he did for a living.

She set the phone down on the counter, went upstairs, put on her bikini, and grabbed a towel.

It wasn't until she was settled in a beach chair that she realized she hadn't picked her phone up on her way out. It didn't matter. She'd put Mercer in the same category as her mother had always been. There was no point in checking her phone to see if she'd heard from either of them.

"I can't eat another bite," Tara said when the waiter asked if they wanted dessert.

"I can. What about you?" Aine asked.

"Sure, what sounds good?" Quinn answered.

Both twins had a sweet tooth, and she never minded having a bite of whatever one or both of them ordered for dessert. She wished they'd hurry it up though; this dinner was dragging along much the same way her day had.

She hadn't been at the beach very long, that afternoon, before the rest of the tribe joined her.

"You left this inside," Ava had said, tossing Quinn's phone on the towel next to her.

"Thanks," she'd muttered, wishing no one had noticed. Not having her phone with her had been freeing. Of course she'd had to look then, to see if Mercer had tried to contact her, and of course he hadn't, which left her in a foul mood for the rest of the day.

She wasn't alone in that either. Her four friends seemed equally grumpy, even Aine, who was almost always in a good mood.

"Too bad your interview is here tomorrow," she muttered. "I'm ready to go back to the city."

Overhearing, Penelope scowled at them. "Thanks a lot."

"It isn't personal, Pen," said Quinn. "It's just…"

What? That it was the beginning of summer and none of them had a promising romance? It made them sound so pathetic. "How long are you staying?" she asked, not finishing her prior thought.

"Through the Fourth of July, at least."

Quinn had no reason to get back to her apartment. Even if her interview went well tomorrow, the position wasn't due to be open until the end of summer. No one was in the city in July or August.

"Can I stay?"

A smile broke across Penelope's face. "Yes!" she practically shouted, and high-fived her.

"I'm sorry, Pen," said Aine. "Can I stay too? I don't know why I said I wanted to go home."

Ava and Tara both chimed in, saying that neither of them had wanted to leave in the first place.

"So it's settled," said Penelope. "Fourth of July party here on Fire Island."

Quinn tried to muster the appropriate level of enthusiasm, but she wasn't staying because she wanted to party.

"Have you heard from him?" Aine asked on their walk back to the house.

She shook her head. "I wasn't very nice when we talked last night."

"Maybe you should reach out to him, then."

She'd been thinking the same thing all day, but every time she picked up her phone to send him a message, she'd decided against it. When he left, yesterday morning, he'd told her he'd stay in contact while he was gone. He hadn't asked Quinn to do the same.

There was no point trying to fall asleep. It wasn't happening. Reading, which usually worked, at least to quiet her mind, wasn't helping at all.

Quinn had always been an insomniac. Her mother told her that even when she was a week old, she didn't sleep. "You'd shake yourself awake. It drove me crazy," she'd tell her. The only time she didn't have trouble falling to sleep was when she was with Mercer.

Her fingers itched with the need to send him a message, if only to say goodnight. It was two here, which meant it was eleven on the West Coast. He'd probably still be awake, wouldn't he? She tossed and turned another fifteen minutes before she finally gave in and sent him a text.

Hi. She held her breath, waiting to see the moving dots indicating he was responding.

Why are you awake, precious?

What would she say now? Because she was worried that he was mad at her for being mad at him?

Before she could decide what to say, Mercer's caller ID showed up on her screen.

"Hi," she answered.

"Quinn," he sighed. "It's good to hear your voice."

She smiled. "It hasn't been that long, although you probably don't want to think about our last conversation."

"We need to talk about it."

"Now, or when you get back?" She got out of bed and paced, too antsy to sit still.

"Both."

"Go ahead."

"Do you remember when I told you to trust your instincts with me?"

How could she forget? It was something he'd said more than once. "Yes."

"I need you to do that now, precious. There are things I can't discuss with you, certain questions I won't be able to answer."

"Because of your job?"

"Yes," he answered simply.

"And that's why there's nothing about you online."

"That's right..." He hesitated, but she didn't speak, waiting to see if he'd continue. "Close your eyes, Quinn."

She sat back on the bed and did as he asked. "Okay, they're closed."

"Tell me what you see when you think about me."

"The first thing is the way you smile at me."

"How does that make you feel?"

"Safe," she said, before she could stop herself. There was more she wasn't sure she could admit. Cherished, but even more than that.

"What else?"

"You're going to think I'm crazy."

"You feel safe, so tell me."

"Loved." She closed her eyes tight and clenched her jaw, waiting for his response.

"Trust that."

"But..."

"Please, precious. Trust your instincts. Trust *me*."

"I want to." She hated doubting him; it made her doubt herself.

"Can you?"

It took her a while to answer. She wanted whatever she said to be honest. Quinn closed her eyes again, and thought about him. Her feelings were the same as they were moments ago. "I can," she finally said.

"I'm glad. Now tell me why you're awake in the middle of the night."

"You."

"I was afraid that's what you'd say. Are you feeling better now? Do you think you can sleep?"

"Can we talk a little while longer?"

"We can talk all night if you want to."

—:—

It wasn't long before Mercer knew Quinn had drifted off. He kept the call active, just in case she woke up, but after a while, he knew she wouldn't, and pressed the "end" button.

He was asking a lot of her, but Paps had been right. He couldn't tell her the truth about himself, or how he knew her, yet. First, they had to figure out what Calder was doing back in the States. When they did, he hoped it would somehow lead them to either find Doc and Leech alive, or confirm they were dead. Either way, at the end of their mission, he intended to take Calder out, and without it being said, he knew Paps and Razor felt the same way.

Mercer couldn't afford this lack of sleep. The next few days could lead to the break they'd been waiting for, and he needed to be rested in order to act on it. He closed his eyes and willed himself to think about Quinn rather than the bad guys he was protecting her from.

When he opened his eyes again, the sun was shining through the bedroom window. He looked at his watch, shocked that it was after ten. How had he slept so late, and why had Paps let him?

He got up in search of a cup of coffee and an answer to both questions.

After he'd had his first cup of legal stimulant and was on his second, he went in search of his partner. He found Paps sitting in a chair on the back deck of the house, staring off into hills behind it.

"It's beautiful, isn't it?" he said when Mercer closed the back door and sat in the chair next to him.

"It is. Is that what you've been doing all morning? Thinking about how beautiful California is?"

"I didn't say California was beautiful. I said those hills were. Good sleep?"

"Yes, as a matter of fact. You?"

"Been up since dawn."

"Why didn't you wake me?"

"No reason to. We're in a holding pattern for the time being. Oh, by the way, Skipper got the job."

"Wait. What? Did she go back to the city?" God, he really hated not getting her reports.

"Tabon decided to interview her on the island instead."

Mercer laughed and shook his head. "Tabon, huh?" He'd rarely ever heard Paps refer to anyone by anything other than by their code name.

"That's who he is when he's her boss."

"He's never her boss."

"You seem in better spirits today."

Mercer told Paps about the conversation he had with Quinn in the middle of the night, and how afterwards, he'd been able to sleep and so had she.

"Tell me what Razor meant when he said history repeats itself."

Paps took a long time to answer, as though he was mulling over whether to tell Mercer the story. "You know that side of Lena you said you saw last night?" he finally asked.

"Yeah?"

"That's how she used to be all the time."

"When she and Doc were together?"

Paps nodded. "He fell pretty hard, but in the end, it wasn't destined to be between them."

Mercer sure as hell hoped Razor wasn't right about the history thing. He was convinced he and Quinn were destined to be together, and he didn't want anything to change that.

"Why not?" As long as Paps was talking, he figured he'd keep asking questions.

"After she was raped, Barbie changed. Who wouldn't have? The bastard literally beat her within an inch of her life." Paps was quiet for another minute, but then turned to look straight at Mercer. "Doc tried, but what could he do? By that point, he was too important to the team for him to quit, not that he would've. Serving his country was everything to Doc. That's who he was. There was no way he could give it up for Barbie, and then years later, for Peyton."

"What about Quinn?"

"That's complicated, and since no one asked my opinion at the time, I can't comment on the decisions they made."

Mercer understood. As hard as he tried, he couldn't bring himself to ask his next question. Did the answer really matter?

Paps continued. "Doc always did what he thought was best for both of them. He supported them in every way he could, although neither of them would've ever hurt for money."

This was part of what Doc hadn't read Mercer in on. He knew the kind of money he, Paps, and Razor made now, but Doc couldn't have made that kind of money before they started K19. Even if he had, it wouldn't have been enough to support Lena and Quinn for the rest of their lives, particularly considering the way they lived. "Why not?"

"It's Elisabetta's money. It always has been."

Mercer recognized the name. "Lena's mother?"

Paps nodded.

"That's how Doc got the land."

Mercer was doing his best to follow along, but Paps' economy of words was making it difficult.

"She left it to him."

"Care to elaborate?"

Paps phone pinged and he looked at the screen. "Maddox and Naughton found the house and the winery."

"Yeah?"

"Barbie is with them now, telling them its history."

It was another example of the woman's humanity. It must've made her happy to be able to talk about her family, her grandparents in particular, who had built the house as well as the other buildings on top of the hill. It was Mercer's understanding that, shortly after they died, Lena's mother was diagnosed with Parkinson's, the same disease that took Quinn's great-grandfather's life. She must've been terrified.

"I feel sorry for her. The way her mother died..." Mercer said out loud, not necessarily meaning to.

"I felt sorry for Leech," added Paps. "Something died inside of him when his wife got sick. All the plans he'd had for his retirement turned to dust. He and Elisabetta planned to bring the vineyards back and turn the property into a thriving wine business. None of that came to fruition. Instead, he simply watched his wife deteriorate."

From what Mercer knew, the disease was not typically hereditary. The research he'd read indicated that only ten percent of Parkinson's cases were genetic. Still, if both his grandfather and mother had died from it, he'd be vigilant about watching for symptoms. He wondered if Lena did. And what about Quinn?

"After Elisa died, Leech retreated. Doc was worried, but Leech acted before any of us could intervene."

"You couldn't have predicted he'd do what he did."

"No? I'm not so certain."

If he were in Paps' shoes, he'd feel the same guilt, logical or not.

"It's time you knew more of the story, but first, I'm hungry. Let's go to Sadie's."

"Sure. I'll just...uh, grab my wallet." He was going to say he'd take a quick shower, but he sensed that Paps wanted to talk now, and he didn't want to miss his chance. In particular, he wanted to know why Lena's mother had left Doc half the estate, and how her daughter, Kade's former wife, felt about that.

Five minutes later, they were seated in the diner. Sadie had taken their order, and they were waiting for their food when Paps started talking again.

"He trained all of us, you know. Me, Doc, Razor, Calder."

Mercer lost his appetite. With every word Paps spoke, the picture became more clear. Leech Hess had recruited Doc, Paps, Razor, and Calder, and the latter betrayed them all.

"Doc and Boiler, that was Calder's code name, back then anyway, they had a love/hate relationship from the start. Some days they were close, like Razor and me. Other days you could tell they wanted to kill each other. Barbie was always in the middle. Even in those early days, it was a tossup as to who she'd end up with. One day she'd favor Doc; the next day, it was Boiler."

"What happened?"

"The Marines. Hell, I don't need to tell you it's all about competition. Boiler was used to being the best at whatever he did. When Doc came along, that changed. You could see it build between them like a tangible energy field. In the end, Boiler lost."

"What did he lose?"

"Everything. Barbie. Delta Force. Leech wasn't even sure if Boiler would be recruited into the NCS."

"Because he saw something."

"Yep. In the same way we see something isn't quite right with Max. We hone those instincts in order to stay alive."

Mercer nodded. Didn't he know it. "How'd they turn him?"

"That's probably the part Leech wished he could go back and change the most. He thought that Boiler would rally, work harder, try harder. I guess that's what they call tough love these days. It didn't work, and that was the beginning of the end."

Paps looked out the window, away from Mercer. "Boiler had always been good with languages, spoke three or four almost fluently, including Russian. I've wondered sometimes if they went after him, or if it was the other way around."

"He couldn't have had much clearance." They'd all been so young, younger than Mercer was when Doc recruited him.

"No, he didn't, but Leech did."

Paps told him that Calder had managed to hack into Leech's system and decode thousands of classified documents, that he then handed off to the Russians. What resulted was the death of at least a dozen US operatives.

"I have to tell you, I'd never guess he was that smart."

"He wasn't."

"Then how'd he do it?"

"He had help from a beautiful, brilliant, and insanely lethal agent."

"What happened to her?"

"Doc killed her. If he'd had another ten seconds, he would've killed Calder too."

"Who stopped him?"

"Leech." Paps shook his head and looked out the front window again. "That's enough for today," he said when Sadie delivered their food.

Mercer moved his food around his plate, piecing together what he could of the rest of the story.

What he didn't know was when the rape had occurred. It must've been after Doc killed the other agent; otherwise, Leech would have let him finish Calder off.

"He'll need a to-go box," he heard Paps tell Sadie.

Mercer looked over to see he'd cleaned his plate and paid the check already.

Paps checked his phone. "It's later than I thought, and we're expecting company."

"Who?"

"Laird Butler."

Mercer stopped in his tracks.

"Come on, Eighty-eight. I'll fill you in on the way back."

"Gunner, it's good to see you," said Laird when Paps invited him in.

When the two men smiled and shook hands, it was evident to Mercer that they'd known each other a long time.

"Burns, this is Eighty-eight."

Mercer stepped forward to shake his hand. "Hello, sir."

"I've heard a lot about you, son. It's a pleasure to finally meet you." Laird pointed at Paps. "He's quite the gatekeeper."

"Sit down, Eighty-eight," Paps said. "You look like you're gonna faint."

Both Laird and Paps laughed, and Mercer did as he'd suggested and took a seat.

"Over breakfast, I briefed him on pretty much everything Doc left out in terms of what happened with Boiler twenty years ago."

Not everything, thought Mercer, there were still a lot of holes.

"Breakfast? At this hour?" exclaimed Laird. "What the hell kind of operation have you turned this into?"

He pointed at Mercer. "It was this guy. I was up at dawn like always."

"Let's take a walk," Laird said to Paps. They left, and neither one suggested he join them.

"How'd he get the code name Burns?" Mercer asked when Paps came back half an hour later and Laird wasn't with him.

"A couple things. You know the Scots, Robert Burns ranks higher than God himself. In addition to that, I've never known an agent who was better at taking out bridges than Burns Butler."

Mercer understood. In the intelligence community, burning bridges meant cutting links in every operational chain if a mission was compromised, so none of the parts could ever be put back together.

"The apple didn't fall as far from the tree as everyone thinks," he commented.

"Hell, no. Doc idolized his father. Wanted to be just like him," said Paps.

"Yet, none of Doc's siblings know about Laird's *other* career."

"That's right. Remember I told you that Leech's dream had been to bring the vineyards back to life, retire, and make wine?"

Mercer nodded.

"Where do you think he got the idea?" Paps shook his head and smiled. "Burns and Leech…well, that's a story for another day. Anyway, when Burns quit the agency and committed himself full time to the ranch, Leech envied him and decided to do the same."

"But Laird was born to it."

"So was Elisabetta. Yet, she chose the life she led with Leech. There were no secrets between them, other than what he was restricted from telling her, and she understood that part."

"What about Sorcha?"

"Have you heard the story about how the two of them met?" Paps asked.

He shook his head. "No, sir."

Paps put his hand on Mercer's shoulder and squeezed. "I'm done telling tales today. Don't you have an asset to check up on?"

"I can't believe you held out this long, Eighty-eight," Razor said when he answered Mercer's call.

"How is she?"

"Skipper?"

"No, the Queen of England."

Razor laughed. "Settle down, son. She's fine. Antsy, but fine."

"How'd the interview go?"

"As you'd expect. She was professional and polite."

"Glad to hear it. Listen, there are some things I need to read you in on."

Fifteen minutes later, Mercer hung up. Razor knew everything he knew, both about what had transpired in the last forty-eight hours, and what Paps had told him about Leech and the team's early days.

When he came back, Paps was outside, having a beer—with Lena. Something told him he shouldn't interrupt. Instead he sent a text saying he had to go into San Luis Obispo.

Yesterday he'd forgotten to pick up the frame he had the artist make for Quinn. Besides that, Mercer needed to get out on the road for a couple of hours, clear his head, and process everything he'd learned today, so tomorrow he could craft the next part of the mission.

He was on his way back to the bike, frame in hand, when he saw someone familiar checking it out.

"This yours?"

Mercer nodded and looked over at the motorcycle parked next to it. "That yours?"

"Sure is." The man extended his hand. "I'm Naughton. Is this a Monster?"

"Name's Mercer. And yeah, a 1200."

"It's a beauty."

"Thanks. Is that an R5?" Mercer walked closer to the vintage bike. "Fifty-two?"

"Yep."

They talked for a few minutes about the new bike versus the old. Both the Ducati and the BMW were equally impressive.

Mercer put his jacket on, tucked the frame inside, and zipped it up. "You up for a ride?" he asked.

"Sure. Got one in mind?"

"Nope. You?"

"How much time you got?" Naughton asked.

"Nowhere I need to be," he answered.

Paps had suggested he engage Doc's younger brother, and it couldn't have worked out better if he'd planned it.

"It'll bring us back here, but the views aren't as good if we don't come up from the south."

Mercer gave him a thumbs up, and followed when Naughton pulled away from the curb.

"Wanna trade for the ride down?" Naughton asked when they reached the top of See Canyon Road and stopped to take in the views.

"Sure," said Mercer, mimicking Naughton's earlier enthusiasm. "In a minute, if that's okay."

"Take your time, no better views in the county."

Mercer set his helmet on the seat of his bike and walked across the road, to the boulder he saw jutting out from the hillside. Naughton was right about the view. Beyond Morro Rock, he could see as far north as the Piedras Blancas Lighthouse, at least an hour away.

"How's the ride down?" he asked when Naughton sat down on the big rock near him.

"Not as hard. More fun."

"Sounds great." Mercer looked back out at the vast Pacific Ocean and felt a pang of regret. If he weren't Doc's younger brother, Naughton would be someone he'd like to get to know better. As it was, establishing a friendship seemed wrong. It would be another relationship based on secrets, with Mercer knowing more about the person than he should—just like with Quinn.

The ride back into town was fun, but like Naughton said, not as much of a challenge. He loved riding the BMW though, and rethought his plan to buy a Ducati to keep in the city. Instead, maybe he'd look for an old R5 like Naughton's.

"Got time for a beer?" he asked.

Mercer checked the time even though he had nowhere to be. "Maybe one."

They went into the same restaurant where he and Paps had met the other day, and sat at the bar. When

Mercer took his jacket off, his shirt pulled to the side, and Naughton noticed.

"My brother had ink a lot like yours," he said.

"Yeah?"

Naughton didn't say anything else, which only made Mercer feel shittier. *I'm sorry about your brother,* he wanted to say. *I knew him well, in fact, I considered him a brother myself.*

"You from around here?" Naughton asked a few minutes later.

"No, the East Coast. Just here on business."

Naughton didn't ask what kind of business, but Mercer hadn't expected him to.

"What about you?" he asked.

"Born and raised here," he answered. "A few miles north, in Paso Robles."

"Wine country," Mercer commented. "In the business?"

He nodded. "I'm a vineyard manager for Butler Ranch."

"I know their wine well."

"Come by some time, and I'll give you a tour of the place," Naughton offered.

"I'd like that."

A few minutes later, when Naughton stood to put his jacket on, Mercer did too. They'd had their beer, and it was time to part ways.

"Good to meet you," Naughton said as they walked out the door.

Mercer turned and shook his hand. "You, too." He waited for the other bike to pull away before he got on the Ducati. He started it up and sat for a minute, rubbing his hand over his chest and missing Quinn.

Tuesday was as quiet as Monday had been, but both seemed like the proverbial calm before the storm. He was on edge, and so was Paps.

"Slow down; I can't understand you," Mercer said when he answered a call from Lena.

"He knows."

"Who knows what?"

"Maddox knows I was married to Kade."

"Tell me what happened."

Lena explained that she'd been showing Maddox photos of the vineyards back when her grandparents were alive. "A photo of Kade and me must've been stuck to one of the others, and he saw it."

"He saw the photo; that doesn't mean he knows you were married."

"I told him."

"It's inconsequential at this point," he said.

"*Shit,*" she gasped.

"What?"

"Calder is here."

"Paps will take care of him."

"What if he followed Maddox out?"

"He didn't."

"I don't trust him."

"You don't trust me either."

"True," she said right before she hung up.

A few minutes later, Paps called to report that Calder was gone. "He showed up right after Maddox left, wanting to know what Lena had told him," Paps said.

"Where is he now?"

"Moving the wine."

By dawn the storm hit landfall. At a little after five, the call came in from the Alcohol Tax Bureau.

Calder had paid some of Naughton's vineyard workers, Max included, to take the wine from the caves, back to Los Caballeros. At the same time, he called the ATB. The only thing they hadn't anticipated was Calder fingering Naughton Butler as the snitch.

By the time Mercer arrived at Los Cab in ATB gear, Gabe Avila was ready to kill, and Naughton Butler was in his crosshairs.

Unable to keep Gabe from going after any of the Butler brothers without blowing their cover, the team was forced to watch the afternoon's events play out, including Alex Avila landing in the hospital when she got between Maddox and her oldest brother's rage.

"Time to go, Barbie," Paps said to her when they got back to the house in Harmony.

Her reaction was palpable. It was like watching ten years come off her age.

"When, specifically?" she asked.

"Nightfall," Paps answered.

Shortly after the sky had turned dark, Mercer pulled up to the estate's main gate and killed the bike's engine. He rolled it inside and waited for Max to show. As he surveyed the property, a vehicle caught his eye, and it wasn't the one he'd expected to be there.

"*Shit*," he spat, recognizing the license plate of the truck. What the hell was Naughton Butler doing here?

He sent a text to Max. *Change of plans, meet me at the south gate.*

"Why? I'm right here," Max whispered behind him.

Mercer pointed to Naughton's truck. "That's why."

"You want me to move it? I thought this was where we were supposed to meet?"

"*That's* the truck you took?"

"Paps said to use the ranch truck."

"*Jesus-fucking-Christ.* Who the hell is that?" he growled as another vehicle pulled through the gates. Thankfully, he'd moved the bike out of sight, and he and Max-the-idiot were under the cover of the woods.

"Maddox," answered Paps, who came out of the woods on the other side of the dirt road after the truck had passed.

"What is he doing here?" Mercer asked.

"Barbie called him," answered Paps, coming out of the woods. "I told her to."

"Why?"

"To tie up the loose ends so he'll back off. I suggested she tell Maddox that Calder was blackmailing her to keep his knowledge of the wine secret."

Mercer's eyebrows scrunched.

"Don't worry, Eighty-eight. I had her tell him that Calder was using her marriage to Kade as incentive to get her to help him."

"Good thinking, Paps." That would make sense to Maddox, and maybe he'd quit sniffing around.

For now, though, they needed to get Naughton's truck the hell out of there.

"*What's that?*" asked Paps, pointing at the very thing Mercer was worried about.

"I got the wrong vehicle," Max confessed.

Mercer knew Paps well enough to know he wouldn't freak out. "No one is going to die because of this mistake," he was known to say, and Mercer tried to remember that when the little shit started piling up.

Before Mercer could suggest Max leave now to exchange trucks, they saw headlights coming back down the dirt road. The three men moved back into the woods.

"Jesus Christ," whispered Paps, watching as Maddox stopped, got out, walked over, and looked inside Naughton's truck.

Once Maddox drove away, Paps pointed at Max. "Get your ass to Butler Ranch, put Naughton's vehicle back where you found it, and get the ranch pickup that's parked to the right of the winery building."

Max left before Paps could say anything else.

"Let me guess, Naughton's was parked on the left side."

"Hell if I know, but how else do you explain it?" Paps started to walk away, but turned back. "Go. I got this. There's a plane waiting at the airfield to transport you to New York."

"What are you talking about? Why?"

"Because I said so."

"Not good enough." Mercer had a hell of a lot of respect for Paps, but recently he'd begun treating him like an employee instead of a partner, and he didn't like it.

"Skipper, asshole."

Mercer wasn't sure what to do. He'd never been in this situation before.

"I'm transporting Barbie myself," Paps added. "And when I get back, I'm hiring a whole new crew."

Mercer laughed. "I'm with you there. You say Razor vetted these guys?"

"With his head up his ass."

"Thanks, sir," he said, slapping Paps on the back.

There wasn't any way he would've gotten a flight tonight if Paps hadn't arranged for the plane. This way, he'd fly all night and land in the morning.

"By the way, Skipper is still on the island."

Mercer already knew that. It didn't matter how much shit went down in the last forty-eight hours; he'd checked in with Razor every chance he had.

11

"Are you bored?" Aine asked Quinn at breakfast.

"A little bit." She wasn't bored as much as she missed Mercer. She hated being *that girl*, but even though she'd vowed not to be, she couldn't help herself; he was all she thought about.

"How mad do you think Pen would be if we went back to the city for a couple days, and then came back for the party."

"She's going to be pissed that we're not staying over the weekend."

"I know, but I can't handle another seven days on this island. It's been fun, but God, we're the youngest people here."

Quinn rolled her eyes and laughed. If they left later today, by tomorrow, everyone their age would be back here to celebrate the long holiday weekend. "We should stay."

"I knew you were going to say that," Aine grumbled. "Have you heard from the mysterious Mr. Mercer?"

"Not really." She'd gotten a few texts, but still no word on when he'd be back. It was one reason she wanted to stay on the island. She couldn't go back to her apartment and sit there, waiting for him. She'd go crazy.

"What should we do today? Wait, I know. Let's go the beach. *Again.*" Aine rolled her eyes and huffed her way back into the bathroom to take a shower.

Quinn got up from the kitchen table and filled a bowl with fruit she'd cut up last night knowing that if she didn't do it before she went to bed, they'd eat crap for breakfast again today. It wasn't that she didn't love the freshly baked croissants they'd had every day since they'd arrived, but if she didn't stop eating them, she'd have to go buy new bikinis because hers wouldn't fit anymore. When she heard the ping, Quinn left the bowl of fruit on the counter and grabbed her phone off the table.

Good morning, precious.

She smiled and did the math. It was six in the morning in California. *You're up early. Hitting the gym?*

Thinking about going for a bike ride.

Sounds nice. Maybe instead of going straight to the beach, she and Aine should ride around the island, get some exercise to help work off all those croissants.

Want to join me?

She'd like nothing better. *Sure. I'd love to.*

Then come outside.

Quinn looked out the breakfast nook window and saw Mercer standing just outside the guest house's gate, with two bicycles.

"*You're back,*" she squealed and ran out the door, through the gate, and into his arms.

"I'm back."

"You didn't tell me."

Mercer cupped her cheek and covered her lips with his. Quinn wound her arms around his neck, kissing him back.

"I left late last night instead of waiting to catch a flight today," he murmured. "I wanted to surprise you."

"You sure did. How'd you know I was...never mind. I don't care. I'm just so happy you're here."

"I missed you, precious," he said, holding her tighter.

"Are you here just for the day?" She knew she sounded disappointed. The solution was easy though, if he was going back to the city later, she'd go with him.

"No. Why?"

"You don't have a bag or anything."

"I have a friend who has a place here."

"Of course you do," she said, laughing.

"I thought you hadn't heard from him," Aine shouted, coming out the same door Quinn had.

"I'm a surprise," Mercer told her right before she hugged him.

"You're too good to be true," Aine said, and then looked at Quinn. "Isn't he?"

She leveled her gaze at her friend, willing her not to say anything about Mercer's lack of internet presence. Instead, Aine went in a different direction.

"Do you have a twin by any chance? I need one of you for me."

"You need one of him for you?" Quinn burst out laughing.

"You know what I meant." Aine laughed too.

"He's got a buddy with a house here."

"Is he single?" Aine asked.

"He's not here; I'm just staying at his place."

"Oh, well." Aine leaned forward and kissed Quinn's cheek. "I'll see you later?"

She looked at him, and he nodded. "At some point."

"Have fun!" Aine waved behind her and walked through the garden to the main house.

"Ready to ride?" he asked.

"Um...sure."

He pulled her toward the bike. "Come on."

Quinn looked down at what she was wearing. "I should change, and I haven't showered yet."

Mercer wrapped his arm around her waist and pulled her close to him. "I thought you might want to take a shower with me."

"I'd like that," she murmured.

"This time we won't be rushed."

"Okay," she said, climbing on the other bike, and trying to slow down her breathing. "Where are we going?"

"Not very far."

"Thank God."

"You weren't kidding about it being close," Quinn said when they pulled the bikes up in front of the beach house.

"We should talk," he said as they put the bikes on the side of the house.

Talk was the last thing Quinn wanted to do.

Mercer put his hand on the small of her back and guided her to the side door. He unlocked it and held the door open for her to go inside.

She stood with her back to the kitchen counter while he locked the door behind him. Her eyes were glued to his when he met her gaze. Mercer stood in front of her and put his hands on the kitchen counter, boxing her in.

"Did you hear me?"

She nodded. "I just..."

He waited for her to finish, but instead, she let out a sigh.

"It would be so much easier sometimes if you'd just finish my sentences for me." She laughed and so did he.

"I know you think I can read your mind, precious. But I can't."

"Can we talk later?"

Mercer shook his head. "No, we can't. Because after we do, our relationship is going to change."

"In a bad way?"

"No, precious. In the best way."

"Oh."

"Come here." Mercer led her over to the front of the house, to a sofa near the front windows, which looked out over the water. They sat, and he put his arm around her shoulders.

"I am affiliated with K19 Security Solutions, Quinn, but I don't work for them; I'm one of the owners."

"What does your company do?"

"Lots of stuff that I can't talk about."

She nodded.

"I'll tell you this much. Most of our work is with the federal government and the national security agencies."

"Like the CIA?"

Mercer nodded. "Yes, and the others."

"Were you in the military?"

"At one time I was."

"I thought so."

Mercer smiled. "Yeah?"

She nodded and smiled too. "You remind me a little bit of my grandfather, not that I knew him all that well. I mean, I did, but I haven't seen him in so long."

"As far as what I do goes, no matter how our relationship progresses, my inability to discuss the details of the work I do with you won't change." He waited again for her to respond, and when she didn't, he continued. "The majority is highly classified. I need to know, Quinn, do you think you'll be able to handle this long-term?"

"It helps that you told me this much. Will it be the same? When you go out of town, will you keep in touch with me? Can we talk?"

"Not always. When I can, I will."

"Oh." She looked away.

"Talk to me, precious."

"I'm not sure how I feel, to be honest. I'll worry a lot."

"That's natural."

"What if something happens to you?" She regretted the question as soon as she said it.

"You'll know in the same way you'd know if I was in a car accident, or something else happened unrelated to the work I do."

"That's fair, I guess. Is there anything else?"

"That I can tell you?"

She nodded.

"Not a lot, except I hope you'll trust me, and believe I only want the very best for you. I never want to hurt you, or even make you unhappy."

"What about your tattoo?" She held her breath, hoping he'd answer.

"A big part of what I do is to protect people."

"You see yourself as a guardian angel?"

"Yes. To a certain extent anyway."

"Okay." She paused. "Mercer?"

"Yes, Quinn?"

"How is our relationship going to change?"

"Let's take that shower and see. Shall we?"

She nodded and crossed her arms, hoping he didn't notice how much she was shaking. The idea that this was it—she and Mercer were about to have sex—overwhelmed her.

"Quinn?"

She smiled. "Yes, Mercer?"

"What happens or doesn't happen between us today or any other day, isn't predetermined. Like before, we'll go with what feels right to both of us."

"Okay."

"Anything else you want to ask me, or talk about?"

"I don't think so. Not talking would be preferable, actually."

He drew her closer to him, and looked into her eyes. When she tried to look away, he put his fingers on her chin. "When I ask how you're doing, I want you to answer me honestly, okay?"

Quinn could feel her face turning ten shades of red, and the tremors in her body worsen. When he didn't look away, she realized he was waiting for an answer. "Yes."

—:—

Mercer scooped her up in his arms, the only way he could think of to alleviate the tension that threatened to derail them before they even got started. Quinn had been bolder than he ever could've predicted when she'd undressed and joined him in the shower six days ago, but now she was cautious, worried, and so anxiety-ridden her body trembled.

He carried her into the bedroom, set her on the edge of the bed, and gently pushed her shoulders back. Then he rested his clothed body against hers.

He covered her mouth with his, soft at first, but then harder. The idea that she was his—all his—made him crazy with want. He slowed again, pulling back to look into eyes that were glazed over, pupils dilated, as she searched his for what would happen next.

Mercer slid his hands under her shirt, gripping her breasts through her bra. He had to taste her; he couldn't wait a minute longer. Quinn's hands pulled at the fabric, and together they got it over her head and flung it to the floor.

"God, you're so beautiful," he growled, burying his face in her neck as, with a flick of his fingers, he unclasped her bra and moved the cups out of his way.

Quinn pulled it from her body, throwing it to the floor.

His eyes took in her perfect, full breasts. His lips followed, and he trailed his tongue down to where he'd feasted only days ago. Now, though, he was breathless in the knowledge he could spend all day lapping their sweetness. Beneath him, Quinn began to writhe, her body reacting instinctively to their shared desire. Her back arched, and she cried out his name as his wet mouth closed over her nipple. She raised one knee, and he stroked her bare thigh with his fingers.

"These have to go," he said, unbuttoning her shorts and easing the zipper down slowly, as though he were unwrapping a treasure.

Quinn lowered her leg, and then lifted for him. He pulled them off with just a glimpse of the pale pink panties that matched her bra. Later, in the days to come, he'd take his time, savoring her beauty as he made her undress before him. Now, though, he couldn't control his urge to have her naked beneath him.

Once every inch of her lay bare before him, he stood between her legs, which hung off the edge of the bed, and drank her in, from her pretty pink toes, up the body he'd had countless dreams about, to her eyes that were locked onto his.

Mercer's nostrils flared and his breathing became more labored as he pulled his shirt over his head and threw it on the floor. She sat up and ran her hands over his chest. Chill bumps covered her body as his tongue swirled and licked trails over her bare skin.

"Breathe, precious," he whispered as he rested each hand on the inside of her thighs. "Open for me."

As his fingers trailed up, so close to her sex, she scooted away, farther up on the bed, but his fingers followed until they touched her heat.

"Oh, God," she cried, and opened her squeezed-shut eyes, embarrassed by her reaction.

He smiled down at her with a mixture of pride and desire. "You're magnificent," he murmured before kissing her again.

She tugged at the waistband of his shorts. Tearing his lips from hers, Mercer unfastened his belt, unzipped, and dropped them and his underwear, freeing his hardness. She leaned forward, trying to reach him with her hand.

"Careful, baby," he sighed, his jaw clenched tight as he moved her hand away.

"I'm sorry. I wish I knew what I was doing."

"Don't ever apologize for wanting me, and what you're doing is perfect," he said, lowering himself so his body stretched out next to hers.

"Please, Mercer. Teach me what to do," she begged.

His eyes trailed over her body, until she flushed again.

"I will, precious, but first I want to look. Whenever we're apart, I want to see you just like this. Open for me, wanting me…I want this every day, Quinn, for the rest of our lives."

She shuddered as he leaned over her and reached between her legs. He marveled at her responsiveness, watching as she bit her bottom lip, pulling at him.

As much as he wanted to be inside her, he held back, taking his time as his fingers explored her body. Her moans of pleasure almost undid him.

"You like that, precious?" he asked, probing deeper.

"Yes," she answered, moving her body against his hand. "I want more, Mercer."

When he gave her what she wanted, her body arched, her thighs quivered, and her mouth opened, letting the sweetest sound he'd ever heard escape from her lips.

Mercer waited for her to come down from her climax, licking the perspiration from her neck and shoulder, until he saw her eyes open.

"Don't you want to..." she murmured.

He loved the way she struggled to finish her sentences, particularly when she knew he wasn't going to do it for her. He watched as her mouth formed words she didn't speak.

"I do," he said, freeing her from her torment. "But you have to be ready first."

She continued to writhe as he explored the depths of her with his hand and mouth, wringing cries of pleasure from her again and again.

He waited again until she caught her breath and opened her eyes. While she watched, he reached over and pulled a condom from the nightstand drawer, and rolled it on.

"Precious," he said and waited until her eyes met his. "This will hurt, but only for a moment."

She nodded, her eyes beseeching, and her body yearning.

Slowly he took her, watching as her eyes rolled back in her head. He swept his tongue into her open mouth and swallowed her cry of pain. He stilled then, waiting for it to ease. When Quinn started to push back against him, he knew she was ready for more.

He thrust harder and harder, his body rubbing against hers, and soon he felt her tighten, clenching him as her body bowed again and her cries escaped. He couldn't stop himself from joining her in the most intense, perfect ecstasy he'd ever experienced.

He kissed her throat, her chest, and her nipples. He ran his tongue around her belly button and then his mouth found hers again. She wriggled under him, and the expression on his face changed.

"Being inside you feels so good, so perfect," he groaned, as his hips began to move again. Mercer wove his fingers in her hair, and his other hand gripped her hip. "I need more of you," he growled. His jaw set firm and his eyes stared into hers as he took her higher and higher, until he knew she'd explode again.

She grabbed his shoulders, digging her nails into his skin, as he withdrew from her body and collapsed beside her.

"My God," he groaned against her neck. He pulled her closer so their bodies were flush against each other.

"I didn't know," she whispered. "I had no idea it would be like this."

He raised his head to look at her. "Only us, Quinn. You and me. It's never been like this for me before."

"It hasn't?"

"Not even close. This is how it's supposed to be, our bodies and souls connected. That's the magic, precious. That doesn't happen without a love so deep that you can feel the other person in your heart, in your bones. When it's like that, you know it's right, and nothing else will ever be again."

She closed her eyes and rested her head on his chest, another thing he loved.

"Precious, precious Quinn," he said before her breathing evened out, and he knew she was asleep.

—:—

When she woke, she was alone in his bed, but she could hear him moving around in the kitchen. She found his t-shirt on the floor, next to her clothes, and put it on. She was on her way through the bedroom door, when she went back and put on her panties too. This was unfamiliar territory for her. She had no idea how to act, and wished she'd woken up next to him.

Instead of going into the kitchen, she ducked inside the bathroom first and looked in the mirror. Her face was flushed, mottled almost, and her hair was frightening. She tried to tame it with water, but that didn't help. She used the toilet, and was on her way to find him when she heard a knock on the door.

"Quinn?"

She opened it and smiled. His voice sounded so sweet, like a little boy almost.

"Are you okay?" he asked, his brow furrowed.

"I'm fine. How are you?"

Could this conversation be any more awkward? What was wrong with them?

"Come here," he moaned and pulled her into his arms, and with that, the discomfort she'd been feeling melted away.

When he kissed her, she whimpered. His lips touching hers sent currents of desire flowing through her. Now that she knew what he could do to her body, she wanted more. A lot more.

"I made breakfast," he said, brushing her hair away from her face. "God, you're beautiful."

"Thank you," she murmured. "Breakfast?"

"I thought I should feed you before I ravish you again."

"I like the sound of more ravishing," she whispered, running her tongue from his ear down his neck.

"Breakfast can wait," he groaned. He walked her backward, farther into the bathroom, reached in, and turned on the shower. "We didn't take our shower earlier."

His t-shirt that she was wearing landed on the floor, along with his shorts. Quinn was about to slide her panties down her legs, when he put his hand on hers.

"No more of these, for the rest of the day," he growled and pulled the thin fabric until it tore.

Quinn thought she'd faint with her desire for him anyway, but when he ripped her panties from her body, her knees went weak, and she grasped his arms to steady herself. "God, Mercer, that was…"

He waited for her to finish in that maddening way he did.

"So…*hot.*"

He pulled her into the shower with him, and backed her up against the tile. The coolness of it felt so good in contrast to her overheated body.

"I asked you before if I frighten you…" he began.

"You don't," she said, finishing his sentence. "Not at all."

"If I ever do, I want you to tell me."

It sounded like he was talking about sex, but she wasn't sure. "Mercer?"

He rubbed his hardness against her as his lips attacked her neck. "I don't want to hold back the way I'm feeling. I won't hurt you, though. I promise."

She grasped his shoulders with her hands, and dug her nails into his skin, leaving marks. "Don't hold back," she groaned. "I want you, all of you."

With his powerful hands, he lifted her bottom, and she wrapped her legs around his waist. His mouth came down on hers, and he kissed her hard.

"Take me, Mercer. Please. Don't make me wait."

The sound he made was between a groan and a growl. "No condom." He gripped her bottom tighter until she was molded against him. "Hold on," he said, carrying her out of the shower and into the bedroom.

He set her on the bed, like he had before. "Don't move."

She watched him walk back into the bathroom and turn the shower off. When he came back in, he opened up the nightstand drawer and tossed a couple of condoms on the bathroom counter. With his teeth, he tore open another one, and she watched as he rolled it on.

"Are you sore?" he asked, lowering himself so he rested between her legs.

She shook her head, but when she felt his fingers, she gasped.

Mercer moved away from her, and she reached for him.

"No, it's okay," she told him, but he slid away from her grasp, down her body, and soothed her soreness with his mouth.

Quinn wove her fingers in his hair, holding him close to her, wanting him closer still. "Oh, God," she hissed between clenched teeth. "Mercer…"

"Let go, precious," he breathed against her, and she exploded, writhing against his mouth, wanting more, but wanting him to stop too. Her nerve endings were raw, exposed, and she pulled at his hair. "Stop," she moaned, but he didn't listen. Instead, he drew every ounce of pleasure he could from her body, until she dropped her arms, unable to hold them up any longer.

Mercer ran his fingers through her damp hair. "I want to be inside you more than I want to breathe, precious," he whispered.

"Why aren't you?"

"Because you're sore, and I promised not to hurt you."

She caught his hand with hers and stopped him from caressing her scalp. "Tell me what you're thinking," she said.

He took a deep breath. "How precious you are to me. How I'd do anything for you."

"Why do you sound sad?"

"I'm not. I'm the furthest thing from sad. It's more that I am so in awe of you, and how strong my feelings for you are."

"Tell me."

He smiled. "You already know."

"Tell me anyway."

Mercer leaned forward and kissed her forehead, and then each of her eyelids, the tip of her nose, and then her mouth. "I don't want to scare you."

"You don't. I feel safe with you, Mercer. I feel loved."

"See? You do know."

"I want to hear you say it."

With each of his palms cupping her cheeks, he took a deep breath, and then kissed her again. "I love you, Quinn. I think I've loved you forever."

"Do I scare you?" she asked.

"Sometimes."

"Why?"

"Because you hold my heart in the palm of your hand, precious."

"I'd never hurt you either."

"What should we do today?" Mercer asked after they'd showered and were in the kitchen, making breakfast, just like they had the last four days in a row.

"You've been so good about doing everything I want to do, even spending time with the tribe. What do you want to do? And don't say whatever I want."

"I want to go sailing."

"Wow. Um...do you know how?"

He smiled. "I've sailed a few times in my life."

"I think there's a place on the other side of the island that rents boats."

"Not the kind of boat I want to sail."

She set down the knife she was using to chop vegetables for an omelet, and turned around to look at him. "You have a boat, don't you?"

He nodded and smiled.

"Here?"

He nodded again.

"Oh, Mercer. Will there ever be an end to your surprises? Where is it?"

"She's docked at Seaview right now, but I want to move her."

"Where?"

"Here."

Quinn looked out at the bay and saw the dock in front of the house. "I didn't notice that before."

"After breakfast we can go get her, sail for a while, and then bring her here."

"Sure you can wait for breakfast?" She smiled.

Mercer wrapped his arms around her waist and kissed her neck. "Just barely."

She loved the way he let her lean back against him, the way her body molded into the hardness of his. It hadn't been an hour since he was last inside her, and yet she wanted him there again.

They'd spent every day here, on the bay front, only going back to Penelope's father's house to get her clothes. They'd gone for bike rides, went running on the beach, spent time with her friends, and more time alone, in nothing but each other's arms.

He'd told her that, if the house weren't so open, he'd rather she never wear clothes, as it was, most times he kept her in as little as possible.

He reached down and cupped her sex with one hand, eliciting her whimper.

"We'll never go get your boat if you start that." She smiled.

Quinn's eyes nearly popped out of their sockets when Mercer pointed to the boat docked in a slip a few feet from them.

"You're kidding, right?"

He shook his head. "That's *Aurora*."

"Wow. She's beautiful." The boat was exquisite. Even from the dock, Quinn could see every detail was well thought out by a fine craftsman, and that she'd been cared for since the day she was launched.

"She's named after my mom," Mercer said as he held out his hand to help her aboard.

Quinn walked from stern to bow, marveling at the condition of the teak deck.

"There are two cabins, aft and forward, and two heads, although only the aft has a shower," he said when she came back by the wheel where he stood. "Shall we go below?"

"Sure," she answered, walking over to the companionway.

The saloon and galley below deck were more spacious than she'd thought they'd be, especially given the two cabins. "Fifty? Sixty feet?"

"Forty-two with a twelve-foot beam."

Quinn raised her eyebrows and ran her hand over the brass plate that read Hallberg-Rassy.

"She was built for comfort and functionality more than speed, but she holds her own. I definitely wouldn't race her," he added.

"Is this a Frer design? I learned to race on Tara's father's F3."

Mercer nodded, impressed that she recognized the builder.

"The F3 was nothing like this, more just a hull with the bare bones below."

The teak below deck was equally well-maintained as above, and the gray, blue, and red used for the cushions and accents in the saloon and cabins matched the yacht's hull colors. "She's really beautiful, Mercer."

He smiled and ushered her toward the stern. "The aft cabin has two berths," he said, stepping inside. "Or one." He folded the chair down that separated them and winked.

"How did you get her here?"

"My brother Hudson and a couple of his friends sailed from Cape Charles here."

"You're kidding?" She laughed. "When did you arrange that?"

"On my way back from California, I called and offered him a lot of money to bring her here. I told him that, once she was delivered safe and sound, I'd treat him and his buddies to two nights in New York City. The wind was on their side, and she arrived late yesterday afternoon."

"How did you manage to keep her a secret?"

"It wasn't easy." He pulled her close and buried his face in her neck. "I wanted you more."

She backed away, knowing that, once they got started, it might be hours before they were under sail. "Do you have any other siblings?"

Mercer grinned. "Trying to distract me, precious?"

"Yes," she murmured.

"Hudson is the youngest, and Owen is between us."

"Two brothers. Any sisters?"

Mercer shook his head. "Mom was really outnumbered."

"Are you close to your parents?" Quinn tried to keep her voice light, as though the questions she was asking were completely innocuous, but she couldn't bury the hurt she felt, thinking about her own mother.

"I was. They died in a car accident fifteen years ago."

"I'm so sorry." And here she'd been feeling sorry for herself because she didn't know where her mother was, at least she was still alive.

Mercer nodded. "Thanks. It was tough."

"You're the oldest, then." No wonder he felt like everyone's protector; it was the role he fell into when his parents died.

"Our aunt, my mother's sister, moved in after we lost Mom and Dad. She's a gem, and kept us in line."

"What's her name?"

Mercer laughed and shook his head. "Her name is Ariana, but we always called her Auntie Air. I guess it started when we were little, and it was easy to say."

He walked back over to the companionway. "Shall we get on our way?"

It was a big boat for them to handle on their own, but since he seemed confident, Quinn didn't argue.

"Wanna take the helm?" he smiled.

"I will after we're away from the docks."

"Deal."

There wasn't a lot of wind, and they weren't going far, so Mercer only raised the genoa, which he could manage on his own.

"You're good at this," he said, joining her at the wheel.

She loved to sail, especially out on open water. She closed her eyes and felt the wind, knowing it was best to keep her touch light.

"You're amazing," he said from where he stood, watching the sail less than he watched her.

"I'm going to let you take her in, though," she told him.

"It's just like parking a car, precious."

She laughed. "I've never driven a car in my life."

"Do you want to learn?"

"I guess so. I mean, I might not live in the city my whole life." She shrugged. "Maybe I should."

"I'll teach you."

"Do you have a car other than your friend's fancy one?"

He shook his head, and an odd look briefly came over his face.

"What?"

"It's nothing."

"Don't do that."

"Sorry. It's nothing. I promise. I think the Jaguar is the perfect car for you to learn in."

"I love the Fourth of July," Quinn said the next morning. "I guess it stems back to when we used to spend it in California with my grandparents. They lived not far from where you were, in Paso Robles. Have you heard of it?"

"I have. I visited several wineries in that region."

"What a coincidence. They owned a vineyard. Several actually, but after my great-grandparents passed away, it fell into neglect..."

"What did you and your family do to celebrate?"

Quinn told him about barbecues and fireworks, but her favorite part was that it was the only holiday where her grandparents invited a lot of people to the estate.

"My grandfather was very patriotic," she explained. "What about you? Did your family do anything special to celebrate?"

"Cape Charles was a great place to spend the Fourth every year. There were parades, both in town and in the water. Like you, our family had barbecues with the neighbors." He paused. "I'd love for you to meet Auntie Air one day."

Quinn cocked her head. "What about your brother? You didn't want to spend the holiday with him?"

Mercer laughed. "More the other way around."

"What are you thinking about?" she asked.

"My family. How I want to spend more holidays with them."

"I don't really have one," she muttered.

"I disagree."

Quinn had been looking out at the water, but turned around. "How so?"

"You have Aine, Ava, Tara, and Penelope. The five of you are closer than most sisters."

She nodded. "True."

"You have me." Mercer put his arms around her. "And I have you."

Quinn smiled. "I like that."

"Me too." He looked over her head at the clock inside the house. "We should get going."

"Already?"

He smiled. "We said we'd be there an hour ago, precious."

"I guess we better go, then."

Instead, Quinn slid her hands under his shirt and kissed up the side of his neck to right below his ear. "I don't think they'll notice if we're a few minutes later."

"A few minutes?"

Quinn nodded and took his hand, pulling him inside.

They got there a little over two hours later than they said they'd arrive at Penelope's father's house, but with the number of people there, Quinn doubted they would've been missed at all if it wasn't for the food and wine they'd agreed to bring.

"There you are," Pen said, taking the large bowl of fruit salad from Quinn's arms.

"Sorry—"

"No apology necessary, girlfriend. We like seeing you this happy."

"Thanks. I like being this happy." Quinn looked over at Mercer who was loading bottles of white wine into the outdoor kitchen's refrigerator.

"He seems like a great guy," said Tara, picking chunks of pineapple out of the salad with her fingers.

"Quit that," Aine said, slapping her hand. "Other people are going to be eating out of this bowl." She thrust a serving spoon into Tara's hand. "Use this."

"What are you all smiles about?" Ava asked Quinn.

"This morning Mercer and I were talking about families. When I said I didn't really have one, he disagreed and said the five of us are closer than most sisters."

"True that," said Aine, starting a round of high fives.

"We're going back to the city in the morning—"

"Tomorrow?" grumbled Penelope. "Do you know how crowded the ferry is going to be, Quinn?"

"It may be, but that isn't how we're going." Quinn told her five friends about Mercer's boat, and relayed his invitation to go back with them. Given the five had raced together on Tara's father's boat, he thought they might enjoy the sail into the upper bay where Mercer had rented slip space at the Liberty Marina.

"He has a Hallberg-Rassy?" Tara gasped.

Quinn beamed. "Yep. Forty-two."

"My dad is going to want to go too. Do you think Mercer would mind?"

"Ask him," Penelope said. "He's right there."

Mercer was leaning against one of the outdoor tables, listening, but not saying anything.

She walked over to him and rested her hands on his chest, loving the way his corded muscles felt beneath her fingers. If they hadn't just gotten here, she'd suggest it was time to leave. "What do you think?" she asked.

"Of course Tara's father can come along. The more on deck, the less I have to do."

"Although…I didn't realize he was bringing his latest girlfriend today. Can we tell him she has to take the ferry?" Tara whispered. "I swear she's my age."

The five girls looked over at the woman in question, who was completely oblivious to anything going on around her, except for Tara's dad. She hung as much on every word he spoke, as she hung on his arm.

"It's sickening," she said, turning away from them. "He'll trade her in for a younger model in a year, tops."

"She doesn't look like much of a deck ape," Ava added. "I predict she'll decline anyway."

Tara groaned. "Let's make it a dads' and daughters' sail."

Aine and Ava's father was at the party, too, and it was being held at Penelope's dad's house, so obviously he was there. He had a date, but the twins' father appeared to have arrived solo.

"You okay with all this, precious?" Mercer asked.

She nodded, turned her head, and kissed him. "As long as you're with me, I'm okay with just about anything."

12

Quinn picked up the framed photo Mercer had given her shortly after they arrived back in the city after the Fourth of July holiday. "Real—Forever," the frame read. The day he took the "selfie," he told her that, soon, she'd know their relationship wasn't a lie and that she wasn't alone.

So far, this had been the best summer of her life, and she hated seeing it come to an end. He hadn't been called away on business since late June, and since she wasn't due to start her job with the historic preservation group until after Labor Day, they'd spent every day together.

As promised, he taught her to drive his friend's fancy car, which she immediately fell in love with. He warned her driving any other car would pale in comparison, though.

Today they were kickstarting the Labor Day weekend a couple of days early by taking *Aurora* out for a sail. Her tribe and their dates were joining them. Mercer was heading out soon to get provisions while Quinn stayed at her apartment where they'd all agreed to meet.

Lately it didn't feel like "her" apartment as much as it did "theirs." Mercer spent every night with her and only went to his apartment to work.

At first it had been difficult not to ask about what he did, but she got used to it. Since she wasn't working yet, it felt like they were both on a summer-long vacation anyway.

There was something she wanted to talk to him about, though, and she'd been putting it off long enough that soon she'd run out of time.

"I'm heading out," he said from the hallway, but when Quinn turned around, he walked over to her instead. "What's this?" he asked, brushing a tear from her cheek.

"I need to talk to you," she said, backing up so he wasn't touching her.

Mercer sat on the couch and pulled her with him. "What's going on, precious?"

"I want to tell you about my mom."

"Now?" He looked at the time. "Your friends will be here shortly."

"You always do that."

"What?"

"Whenever I bring up my mother you change the subject, or, like today, say we don't have time for the conversation."

"I don't do that."

He did, and so often, it bothered her. "Sometimes I don't think you want to hear about my life."

"What? That's crazy."

She raised an eyebrow and folded her arms.

"I'm sorry. That's not what I meant. It isn't crazy, Quinn. I hate that you feel that way. We'll talk about her tomorrow when we have more time. Okay?"

She didn't feel like it anymore. "Forget it."

He pulled her arms apart and kissed her. "I'm not going to forget it. Tell me about her now if that's what you want to do."

"She's—"

The buzzer rang, indicating at least one of her friends had arrived, so Quinn stood. "Perfect timing, right, Mercer?"

He turned away, but she could still see how his eyes looked hooded and how tensely his jaw was set. It wasn't a look she saw very often, usually only after he came back from a few hours spent working.

For now, she'd ignore it. Her friends knew all about her mother, and the last thing she'd do was bore them and their dates with her sad little story.

Mercer was polite but quiet and reserved enough, all afternoon, that it bothered her. He was acting as though he was mad at her. She was the one who had every right to be angry, not him. The longer it went on throughout the day, the more pissed off she became.

When they docked the boat after their sail, and were packing up to go home, Aine approached her.

"We'd love to take you and Mercer out for dinner as thanks for our fabulous afternoon."

Quinn looked over at him. He had obviously heard Aine, but had looked away. "I'm not sure."

Her friend leaned closer. "Is everything okay between you two?" she asked. "You both seemed...tense all afternoon."

"To be honest with you, I don't know what's going on. We were about to have a conversation about my mother when you arrived. When I said we'd continue later, he got weird about it."

"Maybe you need some time apart. You have been joined at the hip all summer."

Quinn shrugged. Maybe they did. She hated the way he was acting. "I'll go," she said to Aine.

"Huh?"

"To dinner. I'll go. He can do whatever he wants to do."

Aine's eyes opened wider. "Are you sure?"

"Yep. Never more sure."

Everyone helped finish packing up, and since all five of them knew their way around boats, they were able to clean and furl sails, batten hatches, and secure the boat for the night.

"Thank you," Mercer said when everything was done. "I appreciate the help." He looked at Quinn. "Ready?"

"Actually...Aine and Ava invited me over to their place tonight for some girl time." She glanced at Ava who hadn't been privy to her conversation with Aine, but she went along with it. This was her tribe, and they'd stuck together since they were in second grade. If one of them let out a cry for help, no matter how subtle, the other four were there to give it.

Mercer scrunched his eyes and studied her. "Okay, then. Have a good night."

He walked away, leaving Quinn stunned and feeling like absolute shit, but this had been what she'd wanted, hadn't it? As Aine said, maybe they did need some time apart.

Once he was gone, she motioned Aine away from the group. "You don't have to do this," she said, looking over at their dates. "I'll let him get ahead of me, and then I'll go home too. Honestly I'd just like a night to myself."

"That's what you want to do?" Aine asked.

"Yes, absolutely. There's a book I started reading at the beginning of the summer that I haven't had time to finish. I want to take a long, hot bath, all by myself, and eat chocolate chip cookies for dinner without anyone judging me for it."

"Okay, if you're sure...at least see if Tom can pick you up."

All five of them had Tom's number in their contacts. He was their favorite cabbie and often made them feel like he sat on standby, ready to come and get them and take them wherever they needed to go.

"Good idea," she said and pulled her phone out. "All set," she said a minute later. "He'll be here in five."

"Sometimes it feels like he follows us around and then waits wherever we are to see if we need a ride," Ava said.

"I know, right? I was just thinking the same thing." Quinn rubbed her chest when a weird feeling came over her. She remembered thinking something similar about Mercer when they first started seeing each other. Inexplicably, it seemed like he knew her so well. It had been weird, just like it was weird that Tom was also always close by.

"Are you sure you're okay?" Aine asked, walking with her to where Tom waited.

"I'm positive," she promised.

"Have a good night, then."

"You, too," Quinn said, closing the door behind her.

"Where to, Miss Skip...Sullivan?"

She laughed. "What did you almost call me?"

"Nothing, sorry about that."

"No, really. What was it?"

When Tom shook his head and pulled away from the curb, Quinn felt a chill. She folded her arms and leaned back against the seat. For a minute she'd thought maybe they'd have a conversation that might distract her from thinking about Mercer's strange behavior, but Tom had slipped right back into his role as taxi driver.

Quinn's eyes filled with tears, and with no reason to hide them, she let herself cry the whole way back to her apartment.

"Everything okay?" Tom asked once, but didn't say anything more when Quinn nodded.

She pulled a credit card out of her wallet, realizing she didn't have any cash. She'd gotten so used to not carrying any. No matter how often she told him she could afford to pay her own way, Mercer never let her.

"Sorry," she murmured as she handed Tom the card.

"It's not a problem, Miss Sullivan," he said, his eyes meeting hers in the rear-view mirror. "I'm worried about you, though."

His kindness only made her cry harder. "I'm just tired. You know, a day out on the water, too much sun..." Quinn stopped herself. Maybe he didn't know. "I'm sorry," she said again, taking her card and climbing out of the cab. "Have a good night, Tom."

"You too, Miss Sullivan," she heard him say before she closed the door behind her.

By the time she got to the building's entrance, her favorite doorman was holding the door open for her.

"Hi, Vinnie," she said. "Long time, no talk."

"You've had a busy summer."

"I have, but it's coming to an end." When her eyes filled with tears again, she tried to hide them.

"What's wrong?" Vinnie asked.

"Nothing." She waved her hand in front of her face. "I'm just tired, that's all. Goodnight, Vinnie."

Quinn held it together until the elevator opened on the eleventh floor and she opened the door to her apartment. Once inside, she rested her back against the foyer wall, slid to the floor, put her head in her hands, and let herself sob.

Mercer's heart was breaking for Quinn, but he didn't know what to do about it. She'd made it clear she didn't want to be around him tonight, and he'd respect that. The two reports from Tom and Vinnie, both saying she was inconsolable, had him tied in knots. He was torn between letting her be, and going over and banging on her door until she let him in, holding her in his arms, and not leaving until she told him what was wrong.

He paced from one side of his apartment to the other, so worried he couldn't sit still. When his phone pinged, he jumped at it, fumbling with the screen in a way he never did, praying it was a message from Quinn.

Instead, it was from Paps, and what he read made him want to punch something.

Calder on the move. Need backup.

He couldn't say no. This was the mission. If Paps was calling him in, he had to go.

The summer had been quiet, and while every day that passed left him more worried about Doc and Leech, Calder hadn't done anything that gave them a lead.

Maybe this was what they'd been waiting for, and if so, they couldn't afford not to take advantage of whatever move he made.

Without needing to ask, Mercer knew the plane would be waiting at the airfield at zero six hundred tomorrow. He had no choice now; he had to go and talk to Quinn.

Leaving town tomorrow, he wrote. *Please talk to me before I have to leave.*

He held his phone in his hand, willing her to reply. A full fifteen minutes later, she did.

I'm here.

Mercer raced to the door, closed it behind him, and rounded the corner in the hallway. Quinn's shoulder rested against the door jamb, and she looked as though she'd been crying for hours.

"Precious," he breathed, cupping her cheek with his hand. "Why have you been crying?"

She walked inside, leaving him standing in the doorway.

"May I come in?" he asked.

She turned around and glared at him. "Of course you can come in," she huffed.

It clearly wasn't the time for him to tell her that he was trying to respect the boundaries she'd put in place today. Maybe he was overreacting.

When she sat on the couch, he sat next to her and put his arm around her shoulders. She didn't rest her head on his shoulder like she usually did, and he felt a chill because of it.

"What's going on?" he asked.

"I'm tired," she said, repeating what Tom and Vinnie had both told him she'd said.

"What else?"

She shrugged.

"Talk to me, Quinn."

"Why? You didn't talk to me all day. Why should I talk to you now?"

"That isn't true."

"Bullshit. You were cordial. That's it."

"I disagree."

"So do I."

He almost smiled at her tone, but stopped himself, thankfully, since she was already glaring at him.

"When are you leaving?"

"First thing in the morning."

"Where are you going?"

When he sighed, she got up from the sofa and sat in one of the armchairs.

"Forget I asked."

"Quinn."

"No, I get it. You don't have to tell me jack shit."

"We've discussed this—"

"Yes, we've discussed the fact that you can't tell me anything. You just forgot to mention that I can't tell you anything either."

"That isn't true," he repeated. "You can tell me anything."

"Bullshit," she said for the second time.

Mercer had just about enough, and stood. "I don't want to leave town with things so off between us."

"Then don't."

"You know I don't have any choice."

"Do I? I know that huh? Interesting that you think so. I don't know *anything*, Mercer. *Nothing.*"

He sat back down and waited, staring into her eyes like she was doing to him.

When she finally spoke, it was to ask him to leave.

"Please don't do this," he begged.

"It's late. You have an early flight. We'll talk when you get back."

Not knowing what else to do, Mercer stood and walked toward the door, hoping she'd change her mind and ask him to stay. He stood with his hand on the doorknob, waiting too long in the silence. He opened the door, walked out, and closed it behind him.

"Give me the rundown," Mercer said to Paps when he answered his call.

"Hey, Eighty-eight. I'm sorry—"

"Stop right there," he snapped. "We're in the middle of a mission."

"Got it." The rest of the conversation was brief and direct. When Lena disappeared, Calder backed off the Old Creek Road property. His plan to exploit the Avila's bond issue, and force them to sell, fell flat when the ATB let them off without as much as a slap on the wrist. He'd been asking around about other wineries at risk, whose owners would want to sell, but didn't have any luck there either.

"You believe he's going to force someone's hand?" Mercer asked.

"It's a gut feeling," Paps answered.

Mercer understood the importance of being vigilant solely because his gut told him to.

"There's a new winemaker coming on board at Butler Ranch," Paps told him. "Bradley St. John."

"What's his story?"

"Her story."

"Huh?"

"Bradley is a woman. Not much to tell. She's the Jensons' niece. They're winemakers whose vineyards are across the road from Butler Ranch."

Mercer had no idea why Paps was telling him this. If this was more gossip, he wasn't interested in hearing it.

"She's involved with Trey Deveux," Paps added.

Why did that name sound familiar? Mercer pulled up the files on his computer and did a search for the name. *There it was.* He was the one Lena had said signed the non-disclosure before Calder came and viewed the Old Creek Road property when it was for sale. Mercer dug a little deeper and found that the Deveux family had a connection to the Calder family by way of a marriage between a sister and one of Rory's younger brothers.

"What else do you know about her?" Mercer asked after telling Paps what he'd remembered and what he'd found.

"I don't think there's anything there. Maddox approached her about the job; evidently, she's an up-and-coming winemaker. I honestly think the connection with Deveux is coincidental, but certainly not something we should ignore."

"What the hell else haven't you read me in on?" Mercer snapped, more angry with himself than Paps.

"I don't like your tone of voice, Eighty-eight. We'll continue this discussion when you arrive tomorrow."

Mercer stared at the phone, incredulous that Paps had just hung up on him. He slammed it down on the desk.

Since there was no way he'd get any sleep tonight, Mercer made arrangements for Quinn's detail while he was gone, and then dove headfirst into the files that hadn't had his full attention since the beginning of summer. He'd let himself get swept away by his relationship, with an asset no less, and because of it, they were no closer to completing their mission.

He vowed not to let Quinn distract him any longer, but after two hours of staring at his screen, crafting absolutely nothing, he accepted the fact that she was all he was thinking about, and went to bed.

Tomorrow would be different, though. From the moment he set foot on the plane, his head would be back in the game.

"Shitty way to spend a long holiday weekend. How are you otherwise, Eighty-eight?" Razor asked when Mercer walked into the house in Harmony.

"Shitty is as good a word as ever." He momentarily held his breath, praying Razor wouldn't say anything about Quinn. He wasn't in the mood, and doubted he could contain his temper if his partner started in on him.

"I wish I knew what the fuck he's up to," Razor muttered instead.

Mercer looked over Razor's shoulder and studied the tracking report of Calder's whereabouts twenty-four hours a day.

"Who's that?" Mercer asked, pointing to a name on the screen.

"Name's Vatos. Lengthy arrest record but mostly piddly shit. Drugs, theft, that kind of stuff."

"What's Calder doing, meeting with him?"

Razor shrugged. "No idea."

"Who's on him?"

"Nobody. Think we should assign somebody?"

"Immediately."

Mercer had a bad feeling, but the worst part of it was he didn't know whether his gut was reacting to the mission or to Quinn, and it pissed him the hell off.

"Deveux is on his way here," reported Paps. "Hey, Eighty-eight, got a minute?"

"Yes, sir," he answered and followed his partner into the other room. "Before you say anything, I'm sorry about my attitude last night. I was out of line."

Paps leveled his gaze at Mercer. "I'm going to say this one time, so you better listen."

He nodded.

"You wanna know why Calder was able to get to Barbie? Because Doc had his head so far up her ass that he lost perspective. He lost his fucking focus. Don't let history repeat itself, Eighty-eight. You hear me?"

"Yes, sir," Mercer said again.

"Enough of this shit," he barked on his way out.

Fuck. Paps was absolutely right, and Mercer didn't know what the hell to do about it. He *knew* he had to get it together, but his brain refused to cooperate.

As usual, Mercer got very little sleep. Calder's association with Vatos weighed heavily on his mind, but not as much as the things Paps had said to him.

He rose with the sun and met Razor in the house's small kitchen.

"I need help," he admitted.

Razor turned around and looked directly at him. "What can I do?"

"Take over Skipper's detail. I'm done."

Razor nodded and offered him a cup of coffee. "It's only temporary, Eighty-eight," he said, but Mercer disagreed.

He walked out on the back deck, where the sunrise in the east enveloped the hills in pink and orange. Paps was right; these hills were beautiful. He was also right about him when it came to Quinn. He'd lost his focus and that was unacceptable.

"Uh, oh," he heard Razor say from the kitchen.

"What now?" he asked, going back inside.

"Skipper's on the move."

Fuck. Mercer looked over his shoulder again. "Where to?"

"Here."

Jesus. Why? What the hell was she up to now? So much for getting his focus back.

13

There was no way Quinn would sit around all weekend feeling sorry for herself because Mercer was gone. Two could play his game. He couldn't tell her where he was? No problem. She didn't need to tell him where she was either.

It had been far too long since she'd been to the place she considered home, even though she'd only visited but never really lived there. Paso Robles was her grandfather's home, and in the last few years, it had been her mother's home too.

For the first time in her life, Quinn was determined to make a connection with the only two people left in her family, whether they wanted it or not. Her only problem was, she didn't know where either of them were.

Maybe she'd find clues at her grandfather's house, and then travel to wherever one or both of them were.

The first flight tomorrow to the West Coast left at six in the morning, and she planned to be on it.

When she landed at the airport in San Luis Obispo, the first person she thought about was Mercer. She'd thought about him on her way to LaGuardia, and for the entirety of the plane ride too, but this time it was different. As she stood at the rental car counter, about to rent her very first car, she was grateful that he'd taught her to drive and even took her to get her driver's license. She couldn't wait to get out on the open road, all by herself, and go wherever, whenever, she wanted.

"I'm sorry, miss, but we don't rent to drivers under twenty-five," the agent said.

"What? I don't understand. I have my license."

"Yes, but due to liability issues, that's our policy."

"There are other car rental agencies; I'm sure another wouldn't have such an absurd policy," she muttered, more to herself than to him.

"No, miss. We all have the same policy."

"Quinn?" she heard a familiar voice say from behind her. She picked up her license and credit card, and turned around.

"Mr. Sharp, what are you doing here?"

"I'm traveling on business. You?"

"Um...taking one last vacation before I start my new job."

He smiled and then looked at the car rental agent. "What seems to be the problem?"

"I'm only twenty-one," Quinn answered.

"I see. Come with me."

"Where are we going?" she asked as he led her out of the airport terminal.

"To the parking structure."

"Why?"

Mr. Sharp laughed. "I hired you because of your inquisitive nature, Quinn. I'm glad to see you haven't lost it."

She felt her cheeks flush. "I'm sorry."

"Don't be. I told you I like it."

He handed her a set of keys and stopped by a parked car. "Hit the button for the trunk," he said, and when she did, he lifted her bag and put it inside, and then closed it.

"What about your bag?" she asked, noticing he hadn't put it in the trunk.

"I'm going out of town. You can use my car while I'm away."

"No, I couldn't. I mean, thank you, but—"

"The way I see it is, you don't have much choice." He smiled. "It's okay. I trust you."

"Do you live here, Mr. Sharp?" she asked, realizing he'd said he was traveling.

"I do, and please call me Tabon. I have a house on the beach, about an hour north of here. Where are you headed?"

"Paso Robles. My...um...family lives there."

"How nice. I bet they're anxious to see you."

Quinn's heart sank. *If only.*

"Did I say the wrong thing?"

Why was everyone so observant? "They aren't exactly expecting me."

"I see."

"You do?" Damn if Mr. Sharp didn't remind her of Mercer. It was as though he could read her mind.

"I've had my own share of…how do I say this…family issues," he said.

Quinn nodded. She wouldn't call her situation having issues, but she understood what he was saying.

"Tell you what. See that key?" He pointed to the only other one on the key fob. "If things don't go as expected, you can stay at my place."

"Seriously?" Quinn was stunned. "I can't. That's so kind, and incredibly generous, but, really, I can't."

"It's up to you. It'll be empty for several weeks, since I have a new employee starting in a few days, I'll be spending more time on the East Coast." He winked. "No pressure. If you find yourself in need of a place to stay, it's all yours."

"Thank you. Um, where is it?"

Mr. Sharp—Tabon—laughed. "An address would help, wouldn't it?" He pulled a pen out of his pocket and a card out of his wallet, and jotted the address on the back. "All set?" he asked.

Quinn nodded. "Thank you again, so much."

"You're welcome. Enjoy your time here, and Quinn?"

"Yes?"

"Stay out of trouble."

Mr. Sharp walked away, leaving her slightly stunned. It was just an expression, right?

It took her several tries to back the car out of the parking space, and then she got lost trying to find the exit in the parking structure, and then the highway, but now that she was on her way, she'd never felt more free.

She pulled up the directions to Paso Robles on the car's navigation system and turned the volume up on the satellite radio, enjoying her future boss's choice of jazz.

Maybe when she arrived, her grandfather would be home, and she wouldn't need to stay at Mr. Sharp's house after all.

"Can I help you?" asked an older man when she parked just inside the gate.

"I'm looking for my grandfather, John Hess."

The man raised an eyebrow. "Your grandfather isn't here, young lady."

"Oh, um, do you know when he'll be back?"

"He no longer owns this property. My sons do."

Quinn's eyes immediately, and unexpectedly, filled with tears. Not only were he and her mother not here, they'd also sold it. "I see...it's been so long," she muttered as she wiped her tears away. "My name is Quinn, by the way. Please excuse my bad manners."

"It's quite all right, and I'm Laird Butler."

Quinn extended her hand, and they shook. "It's nice to meet you, Mr. Butler."

"Please, call me Laird, and it's nice to meet you as well."

Quinn looked around, unsure what to do next.

"Would you like to look around?" he offered.

"I would, thank you. Your sons wouldn't mind?"

"Not at all. In fact, they've just recently taken possession of the property, so at the moment, they aren't here."

"I won't be long..."

"Take all the time you'd like."

"Thank you, Mr. Butler, I mean, Laird. I do that a lot...I'll just...um...take a walk," she stammered.

Laird smiled in a way that reminded her of her grandfather, even though it had been years since she'd seen him.

"Enjoy your day," he said and walked away, down a path that led through the woods.

Quinn walked back to the car, opened the trunk, and dug sunscreen out of her bag. It was so hot here; it had to be over one hundred degrees. It was less humid than New York City, though, and so wide open, it didn't feel as oppressive.

She could only see one structure from where she stood, and that was the house her grandparents had lived in when she was last here, and probably where her mother had lived before she'd left to go wherever she was.

Quinn tossed the sunscreen back in the trunk, closed it, and walked toward the house, wishing she had asked Laird if she could peek inside. As she walked past on the dirt trail that she remembered led to the vineyards, she sneaked a look inside through one of the windows. It appeared, from that vantage point, that the house was empty. Laird had said his sons had only recently taken possession of the property, so it made sense.

Maybe if she ran into him again, she'd ask if she could go inside, considering no one was living in it.

The house wasn't what held the most interest for Quinn though. She was looking for something much smaller, something she could barely remember, but it had been a special place for her and her grandfather.

The little wooden structure was on the far edge of the property, near the westernmost vineyard, that much she remembered, but only because they'd watched the sunset from there one night.

If she closed her eyes, she could see him, and even hear the words he'd spoken to her. She couldn't have been more than seven at the time, since it was right before she left for boarding school.

"From now on, I'll call this 'Quinn's cabin,' because every time I'm here, I'll be reminded of watching the most perfect sunset with my only grandchild."

She'd never dreamed that would be the last time she watched a sunset with him, or even set foot on this property. She remembered thinking, at the time, that she'd be back the next summer.

Her sense of direction was much better on foot than it had been in the car, particularly since it was easy to tell which way was west. There was a light breeze, and every once in a while, Quinn could smell the ocean and feel the chill it carried away from the water and over the hills.

It was part of the reason grapes were able to grow here so plentifully. The heat of the sun during the day, and then the temperature drop at night, allowed for the grapes to ripen, but not too quickly, ensuring the juice that was eventually pressed from them was complex and full of the sugars that yeast would eventually turn into wine.

She shook her head, marveling at the things her memory kept hidden most of the time, but brought back to the surface as she walked the land, feeling the sun on her face, and breathing in the scent of the earth.

—:—

"How did it go?" Mercer asked Razor, who raised an eyebrow.

"Fine."

"Is she staying at the house?"

Razor folded his arms. "Which way is it going to be, Eighty-eight? Are you done, or do you want to take back over Skipper's detail?"

He couldn't help himself. As soon as Razor had told him she was on her way here, his mind had raced with what that meant. Within minutes he'd rented a house in Cambria, where it wasn't as hot, and she could enjoy being by the ocean in the event she needed a place to stay.

"How's she going to get around?" he'd said to Razor, thinking through what else she'd need while she was here.

"Auto-mo-bile?"

When Mercer had said, "She's twenty-one." Razor conceded he hadn't thought of that.

They'd tracked her flight and made arrangements for Tabon to be at the airport when she landed, although he'd thought Mercer was overdoing it, making him take a bag along.

"She's smart," he'd said, as though that explained his overzealousness.

All the while, Paps watched, but didn't say anything, although the words he'd said a couple of hours ago still resonated in Mercer's head.

It wasn't until Razor left for the airport that Paps approached him.

"Burns will wait on Old Creek Road," he'd said. "Just in case that's where she's headed."

Mercer was stunned. "Thank you."

"I was too rough on you earlier," Paps said, walking away.

"No, you weren't."

Paps turned around. "It isn't the same."

Mercer wasn't so sure. He'd lost his focus; that was the biggest problem, and if Doc had too, then the inherent problems were exactly the same.

"She's there," Paps told him a little over an hour later. "Burns made contact, and she's walking around the property. Fortunately, Maddox and Naughton already left."

That's right, he'd heard they were in the vineyards earlier, with Alex and the new winemaker. "Thank you for letting me know." Mercer nodded, but his mind was on something else, and he was troubled.

"What's going on?" Paps asked.

"Calder and Vatos." Mercer handed Paps his phone.

"This is their third meeting," he commented.

"They're up to something." That was obvious, but the trouble was, each time the two met, it was out in a vineyard where whomever they had tailing them, couldn't get close enough to hear their conversations.

"We could engage Vatos," Paps suggested.

Mercer nodded. He agreed, but wished they'd done it after the second time they'd met. It would still be possible to get him to talk by offering more money than they knew Calder was giving him. He leaned back in his chair and scrubbed his face with his hand. Vatos was about to act; he could sense it, but he had no idea, no leads, and no clue as to what he might do.

When the next message appeared on his phone, Mercer jumped up from his chair. "*Fu-u-u-ck!*" he shouted. "*Fuck, fuck, fuck.*"

Paps came running from the other room. "What's up?"

"*Calder is on Old Creek Road.*"

"*Go!*" Paps yelled. "*I'm right behind you.*"

"*Engage Burns and whoever the hell else we can get on the ground,*" he yelled on his way out the door leading to the garage.

"*Roger that,*" he heard Paps answer right before the Ducati roared to life.

At best, he was thirty minutes away, and as he drove, every one of them ticked by like an hour.

Once he pulled up to the gate, Mercer didn't give a shit whether he came face to face with Calder, all he cared about was making sure the bastard didn't come in contact with Quinn.

Paps messaged that Burns was expecting him and that Calder was in the caves while Skipper was still in the western vineyards. In between, there were two operatives ready to intercept if necessary.

"Where is she exactly?" Mercer asked when Burns came out of the woods near where he'd parked.

"I've sent you the coordinates," Burns answered.

"And Calder?"

"Still in the caves."

"Who's on him?"

"Gunner."

Mercer was momentarily confused as he walked toward the bike, but then realized Burns meant Paps, who had obviously arrived before he had. He brought the coordinates up on his phone and briefly studied the best way to go. It was hard to tell how far he'd be able to get on the bike.

"Come with me," Burns said, already walking toward the trail. "You won't get through on that, and you don't want to alert Calder that you're here."

He looked at the coordinates again. It was a good fifteen-minute walk from where they stood.

"Can you ride?" Burns asked. "Horses?"

Mercer nodded. It had been awhile, but he'd manage. When he saw the two horses in the pasture, he hoped Burns meant the Appaloosa because there was no way he'd get on the enormous draft horse.

"That's Shazam, Maddox's horse. The other is Huck, who belongs to Naughton."

Shazam, the only one saddled, walked over to the gate when Burns whistled and called to him. He appeared gentle enough, but Mercer didn't care as long as he was fast and didn't try to throw him.

"Here," said Burns, handing him a big bag of red licorice. "He loves the stuff. Give him one piece at a time, and he'll do anything you want him to." He opened the gate and motioned for Mercer to follow. "She isn't in any danger presently. The trail is rocky; don't push him too hard."

Mercer nodded as he ran his hand from the horse's shoulder up to his flank, letting Shazam get comfortable with him.

"Thank you, sir," he said to Burns, and held out a piece of the licorice.

The horse took it, and then nudged him with his muzzle.

"You'll get more in a minute," Mercer told him, throwing his leg over and finding his seat.

"You're about the same height as Maddox, I reckon," said Burns, checking out the stirrup's adjustment. "Ready?"

Mercer nodded and led the horse through the open gate.

As he rounded a bend on the dirt trail, he could see one of the structures he'd been looking for but hadn't been able to find when he was here in June. Burns had told him that's where she was, and as he got closer, he could see the door was open.

He dismounted when he was close enough that Quinn might hear him approach, and tied the horse off to a tree branch. "You'll be good in the shade," he whispered, handing over another piece of licorice. "I should've thought to bring you some water."

When the horse neighed, Mercer froze. There, in the doorway, stood Quinn, holding several papers, tears streaming down her cheeks, with a look on her face he'd never seen before.

"I knew it," she said when he got close enough to hear.

"What did you know?" he answered, glancing at the papers in her hand.

"That you'd show up here."

"What have you got there?" He moved closer.

Quinn opened her hand, and he took the papers that had been scrunched in it.

As he studied them, she went inside, so he followed. She sat in an old, rickety-looking rocking chair and put her face in her hands.

"Did you know?" she asked.

He didn't answer right away; he was still trying to process what he was reading.

"Answer me, dammit. Did you know?"

Mercer looked into her eyes and nodded. "Some of it."

"Who is Angus Sullivan?" she asked.

Since the paper on top of the pile she'd handed him was a birth certificate, he understood what she was asking.

"A fictitious name."

She nodded and kept rocking, tears still streaming down her cheeks. Near the stone fireplace of the cabin, Mercer saw an opening cut into the rough, and dirty planks of the floor.

Mercer looked back at the birth certificate. In the box labeled "Father's name," it said Kade Butler, but that wasn't the worst of what she'd read. It was the next document that worried him more.

"She was raped," Quinn whispered through her tears, noticing that he was reading the police report.

When Mercer knelt on one knee in front of her and put his hand on her arm, she jerked it away from him.

"Yes, precious, she was."

"Don't call me that."

"Quinn, please. Let's—"

"Let's what, Mercer?" she spat, glaring at him.

He shook his head.

"This should be good," she mumbled. "Go ahead say whatever you were going to say."

"I'm sorry…"

"Who is Kade Butler?" she asked when he didn't say anything more.

"Your mother was married to him."

"I see. Not my father, though, at least not based on the date on the police report."

"I don't know."

"But you do know my mother."

Mercer nodded. "Yes."

"Do you know where she is?"

"I do."

He saw her hand coming, but did nothing to stop her from slapping his face. He deserved that and more for everything he'd kept from her. The slap stung, but he didn't react.

"What happened to the man who raped my mother?"

"I don't know," he said again, lying through his teeth and hating himself more with every word she spoke.

Quinn studied him. "*One question.* That's all you offered me, and yet, you know everything about me, don't you?"

He nodded, but didn't speak. The sound of his own voice admitting how he'd deceived her was something he didn't want to hear.

When she stood and walked out of the cabin, Mercer didn't follow. He expected to hear her walk away, but instead, she came back inside.

"I almost didn't see it," she muttered, pointing to the opening in the floor boards. "I was leaving. I never would've come back, either, but then something caught my eye. I walked over and ran my finger along the edge. It came up, just like that. You'd think the boards would've been stuck, but they must've warped." Quinn wiped at the tears that continued to stream down her cheeks.

She walked back out again, her shoulders hunched over in a way that shattered his heart.

He'd go after her, but what could he say? She had every right to feel the way she did. What had Paps said to him? "Let her hate you if it's gonna keep her safe." Now, keeping her safe was all that mattered, and he couldn't be the one to do it.

He called Razor. "Where are you?"

"I'm here on the estate," he answered.

"Have you seen Quinn?"

"Yes, Eighty-eight. I have."

"She's yours now. Take good care of her."

"I'll keep her safe, Mercer. You know I will."

Razor's use of his given name said a lot. He appreciated his reassurance, especially now, when he had to face that he'd failed her irrevocably.

If only he'd never...there were too many things he shouldn't have done, and now he understood why.

Never fall in love with a source, a target, or an asset. He knew better. It would never happen again, that he was certain of, because Quinn was it for him. She was the only woman he'd ever loved, and she would continue to be until the day he died.

14

Quinn stumbled her way back through the woods, stopping every so often when her sobs became so overwhelming she couldn't keep going. She'd lean up against a tree, or rest her hand on the trunk, until her tears subsided enough that she could focus on where she was going.

Where *was* she going? Back to New York? Or should she stay here and try to get answers to her questions? There were so many, though, she didn't know where to begin. She'd come here in search of clues about her mother's whereabouts, and instead she'd stumbled on a life she knew nothing about. *Her life.*

Thoughts flew through her head faster than she could process them. Memories flooded her brain, so many of them taking on new meaning.

She passed the house she'd wanted to explore a couple of hours ago, without looking inside, afraid that if she did, she'd unearth more secrets she couldn't handle.

Standing near her car with her hand gripping the door, she noticed a bench near a creek and walked over to it. She sat down and put her head in her hands, contemplating again what her next move should be.

"Quinn?" she heard a voice say. When she looked up, the man who had introduced himself as Laird *Butler* was standing near her.

"Did you know?" she asked him.

He stepped forward. "May I sit?" he asked.

Quinn nodded, scooted over, and waited for him to answer.

"I did," he said.

She turned to look at him. "How do you know what I'm asking about?"

"I just do."

"More *secrets,*" she muttered. "Who is Kade to you?"

"My oldest son."

Quinn folded her arms, waiting for words Laird didn't say. Obviously, he didn't think Kade was her father any more than she did.

"I have a lot of questions..."

"You may ask them."

"I'm not ready yet."

Laird nodded, pulled out a pipe, and filled it with tobacco. He lit it, and Quinn breathed in the aroma. She loved the smell of pipe tobacco.

"*Oh, my God,*" she cried, suddenly realizing why. "You know me, don't you? You've met me, and I've met you." Tears streamed down her cheeks again, although she didn't know how she could possibly cry any more than she had.

"Yes, I have."

Quinn wrapped her arms tighter around her stomach, leaned over, and let her tears fall. All she'd ever wanted in life was a family, and she'd had one, except they'd never wanted anything to do with her. The pain of it was ripping her to shreds. At least now she understood why. She was the child of a rapist. It explained why her mother hadn't been in her life all of these years. Quinn was a constant reminder of a horrific thing that had happened to her. Obviously, her mother's parents had felt the same way since, once she'd been shipped off to boarding school, she never saw them again.

"How old was I?"

"You were a baby, and then a little girl. We used to visit you and your mother quite often."

"Why did you stop?"

"We believed it was no longer safe."

"Because I'm some kind of monster? You feared for your safety from a *little girl*?" Quinn stood and turned away.

"We believed it was no longer safe for *you*, Quinn."

"Why?"

"Please sit back down."

She considered not doing as he asked, but gave in. If she wanted answers about her life, it sounded as though Laird Butler could give them to her.

"There are things that have happened over the course of your life that have necessitated certain decisions to be made in order to keep you safe."

"You already said that. My question was why?"

"The danger hasn't gone away, Quinn. If anything, you need protection more now than ever."

Quinn shook her head, furious with herself for thinking, only moments ago, that Laird might tell her *anything*. He was just like Mercer. *Wait.* Was he?

"How well do you know Mercer Bryant?" she asked.

"Not well."

"But you know him."

Laird nodded.

"He won't tell me anything either. Of course, I didn't realize, until today, that the things he wouldn't tell me were about *me*. I believed he couldn't talk about the work he did." Now she knew the two things were essentially the same.

"Does whatever I need to be protected from involve my mother?"

"It does."

"Do you know where she is?"

"I do not."

"Mercer does."

"He plays a role different than I do."

Quinn stood back up and rested her forehead against a tree. "I'm twenty-one years old. Don't you think it's time that I know *the truth?* It's *my* life."

"I believe, one day soon, you will, Quinn. But for now, I'm asking that you trust the people who have been protecting you."

Trust. How many times had Mercer told her to trust her instincts? How many times had he asked her to trust him? And all along he'd been lying to her. How could she trust her instincts when she hadn't even suspected he was lying to her?

"Mercer knows everything about me," she muttered. "He's been the one protecting me."

"There's more to it, dear child. He cares for you very much."

Quinn shook her head. "I can't do this. Not again."

It didn't matter if he'd been protecting her, and it didn't matter if he cared about her. What they'd had was a lie. That's what she'd told him when they were in her apartment and he'd asked why she didn't have photos. He'd taken one of them together, and then gave her a frame that said they were real. But they weren't.

"What should I do?" she asked him.

She could tell by the look on his face that he hadn't anticipated the question, and it took him a while to answer.

"Go home," he finally said. "You're safer there than you are here."

She nodded and walked toward the car. He stood and followed, and then handed her a piece of paper. "If you need *anything,* call me at this number."

Quinn thanked him and got in the car. She wasn't ready to go home yet, but thankfully she'd run into Tabon Sharp at the airport and had a place to stay.

She rolled down her window before she backed out. "I have another question," she said to Laird who hadn't moved from where he was standing. "Do you know someone named Tabon Sharp?"

Laird rested his hands on the roof of her car. "You cannot afford to resist protection at this time, Quinn. If you haven't listened to anything else I've said, know this: *you are in danger.* People like Mercer and Tabon, and several others, will keep you safe."

Quinn's eyes filled with tears again. She'd lost track of how many times they had. "That's a lie, too," she murmured. "Is there a single truth in my life?"

Her question had been rhetorical, but he answered anyway. "There are many."

"I'm not leaving yet. Since the house I'm staying in belongs to Tabon, I'm assuming I'll be safe there, even if only for a couple of days."

"You will be, although New York is safer."

"How do you know where I live?"

She didn't give him time to respond before she backed up the car and drove away. She hadn't gotten to the highway yet, when she pulled the car over. She opened the compartment between the two seats, but it was empty. She reached over to the one in front of the passenger seat and opened it. Inside were two pieces of paper. One said it was the registration, the other listed insurance information, both were in the name of Tabon Sharp.

For a reason Quinn couldn't explain, that made her feel better. She wiped her tears, pulled out on the road, and drove to the beach. Someone was following her; she knew that now, even though she hadn't been able to figure out who.

When she pulled in the driveway, she saw Tabon sitting on a bench near the front door of the house.

"Hi, Quinn," he said when she got out of the car. He took the key from her hand and popped open her trunk.

"What are you doing?"

"Helping you with your bag."

"I don't need any help," she said, trying to take the bag from him. She was no match for his strength, so she gave up and stood with her arms folded. "Why are you here?"

"I have a few things to discuss with you."

"Wait. You're actually here to tell me *the truth*? I'm stunned, *Tabon.*"

He smiled, and it melted her heart a little. "First of all, no one calls me Tabon except my mother. And you for a short while. I go by Razor. Next up..." he looked around them. "Let's go inside."

It was almost sunset, and Quinn didn't know much more than she had when she arrived, except that, while Razor had been the one to interview her, Mrs. Patchett, the managing director, and the preservation group were real, and if Quinn still wanted the job, they wanted to hire her.

"Have you eaten recently?" Razor asked.

"No."

"Meaning?"

She sighed. "I don't remember."

"Let's see what Mercer stocked the refrigerator with. I'm starving."

Quinn lost what little appetite she had, and stayed where she was when Razor went into the kitchen. He came out a few minutes later with two plates of sandwiches and some chips.

"Eat," he said, putting one of the plates in front of her.

"I'm not hungry."

"Sure you are, and while you eat, I'm going to tell you about our Mr. Mercer."

"Now I'm nauseous. *Jesus,* you know what I called him?"

"Settle down. I thought it was cute. By the way, I don't know anything about the time you spent together. *Nothing. At. All.* Got it?"

She nodded, wishing it was easier to hate Razor, or at least not like him. Instead, she felt the same way she had with Mercer when they'd first met. She felt safe. The other things she'd felt for Mercer, like attraction, obviously weren't there. He reminded her more of Tara's big brother. He was always funny, always sweet, and would lay down his life for his sister.

"*Oh, no,*" she gasped, putting her head in her hands.

"What?" he asked between handfuls of chips.

"What about Aine and Ava? And Tara and Penelope?"

He shoved another handful of chips in his mouth. "What about them?"

"Didn't your mother ever tell you not to talk with food in your mouth?"

"Sure did, but she isn't here, is she?"

Quinn's smile quickly went away when she thought about her own mother.

"Knock that shit off."

"What are you talking about?"

"Quit feeling sorry for yourself."

"Like you have any idea how I feel."

"Here's the thing, I do. At least I know how you should feel."

Quinn felt like walking out, but she was too curious to hear what he had to say. "How should I feel?"

Razor set his plate down on the table and leaned forward, looking into her eyes. "I get why you're pissed off, but you're missing the big picture." He scrubbed his hand over his face like she'd seen Mercer do so many times. "Mercer, me, other people you don't even know—we all protect your ass, little girl. Do you know what that means?"

Quinn shook her head.

"If someone walked in the front door of this place, and he or she had a gun, I'd take every bullet fired before I'd let anything or anyone harm a hair on your pretty little head."

"Thank you," she whispered. "I don't understand, though."

"Which part?"

"Why do I need to be protected. I'm nobody. I'm *nothing*." She'd continue, but she was back to feeling sorry for herself, and after what he'd just told her, she had no right to.

"To a lot of people, you're everything." His tone of voice had changed so drastically, she was stunned. Instead of sounding angry, he was sad.

"Why are you here?"

"I'm taking Mercer's place." He laughed. "Well, not in *that* way. I'm your new lead."

She had no idea what that meant.

"Oh, back to your other question, the one about your friends. They're your friends and that's it. We may know everything there is to know about them, straight down to their favorite breakfast cereal, but they know nothing about you other than what they've learned from spending the last fourteen years with you."

"Thank, God," she mumbled.

"Mercer's the real deal too, sweetheart."

The real deal? What did that mean? She shook her head, too conflicted to be able to sort through her feelings.

"He loves you, and while he'd kick my ass across this fine country of ours for saying so, I'm tellin' you anyway. And you know what else? Doc loved your mother too.

Wanna know how I know that?" He didn't wait for her to answer. "I was *there*. That's how I know."

The tears were back, and Quinn had no idea what to say.

"Every single thing that woman ever did was *for* you, Skipper. Not because of you."

"What did you call me?"

Razor laughed. "Not the most original code name, I'll admit, but I didn't come up with it."

"Why Skipper?"

"You're gonna hate this." He was still smiling which made it so hard to be mad at him.

"That hasn't stopped you so far."

Razor laughed harder. "Damn, you remind me of her sometimes. Anyway, your mother's code name is Barbie."

"Barbie and Skipper?"

Razor cringed. "Yep."

"Skipper is Barbie's *sister*, not her daughter."

"No shit? I am gonna have fun telling Paps that."

"Who's Paps?"

Razor's expression changed again. He was no longer laughing. "Out of all of us, he's the one who has taken care of you and your mother more than anyone else. Even Mercer."

Something occurred to her. Was that what Tom had almost called her?

"What now?" he asked.

She hated how easily he read her. "Tom."

"Yep. Tom too. And Vinnie." Razor pulled out his phone and looked at the screen. "Shit," he said under his breath.

"What?"

For a moment it looked as though he was trying to decide what to tell her. "Butler Ranch is on fire."

"Oh, my God," she gasped and jumped up from the sofa. *"Is everyone okay? What should we do?"*

"We sit tight, Skipper."

"Don't you need to leave?"

He shook his head. "No, that would be the last thing I'd do in this situation."

15

Calder's connection to Johnny Vatos was driving Mercer crazy. There was something there, he just couldn't put his finger on what it was. No matter how hard he tried to focus on sorting through the shit-ton of crap that had been hidden in the floorboards of Leech's cabin, his mind kept drifting back to two things: how Quinn was, and what Calder and Vatos were up to. Both ate away at him.

"Hey, Eighty-eight." Paps joined him in the kitchen. "Find anything?"

"Haven't scratched the surface." Mercer pointed to the box sitting at his feet. "Who's on Vatos?"

"Right now? Max. Why?"

Mercer pulled out his phone. "Where are they?" he asked out loud, but didn't expect Paps to answer, he was sending his own message to Max. At the same time, Paps was pulling up the operative's tracking report.

Mercer stared at his phone, waiting for a response, but when none came, he looked at Paps.

Paps stood. "He's at Butler Ranch. Let's go."

They took one truck instead of Mercer taking the bike, since it was after dark. Neither spoke on the way.

Mercer continued to check his phone, but so far, Max hadn't responded. "I don't like this," he muttered when they pulled up on the side of the road outside the ranch's perimeter. "Coordinates?"

Paps sent them to Mercer's phone, and both men jumped out of the truck.

They were past the first set of vineyards on the north side of the ranch when they smelled smoke.

"Call it in," Mercer yelled and ran.

By the time he reached the fire, it had spread to the point where there was nothing he could do.

"*Body!*" Paps yelled, running from the other direction. He pointed and Mercer saw it too.

Paps got there first and pulled the body away from the flames. "*It's Max.* I've got a pulse," he yelled.

"I've got him," yelled Mercer, who picked Max up and threw him over his shoulder. "You go ahead and get the truck as close as you can." Paps was already out of earshot by the time Mercer finished his sentence.

He drove through an open gate and met Mercer and Max part-way in.

"He hasn't gained consciousness," Mercer told him as he laid the operative on the back seat.

When they heard sirens in the distance, Paps pulled the truck out on the road, and went in the opposite direction.

Once in the truck, the first call Mercer made was to Laird Butler. The fire was still quite a distance from the main ranch buildings, including the houses, but he told them they should evacuate anyway. Mercer knew he and Sorcha were the only two on the property; the rest of the family had been reported together at Stave, Alex Avila and Peyton Wolf's place in Cambria, which he told Laird.

"Is anyone else there? Any vineyard workers? Anyone else?"

Laird said there wasn't anyone else he was aware of, and that he'd stop and get Lucia on their way to Cambria.

"Where are they going?" Paps asked when Mercer hung up.

"Alex's place at the beach."

Paps nodded and Mercer sent another message, this time to Razor.

They heard Max cough and sputter in the back seat. "What the hell happened?" he groaned.

"We found you passed out near the edge of a fire," Paps told him.

"Vatos," Max groaned. "He started it. When I tried to put it out, someone knocked me out." He rubbed his head.

"Someone? Not Vatos?" Mercer asked.

"It wasn't him. Someone nailed me from behind." Max rubbed the back of his head with his hand. When he looked at it, there was blood on it, but not much. Head wounds were notoriously bloody, so if that's all there was, he wasn't going to bleed out.

"How do you feel?" Mercer asked when Max sat up.

"Head hurts. Otherwise okay."

Mercer looked at Paps who seemed as concerned as he felt. If Calder was the person who whacked Max, then he knew someone had been tailing either him or Vatos.

"Where're we headed?" Mercer asked.

"Alex's."

"Why?"

"Sorcha's there."

"And?"

"She has medical training."

That answered one question. If they were going to Alex's place to have Sorcha take a look at Max's injuries, that had to mean she was well aware of why the K19 team was here.

"*¡Dios mío!*" Lucia Avila gasped when they came inside.

While Max was the only one of the three hurt, he and Paps were covered in soot, grime, and dirt.

Sorcha Butler grabbed Max's hand and pulled him into the bathroom. "Come with me."

"What happened?" Lucia asked.

Mercer filled her in as minimally as he could, while Paps and Laird went outside to talk.

"You tell him, he tells her, and she tells me," Lucia told Mercer.

"Oh, yeah?" Mercer knew better. There were too many lives at stake for Burns Butler to be that sloppy.

"I'll check on the fire," Paps said when they came back inside.

"Come with me," Laird said to Mercer.

They went down the hallway and into the bedroom, where Laird filled Mercer in on everything he and Quinn had talked about that afternoon, and told him that she wasn't planning to leave for New York right away. That part Mercer already knew, Razor had told him.

"Do you have ongoing access to her phone?" Laird asked.

Mercer nodded. "Affirmative."

"Have Razor take a look at what's on it."

"What are you thinking?" Mercer asked.

"She came back empty-handed."

"Right."

—:—

"What's happening?" Quinn asked Razor, who had been checking his phone non-stop since the first report came in.

"The Butlers have been evacuated, and there are several crews working on containing the fire."

"Don't make me ask you," Quinn said a few minutes later.

"Eighty-eight is fine. He and Paps are here, actually."

"*Here?*"

"Relax, Skipper. Here in town."

Razor was still studying his phone. "Yeah," he said absentmindedly, not in answer to anything she'd said. He stood and grabbed her hand. "Let's take a ride."

"*What?* Wait. Where are we going?"

Razor led her through a door and into the garage. "Get in the back seat, and lay on the floor," he barked at her.

"*Now!*" he yelled when she hesitated.

"What's happening?" she asked after they'd been on the road for more than fifteen minutes.

"I'm hungry."

Quinn waited for Razor to say more, but he didn't.

"I'm getting car sick," she told him.

"You can get up now."

She sat up and held her stomach. This wasn't going to help. "Can I sit up there?" she asked.

"If you can climb over the seat."

She did, and then put her seatbelt on. "Are you going to tell me what this is all about?"

"Nope."

"Where are we going?"

"South."

Quinn rolled her eyes, but didn't ask any other questions. She was beginning to grasp the severity of what Laird Butler had told her this afternoon, and what Razor told her tonight. She was in danger, and they were keeping her safe. Instead of being a pain in the ass, from now on, she'd try hard to do whatever they told her to do.

"Can I ask you a question?" she said later. "It isn't about where we're going."

"You can ask."

"But it doesn't mean you'll answer, right?"

Razor smiled for the first time since the call came in about the fire.

"Mercer is Eighty-eight, right?"

"Yep."

"Why do you call him that?"

Razor didn't answer for long enough that Quinn figured he wasn't going to. She turned her head and looked out at the moonlight on the Pacific Ocean. It reminded her of that night in Southampton, when she'd been sitting by the water, looking at a similar moonlight, wondering who had sent her roses for her birthday.

"He calls me precious," she murmured, remembering how safe she'd felt with him, even though it had puzzled her at the time.

"Doc was the first to call him Eighty-eight."

Quinn stayed quiet, hoping Razor would continue.

"What do you know about the planet Mercury?" he asked a few minutes later.

She shrugged. "Not a lot that I remember."

"It's the closest planet to the sun, and the smallest in our solar system."

"It has the shortest orbit," she added.

"Exactly."

"*Eighty-eight* days."

Razor nodded.

"Is that it?"

"Nope."

Oh, Lord, he was going to make her figure it out.

"Can I use my phone?" she asked.

"You don't have it."

Quinn felt her pockets and then looked over the seat and to the floor. She didn't have her phone or her bag. They'd left so quickly she hadn't even thought to grab it.

"It hasn't worked since you landed at the airport."

"Why not?"

Razor didn't answer, so she didn't ask any more questions, as hard as it was for her not to.

"What else does Mercury refer to?" Razor asked after a long period of silence.

"The element."

He nodded. "What else?"

"The Greek god."

"Bingo."

"You say that, but I don't know how it relates. Is Mercer a Greek god? Is he Greek?"

Razor smiled at her again. "Hermes is the Roman equivalent to Mercury."

Quinn rolled her eyes again. "While this is *really fun,* I'm not getting it, Razor."

"Hermes was considered the messenger of the gods. He also guided evil souls to the underworld."

"Mercer guides souls to the underworld?"

Razor didn't have to nod for Quinn to know she was right. He didn't just guide them to the underworld, he protected her from those evil souls.

"Doc picked him. Not me and not Paps. He picked Mercer."

"To protect me?"

"Yep. Before he left on his last mission, Doc made Mercer promise that he'd never let anything happen to you."

Quinn rested her head against the SUV's window as more tears streamed down her cheeks. "Thank you, Razor," she whispered.

Razor pulled off the highway in Santa Barbara. Quinn wanted to ask why, but didn't. She'd already asked too many questions for one day, and it had wrung her out. At this point she didn't care.

"Let's go," he said when he pulled into the parking lot of a grocery store. She got out and followed him.

"What do you want?" he asked once they were inside.

"For what?"

"To eat, Skipper. Jeez. Eighty-eight said you were smart."

"Peanut butter and jelly."

"Really?"

"Oh. My. God." Quinn stopped in the middle of the aisle and put her hands on her hips.

"What?"

She got closer to him and whispered, "You won't tell me where we're going or what we're doing. You asked me what I wanted, and I said the first thing that came to mind. I want a damn peanut butter and jelly sandwich. Is that okay?"

Razor held up his hands. "Sure is." He didn't ask any more questions while they were in the store, but filled the cart with enough food to last them a week.

They didn't get back on the highway, and as dark as it was on the back roads, Quinn had no idea where they were, until they pulled up to a gate and waited for it to open.

"I used to live here," she gasped.

Razor nodded and pulled through. The lights of the SUV shone on the garage of the house, and she saw him standing in the driveway, hands at his sides, not taking his eyes off hers. *Her Mr. Mercer.*

—:—

It had been Paps' decision to alert Razor to get Quinn out of town. The tail said Calder was headed to the coast, and while there was no reason for them to suspect he knew anything about her, if he started paying attention, by now he'd know he had a tail, and he would immediately deduce that Paps and Razor were behind it.

Worse would be the possibility he'd figured they were onto him shortly after he showed up in Paso Robles, back in June. If that was the case, Quinn being here put her in the exact danger they'd been protecting her from for the last twenty-one years.

Doc's fear, and theirs too, had always been what a psychopath like Calder might do if he found out Lena had a daughter who was born ten months after he'd raped her. He'd also know there was a chance the child was Doc's too, which put Quinn in the same amount of danger, or worse.

"By the way, Razor is transporting Skipper to Casa Carrizo," Paps had told him.

"She doesn't want anything to do with me."

"Go anyway. It's about protecting her, Eighty-eight. Don't lose sight of that."

"Yes, sir," he answered.

"Stay away from Calder, too. You come face to face with him; you get the hell out."

Paps was right. The way he felt right now, if he and Rory Calder were in the same place at the same time, he'd kill him without thinking twice about it. And then any hope they had that he'd somehow lead them to Doc and Leech, would be lost.

An hour and a half later, Mercer stood in the driveway of the house where Quinn and Lena had lived right after she was born.

While her mother hadn't lived in it for several years, she hadn't actually sold it, like she'd told Maddox she had. As with her parents' estate, it wasn't Lena's to sell. It had belonged to Kade.

When he saw the SUV pull in the gate, Mercer wondered if she'd remember anything about it.

He could see her clearly through the windshield, and once she saw him, her eyes didn't waver from his.

He had a lot to talk to her about, and after they were finished, her opinion of him may not change at all. He had to try though. He couldn't stay away from her, and it was time he accepted it as fact.

He slowly walked over to where Razor had parked, and waited for Quinn to open her door. She stared at him through the glass, and he waited.

"It's unlocked," Razor, who was carrying bags of groceries into the house, shouted to him.

Mercer put his hand on the door at the same time Quinn opened it. She slid out as much as climbed, and landed in his arms. He stroked her hair with one hand while the other held her close to him. Her head rested against his chest, and he could feel the dampness from her tears seep into his shirt. He didn't know how long they stood where they were; he only knew he wouldn't move as long as she was still crying.

He looked up at the house and noticed Razor on the second story, opening windows and turning on lights. Warmth exuded from the Spanish Colonial Revival house now that it was lit from inside. The exterior was white stucco with dark brown shutters and a red tile roof. Balconies with wrought iron railings extended from every upstairs room, where Razor had thrown doors open to air it out. Massive palm trees, which looked old enough to have been planted before the house was built, stretched high above the roof line, and bright pink bougainvillea grew up the side walls of the five car garage.

With her arm still around his waist, Quinn turned and looked at the front of the house.

"Do you remember it?" Mercer whispered, so afraid to break the spell between them.

She nodded. "I used to have a bike that I'd ride around here." Quinn pointed to the circular driveway made of Mexican pavers. Pots that had probably once held beautiful flowers, sat empty, and were placed on the edge of the drive and along the walkway.

"At first it had training wheels, and then..." Quinn started to tremble.

"What is it, precious?"

"He took them off and said he'd hold onto me. He promised not to let go until he was certain I was riding on my own."

"Who?"

"I have no idea," Quinn whispered so softly Mercer could barely hear her.

"Do you want to go inside?" he asked, and she nodded.

They walked slowly through the main entrance and into a room with massive, dark wood beams on the ceiling, and a fireplace that matched the color of the home's exterior at the opposite end of the room.

Dark leather chairs and sofas sat on the tile floors and Mexican rugs. They walked from that room into the kitchen, the dining room, out a double door that led to an outdoor patio bigger than the first floor of the house itself.

As they explored, Quinn's pace steadily increased. When they got to the stairs, she took them two at a time, racing ahead of Mercer. He watched as she went to the end of the hallway, and stood in the last doorway she came to. She turned and looked at him.

"This was my room," she said.

Before he could join her, she'd entered the room, and he found her sitting on the edge of the still-made bed. Like her apartment, beautiful artwork adorned the walls. There were paintings of horses in meadows and of the sea.

Mercer walked over to the window and waved at Razor who was getting in the SUV.

"Where's he going?" Quinn asked, walking to the door that opened to the balcony. "I was never allowed out here," he heard her murmur.

"He's leaving," Mercer answered.

"Why?"

"So we can be alone. Are you okay with that?"

Quinn nodded and walked back over to the bed. "I don't feel like talking right now," she told him.

"We don't have to." It was close to midnight, and after the day they'd both had, he could only imagine she was more exhausted than he was.

She toed off each of her shoes, and then pulled back the comforter and sheets of the bed. Mercer stood where he was, by the window, waiting. She undressed slowly, her eyes on his, until she stood before him completely bare.

"I don't know what to do, Quinn," he practically cried.

"We'll talk tomorrow." She held her hand out to him.

"Are you sure about this?"

"I need to sleep, Mercer. I can't sleep when I'm not with you."

He put one foot in front of the other, gauging her mood as he made his way to her. She climbed into the bed and scooted over to the other side. "The sheets are so cold," she said.

"Would you like me to close the windows?" he asked.

Quinn shook her head. "It's a beautiful night. Let's leave them open."

Mercer pulled his shirt over his head and toed off his shoes, like she had. He hesitated before unfastening his belt. Reaching behind him, he put his gun on the table near her bed, and watched her watch him. When she nodded, he continued and slid his pants to the floor.

When he joined her in the bed, she scooted over and rested her head on his chest. It was only a matter of minutes before her breathing evened out, and he knew she was asleep. Only then did he allow himself to drift off too.

16

When Mercer woke, it was still dark outside, and Quinn wasn't in bed next to him. He was as shocked as he was concerned that he'd slept soundly enough for her to get out of bed without waking him.

He saw her then, sitting in a chair near the window.

"Everything okay, precious?" he asked.

"I remember him," she said quietly. "Just bits and pieces, though, like the training wheels."

"What else have you remembered?"

"My mother crying a lot."

That made Mercer's heart hurt.

"He wasn't here very much. I'm not sure how or why I know that, but I do."

"If it's Doc you remember, he was still active duty then, so he would've been gone a lot."

"Tell me more about them." She stood, walked back over to the bed, and cuddled next to him.

"I can't, and when I say that, it's because I don't know anything at all about that part of Doc's life. What I do know, I've only learned recently, and most of it took place before you were born."

"Thank you for being honest with me about it."

He could only see her face by the light of the moon, so he couldn't tell whether she was angry or sad, or neither.

"I'm sorry. I'd say what for, but there's so much I regret."

Quinn shrugged and rested her head on his chest. "I don't know how you could've handled anything differently."

"I wish…"

"Me too," she said when he didn't finish his thought out loud.

What he wished was that she was still in New York, that the only thing that stood between them was the argument, if he could call what happened before he left that.

He wished she knew nothing about her mother's rape, or that her father was anyone other than Angus Sullivan. And as much as he loved having her in his arms, he wished he could put her on a plane home later today.

"Can you go back to sleep?" he asked.

"I don't think so. Can you?"

"Not if you're awake. What time is it?" Mercer sat up and looked at his phone. It was almost five, which meant the sun would be coming up soon. "I have an idea. There's somewhere I want to take you."

They put the same clothes on they'd worn the day before. Mercer tucked his gun in his waistband, and they went downstairs. "Do you want some tea or anything?" he asked, wondering too if she'd ask about the gun.

Quinn yawned. "I don't think I'm awake enough yet."

"We don't have to go. You can go back to sleep."

Quinn studied him, and he thought he saw the glimpse of a smile. "You sound like me now. Let's go."

Mercer opened the garage and realized he only had the bike, and no second helmet. Near the other end of the building was a vehicle, but it was covered, so he had no idea what it was, if there was a key anywhere, or even if it ran. He could probably rent a car, but not at this hour, and where he wanted to take her was too far to walk.

"What's that?" Quinn was walking toward the car he'd noticed.

Mercer followed, and when they got close, he pulled the cover off of one side of the front part of the car. He could tell it was a Porsche, but he had no idea what model. The pale yellow paint looked to be in perfect condition. Quinn pulled from the other side and exposed the black convertible top.

"There's a key in it," she said, looking through the driver's side window.

"Let's see if it runs," said Mercer, not optimistic that it would. He pulled the cover the rest of the way off, and found the button to open the garage.

He climbed inside and saw that it had a manual transmission. If it hadn't, and he was successful in getting it started, he would've asked Quinn if she wanted to drive.

She got in the passenger side and opened the small glove box in front of her. She pulled out a piece of paper and handed it to him.

"I can't look," she whispered.

Mercer pulled out his phone and shined it on what he discovered was the registration. It had expired a year ago in June, which meant it had been registered a year prior to that, and the name of the owner was Kade Butler. He looked at Quinn, who had seen the same thing he had.

"That means he was here."

"More than likely."

Mercer put his foot on the clutch, turned the key, and the car started right up. He put it in reverse, backed it out, and shifted into first.

"What is that?" she asked, pointing to the gear shift.

"It's a manual transmission. I'll teach you how to drive it later."

"Oh," she said, looking away from him.

Mercer put the car back in neutral. "If you want me to."

She didn't look at him or answer.

"I know I'm pretending that everything is the same between us, but it's because I don't know what else to do, Quinn."

"I know," she said, but still didn't look at him. "Let's just go, okay?"

Mercer drove the short distance from the house, over the highway, and down a road where he knew there used to be three public parking places. The sun still hadn't come up, so he doubted many people would be there yet. Sure enough, when they rounded a bend, all three spots were empty.

"It might be chilly." He looked in the jump seat and found a rolled-up Mexican blanket. He walked to her side of the car, and when she got out, he put it around her shoulders.

"You don't get cold," she murmured.

He smiled. "Not in the summer."

"Why not?"

Mercer shrugged. "I don't know. Too much time spent in places like Afghanistan where it's so unbearably hot. Although, my dad was like that, too."

Her hooded eyes drooped, and he put his hands on her shoulders. "Listen, I don't know who Doc was to you biologically. I'm sorry to be blunt, but it's the truth. What I do know is that he cared enough about you to not just keep you safe, but to make sure you had the best life he could give you."

"What happened to him, Mercer?"

"I don't know."

Quinn looked into his eyes. "Is he dead?"

He looked away from her. "I pray he isn't."

"But you think he is."

"He was reported killed in action." He answered her questions, refusing to let his conscience convince him he shouldn't. He couldn't tell her everything, but whatever he believed wouldn't put her or Doc in more jeopardy than they already were, she deserved to know.

"I see."

"Let's go," he said, putting his hand on the small of her back and leading her out on the sand.

"We used to surf here," he told her.

"Who?"

"Me and Doc. He was a good man, Quinn. One of the best I've ever known outside of my own father, Paps, and Razor."

"Tell me more about him," she said, sitting down on the sand.

When Mercer sat next to her, she brought the blanket around his shoulders too.

"Thank you," he whispered. She might think he was thanking her for making sure he was warm, but he wasn't. He was thanking her for still caring about him.

He told her that the first time he'd met Doc was at Stanford, and about the first time he'd brought him to this beach. He told her about many things they'd done over the years that weren't connected to their missions. He wished he could tell her more about Doc and her mother, but maybe someday he could convince Razor or Paps to.

"Razor told me Kade loved my mother," she said, as though she were reading his mind.

"What else did he tell you?"

"Not very much, *Eighty-eight*." She smiled and so did he.

"That was Doc too."

"I know. Razor told me when he made me guess what it meant."

Mercer laughed because she was still smiling. It sounded as though she and Razor got on okay. He wanted to ask how she'd felt when she found out he was someone other than the Tabon Sharp she knew, but he didn't.

"There are so many things I want to ask you."

"I know, and maybe someday I'll be able to give you answers."

"Mercer, tell me what happened to the man who raped my mother."

"Quinn—"

"It's my question."

The one he promised he'd answer truthfully, to the best of his ability. He'd told her then to make it a good one, and she had. If he answered, she'd know the worst of what he couldn't tell her.

—:—

Her insides were screaming at her to tell him to forget it, but Quinn couldn't. She had to know. "Is he the reason I'm in danger?" she asked.

"He is the danger, precious."

She knew it without him saying it. "Is he here?"

"Yes."

"Did he go to jail?" The police report she'd read only gave details about the rape itself, not what had happened to the man afterwards.

Mercer didn't answer.

"I saw his name."

"Don't speak it, Quinn."

His statement surprised her, but she got it. That man would be one of the evil souls Mercer would deliver to the underworld if given the opportunity.

"I'm worried about my mother."

"She's in a safe place."

The tears she'd thought she'd cried out in the last couple of days, rolled down her cheeks. She bent her legs and rested her head on the arms she'd folded and rested on her knees. The questions she'd been able to quiet enough to sleep last night, screamed inside her head. *Did her mother hate her? Was it that she couldn't stand the sight of her? Did she look like him?*

When her tears turned into sobs, Mercer pulled at her arms and put his around her. She buried her face in his neck and cried harder than she remembered ever crying before.

"God, Mercer. I don't know who I am," she cried. *"Is that why no one wants me?"*

He shifted so he could grip her chin with his fingers, and forced her to look up at him. "You're wrong, precious. That isn't how it is. You're wanted, and you're loved."

"But my mother—" she cried, choking on her own words.

"You're here, with me, because of your mother. You have a college education, and you've had a decent, care-free life to this point. It's because of her. Don't ever doubt that everything your mother ever did for you was out of love."

Her sobbing subsided, and she took several deep breaths. "I wish I could see it that way."

"I think you will. Eventually."

"Razor told me to quit feeling sorry for myself. He said that you, someone named Paps, and other people I would never know, put your own lives at risk in order to protect mine."

Mercer nodded.

"Have you risked your life for me, Mercer?"

"I have, and I'll continue to until the day I die."

Another cry took her breath. "I'm so sorry," she said before she couldn't say anything else.

"Don't be sorry, precious. You have nothing to be sorry for." Mercer soothed her.

"Can we go back to the house?"

"Of course we can." Mercer stood and offered her his hand.

When they got to the car, there were several others, with surfboards strapped to the top, vying for their parking spot.

"Must be a good place to surf," she said.

"One of the best in the world." He opened her door and waited for her to get in.

She looked up and saw his eyes dart between the waiting vehicles. His right hand not far from where she'd seen him tuck his gun.

"So many things make sense to me now," she said when he got in the car. "I remember when we walked to the Indian restaurant. I asked you if you were a spy."

"I told you to trust your instincts, Quinn." The way he smiled at her was part of why she did.

Yesterday she couldn't imagine ever speaking to him again, and now, less than twenty-four hours later, she knew that no matter what he did, she'd still love him, which meant she'd also forgive him.

"I want you to tell me as much as you can, Mercer. If something is going on, I want you to tell me. If you have to leave, or if something happens to my mother, or even if I'm doing something I shouldn't be, something that makes your job harder, I want you to tell me."

He started the engine and backed the car out, but pulled over once he was out of the way and someone else could take the spot. "There will be reasons I can't always do that, Quinn."

"As much as you can," she repeated.

—:—

"Are you ready for some tea? Hungry?" he asked right before they drove through the small downtown section of Montecito.

"I'm starving. I didn't even get to eat my peanut butter and jelly sandwich last night."

"My guess is that has something to do with Razor."

"He'd make a good big brother," she said and then added under her breath, "He wouldn't let me get away with anything."

Mercer smiled. "He's a good man, too."

"Yeah," she murmured, looking out the window. "I can't believe how much I remember about this place. I haven't been back here for almost fourteen years. Oh, wow!" she exclaimed when he pulled up in front of Jeannine's Bake Shop. "They have the *best* apple pancakes."

"I'm partial to the lobster benedict."

She rolled her eyes. "Seven-year-old girls don't eat lobster benedict, Mercer."

Quinn ate every last bite of her pancakes and had part of Mercer's breakfast too.

"Feel better?" he asked on the way back to the car. She shivered.

"Get in the car," Mercer told her, and quickly shut the door behind her. He surveyed the street, the surrounding buildings, the car itself, and nothing caught his eye, but the fact she'd shivered when it was almost ninety degrees outside alarmed him.

"Can we go home?" she asked when he got in. "I mean back to the house."

"Yes." He nodded, thankful it was only a couple of blocks away, gated, and under constant surveillance. Once they arrived, he'd ask her what she was feeling, but for now, he had to stay alert and focused. His phone pinged as they approached the gate.

"Hurry up," he muttered, willing it to open more quickly. If she was going to spend any time here at all, they needed to have a new one installed. He stopped just inside and waited for it to close behind them, and then pulled into the garage. He closed that too, and told Quinn to wait where she was. He got out and checked his phone before going in to check the house.

Evacuate. Transport situation? the text from Paps said.

Car. Safe now?

Five minutes max. Backup just arrived.

17

"What's going on?" Quinn asked when he got back in the car, opened the garage, and pulled out.

"We're leaving."

"Why?"

"Because." Mercer eased through the gate, and made eye contact with his backup.

One SUV pulled out in front of them, and another followed. Mercer didn't know what was going on any more than Quinn did, but it was bad, whatever it was.

He followed the lead vehicle through the twisting, turning backroads of Montecito, until it pulled up to another gate, waited, and then pulled through. Mercer followed.

"Hey, Eighty-eight," said Razor, getting out of the SUV after the gate closed behind the Porsche. "Damn nice ride you got there. I always loved that car. Hey, Skipper." He waved when she climbed out.

She waved back and stood by the car.

Good girl, thought Mercer as he approached Razor. "Give me the rundown."

"Surveillance picked up someone we didn't recognize, paying too much attention to the house. Ran the car, facial recognition, and nothing came up."

"Could be nothing, but I still want her gone."

"No can do. She's staying put, meaning with us, until further notice."

Mercer looked Razor in the eye. "Who's in New York?"

"Who do you think?" he answered, looking in Quinn's direction.

"Roger." Mercer turned and waved her over. "We have to leave. I'm sorry we can't stay longer."

"We, meaning me too?"

Mercer nodded.

"Good. Should I get in?" She motioned to the SUV.

"I like her," said Razor, putting his hand on the back of her neck. "She's getting better at doing what she's told."

Quinn rolled her eyes, but she also had her arms folded tightly in front of her. She was afraid, and those were her instincts doing what they were supposed to. "Do I have to lie on the floor?"

Razor nodded, and she climbed in the back.

"I hate this part," Mercer heard her say. He closed the door behind her and walked to the back of the vehicle.

"Who's in New York?" he asked again.

"Russians."

"*Fuck*. Where?"

"Nowhere important yet, but if you're here, she's going to be too."

"Roger that."

"Carsick yet, Skipper?" Razor asked after they'd been on the road for a few minutes.

"Can't you take the highway? It goes straight, you know."

"You told me that made you sick the other night."

"Oh, yeah."

Razor smiled, but Mercer didn't feel like smiling. Things were about to come to a head, and he didn't want any of it to touch Quinn.

"What about the car?" she asked.

"What's that?" Mercer asked.

"The car," she said again, louder than she needed to.

"You can get up now," Razor told her. "She doesn't like sitting in the back seat, either," he said to Mercer.

"We'll switch when we can."

"So the car," she said again. "You just left it at that house."

Razor shook his head. "She doesn't want to know anything else, just what's gonna happen to the Porsche."

She asks the questions she can, thought Mercer.

"It's back in the garage by now," he told her.

"What kind of car is it?"

"A Porsche," Razor answered.

"I know that much. What kind of Porsche?"

"A 1962 Porsche 356B T6 Twin Grille Roadster."

Mercer could hear their banter, but his mind was racing, crafting a plan. Tonight he'd finish sifting through what he'd taken out of the cabin. Maybe, with Paps and Razor's help, they'd find more on Calder that they could do something with.

"A shit-ton of money," he heard Razor say.

He'd missed whatever Quinn had asked.

"How much?"

"Almost a half a mil."

"Oh."

"That shut her up," Razor muttered to Mercer.

"I can *hear* you, you know."

When Razor laughed, Mercer zoned out again, happy that his partner was giving him the time he needed to think.

A few minutes later, Razor pulled to the side of the road. "Time to switch," he said. "You drive. I'll get in back."

Mercer nodded, got out, and opened Quinn's door. He ran his fingers through her hair when she stood in front of him. "How are you holding up?"

"Scared shitless," she answered, surprising him.

"You're covering it well."

"I'm learning."

He kissed the side of her face, and then her forehead. "Do you know how amazing you are?"

She shook her head and looked away from him, but he turned her face back toward him. "So fucking amazing."

Razor let out a whistle. "Come on, let's go."

It wasn't long before Quinn fell asleep, giving Mercer more time to think. Who were the Russians in New York, and why were they on Paps and Razor's radar?

"Don't pull off in Harmony," Razor told him.

"Where am I going?"

"Little place called Cambria Motor Lodge."

Mercer knew it. It had been updated not too long ago, but the layout of the place was ideal. It backed to the highway and was well-lit, and the frontage was wide open to the Pacific Ocean.

Mercer looked over at Quinn who had shifted in the seat, but was still asleep. "I wanted to go through the contents of the box today."

"Paps is elbows deep. Plans to get to the bottom by the end of the day."

"Did he find anything?"

Mercer could see Razor's nod from the rearview mirror.

Razor went inside so Mercer didn't have to, got the room key, and then pointed to where he should park the SUV. "Your transport should be here any minute," he told him.

Mercer nodded, not paying much attention. They moved cars around like checkers in their line of work. He didn't really care what he got, as long as it was safe, and he could get Quinn wherever he needed to take her.

"What the hell?" Mercer muttered when he saw the pale yellow Porsche pull in the space next to them. "How'd you manage this?"

"Practically flew the damn thing up here." Razor motioned to Quinn. "She likes it."

"You like her."

"Yeah, I do."

"Me too," said Mercer, leaning over to wake her up.

"We're here," he said, stroking her cheek with his finger.

She sat straight up and looked around. "I always do that. I'm sorry." She looked out the back of the SUV. "Are we back in Cambria?"

Mercer nodded, and then saw her eyes light up when she looked past him and the car registered.

"It's here!" She clapped her hands and looked at Razor. "Thank you."

"Hey, how do you know I didn't arrange for it to be here?"

Both Quinn and Razor laughed. He didn't get the joke, but he was too happy to see her smile to care. He got out, walked to her side of the SUV, and opened her door.

"Thank you," she whispered.

"For what? Evidently, you know I didn't have the car delivered," he joked.

"Not for the car, Mr. Mercer, for loving me enough not to let me go."

Razor tossed him the key to the Porsche, got in the SUV, and waved. "Be in touch shortly."

The room was small, but had everything in it they needed—a king-size bed, a fireplace, and a shower. On the table near the window, there was a bottle of wine, and two glasses, and a plate with fruit, different types of meats and cheeses, and bread, which looked as though it had just been delivered. Next to it was a menu from the Sea Chest, which was a short walk from the motel, with a note attached telling them to call a certain number when they were ready to order dinner.

Mercer turned around and saw Quinn sitting on the bed, staring into space. "Everything okay?" That was the best he could come up with? Of course everything wasn't okay. Her life had been turned upside down and sideways in the last few days.

"I'm fine, Mr. Mercer," she smiled. "I just want to take a shower." She got up and looked in the bathroom. "At least there are robes."

His first thought was that he didn't intend to let her wear clothes after their shower anyway, but he took a couple of steps back from that. While he'd loved having her naked body next to his last night, they needed to talk about where their relationship stood before he ravished her. Plus, he'd gotten a text from Razor, saying both her and his bags would be delivered within the next hour.

"What are you thinking about?" she asked.

"Clothes," he answered.

"I was kind of hoping I wouldn't need any right away."

Mercer raised his eyebrow. "We should talk, Quinn."

"No, we shouldn't. And I prefer 'precious' over 'Quinn.'"

"Yesterday you told me not to call you that."

"That was before I knew how much you love me."

"You didn't know that before?"

"I did, but today I felt it in a different way. I get it, Mercer. It's hard because I'm still pissed that you lied to me, but I know *why* you did—because you love me so much."

"I do."

"So show me."

—:—

"You told me that sex hadn't been this good for you before. That's not really what you said, but something like that. Something about a love so deep that you can feel the other person in your heart. When it's that right, nothing else will ever be again."

"That's right, precious. What we have, has never and will never be just sex. It's love."

"I know." She trailed her fingers over the tattoo on his chest, knowing the true significance of it for the first time. Mercer was her guardian angel and her protector, just like she'd said so many times.

"What are you thinking about?" he asked.

She smiled. "You."

"Are you hungry yet?"

She nodded. "Starving, actually."

They spent the afternoon first in the shower, and then in bed, taking their time exploring each other's bodies. Each time he'd ask before if she was hungry. They ended up feasting on each other rather than the food that sat on the table, waiting to be eaten.

"Where is the restaurant?" she asked.

"Just down the road, but they'll deliver."

"We could—"

The look on Mercer's face told her that whatever she was going to recommend, was out of the question. Which meant a walk on the beach was probably out of the question too. When she turned around, Mercer was studying her.

"Can I ask you something?"

"Of course."

"Is my mother somewhere safe?"

"She is."

"Somewhere she doesn't have to hide out in a room?" The question sounded harsher than she'd meant it to. "I'm sorry."

"Don't be." Mercer was looking at his phone. Maybe he hadn't even heard what she said.

Quinn pulled the curtains back and peeked outside. The Porsche was covered up like it had been in the garage. Razor must've done that when he dropped off their bags.

"Let's get dressed." Mercer set his phone down and walked over to where she stood by the window.

"Why? I mean, we can't go anywhere, right?"

"Wrong. I've made arrangements for us to be able to have dinner out."

"Where?"

"It's a surprise."

"Do we need a reservation?"

"Everything is taken care of."

"Let me ask a different way. Do we have time for another shower?"

Mercer smiled, pulling her toward the bathroom as she slipped the robe off her shoulders.

—:—

Hiding wasn't something Quinn would be good at. She hadn't spent her life looking over her shoulder like her mother had. He'd sent a text to Razor, asking if he could make arrangements for him to take her somewhere for dinner. He'd answered within seconds, saying he'd take care of it.

I'll arrange for transport too, he'd added.

That sounded good. Bringing the Porsche here for Quinn had been sweet, but completely impractical.

Plan to relocate in the morning, he'd added, which was also welcome news.

He knew that bringing them to the motel had been necessary, but it couldn't work for more than one night.

Mercer knew that, between the time Razor dropped them off and tomorrow morning, a safe house would be set up for Quinn. Until they took her there, Mercer would have no idea where it would be or what kind of freedom she'd have while she was there.

What he really wanted was for her to be able to go back to the house in Montecito. The place had been designed as a fortress, albeit one with outdated technology. Maybe tomorrow he'd offer to oversee a security update on the property, so eventually, she could stay there until it was safe for her to return to New York.

By the time his phone pinged, Quinn was antsy.

"Are you okay, precious?" he asked before he opened the door for them to leave.

"Can I have my phone back?" she asked.

"Of course you can," he answered.

"Will it work?"

"Why wouldn't it?"

"Tabon told me that it stopped working when I landed at the airport in San Luis Obispo."

"I'll make sure it's working, Quinn, and if it isn't, we'll get you a new one."

He watched as she went from antsy to agitated.

"I don't want a new one. I want my phone."

"You got it."

Quinn looked into his eyes. "Do you promise?"

Mercer nodded. It was an easy promise to make. Copies of the photos she'd taken at the cabin had been downloaded.

18

"It's got to be you, me, or Paps on Quinn's detail," Mercer said to Razor the next day. "I don't trust anyone else."

"What about Burns?"

Someone Mercer hadn't considered, but certainly a possibility, although would he be up for it, both in willingness and in ability?

"Last resort, how's that?" Razor added. "By the way, Naughton saw Burns in Harmony this morning."

"Is it something we need to be concerned about?"

"Not sure."

Mercer asked for an update on Calder.

"Paps thinks he's getting ready to move. He's picked up some chatter on another vineyard scheduled to be hit, but hasn't been able to pinpoint who, what, or when."

The news wasn't a surprise. Mercer's gut told him Calder was going to do something for his *coup de grâce* after the relatively spectacular failures his last two attempts at sabotaging a winery had been.

The bond issue had gone nowhere with Los Caballeros, and while the fire at Butler Ranch had caused damage, there were enough vineyards spared that, combined with the insurance on those that were destroyed, the family wouldn't take too great of a financial hit.

Based on what he'd learned from Paps, Calder had to be seething, particularly over Butler Ranch. Once again, Doc had bested him, whether he was still alive or not. It was Doc's team—Paps and him—that called the fire in early enough that it was contained quickly.

Acting on a tip from Paps, the California Bureau of Investigation had arrested Vatos for arson, although the news would not be made public until tomorrow at the earliest. By then, the local sheriff's department would be the agency of record for the arrest. While Vatos was too well known in the area for the CBI to spin a story that would stick for very long, for the next twenty-four hours at least, word on the street would be the fire was started by a migrant farm worker.

"Can I come out?" Quinn asked, peeking through a crack in the hotel room door.

"Good morning, Skipper," Razor answered, motioning for her to join them.

The house they'd arranged for Quinn to stay in was between Cambria and Paso Robles, on a large ranch in the hills off Green Valley Road.

The property was owned by one of Randolph Hearst's grandchildren, who'd been abducted as a teenager. Years after her release, she'd had a compound built with the same security one might see at a prison, only this kept the bad guys out rather than in. Not only was the place secure, there were miles of dirt roads where Quinn could learn and practice driving a manual transmission car. The woman had named it Happy Valley Ranch, and Mercer hoped it proved to live up to its name for as long as they needed to keep Quinn holed up there.

"It can't be that difficult. Have you ever learned yourself?" Quinn asked, teasing Razor in the same way he teased her. She'd mentioned something about him making a good big brother, and the two of them had sibling rivalry down pat.

"By the way," Mercer heard her say. "Thank you for arranging dinner last night."

Razor had contacted the owner of the Sea Chest, and convinced him to open a private room in the back for them. They'd had to enter through the kitchen, but once they were inside, it was private and romantic.

"He's only done it one other time," Razor had told Mercer. "It was for Barbra Streisand and that guy she married. But don't tell Skipper. She'll get it into her head that she ranks as high as a Hollywood superstar."

Once outside, Quinn continued to prod Razor. "Do I get to know where we're going? Or do I have to hang out on the floor of your SUV again? You might want to consider keeping barf bags back there." She put her hands on her hips and frowned when she noticed the empty parking space next to his SUV. "Where's the Porsche?"

"Already transported. Let's roll."

Mercer suggested Quinn sit up front, with Razor, on the ride to her new accommodations, so he could get some work done.

"Mercer said I could have my phone back," he heard her say, and watched Razor toss it to her.

"Even charged it all up for you."

Quinn was too busy checking text and voice messages to respond. Mercer knew her friends had attempted to reach her, because Aine had left him a message asking if she was okay.

Mercer had wanted to go to Harmony today and get with Paps about the stuff Quinn had unearthed at the cabin, but decided it was better to spend time with her instead.

So far, they hadn't found anything significant enough to be what Calder might be looking for. "It's mainly information Doc wouldn't have wanted him to have. We're looking for something Calder himself wouldn't want exposed," Paps had told him about what he'd looked through so far. "There is one more possibility," he'd added. "And that is Doc may have found it and moved it, leading Boiler to have reason to target Butler Ranch and the closest properties to it."

Mercer pulled up a map of Adelaida Trail, where Butler Ranch was located. Closest to them was Los Caballeros and Wolf Family Vintners. While he doubted Doc would've put Peyton Wolf or her family in danger by hiding something on their property, knowing he'd been involved with the woman who was now his brother Brodie's fiancée, might lead Calder to target them next. He sent a message to Paps to see if he concurred. If so, they should consider adding surveillance.

When Razor pulled up to the gates of Happy Valley Ranch, he stopped and handed Mercer and Quinn bracelets. "Put these on," he told them.

Mercer knew the bracelets kept the security system from triggering when residents moved about the ranch. They also tracked the location of each of the apparatus, probably developed specifically because of the kidnapping.

Mercer surveyed the security checkpoints as they showed up on the software he had developed for K19 as they drove through the gates and to the main house. If there was ever a place more secure than he thought necessary, it was this place.

"I'll stick around today," Razor told him when they exited the vehicle. "Maybe I'll initiate driving lessons."

"Appreciate it, but I want to spend the day with her."

"Roger that."

"Tomorrow."

"You got it, Eighty-eight."

Quinn joined them. "What is this place?"

"Where we'll be for the next few days, at least."

"It's nice," she said, looking around. "Are those horses?"

Mercer looked where she pointed. "Do you ride?" he asked.

She nodded. "Like sailing, it was something the tribe and I learned together."

"I can check and see if they're available to ride if you'd like."

"Maybe." She looked over at the car.

"After driving lessons, of course. You're very taken with that car."

"You're going to think this is silly, but I feel connected to him when I'm in it."

She didn't need to tell him who she was talking about when she said "him," and it made him happy that something good had come from her birth certificate discovery.

"The Jaguar is his too."

"I thought so. And I'm glad you said 'is.'"

Mercer ran his finger down her cheek. "Until we prove otherwise, Doc is alive to us."

They spent the rest of the day as normally as Mercer could make it for Quinn. Her first driving lesson in the Porsche lasted almost three hours. When he asked if she wanted to look into riding the horses, she declined.

"I just want to be with you. Close to you."

"I feel the same way, precious."

They made love, made food, and then made love again. They found a library full of books, and sat on the front porch, reading until the sun went down.

"Thank you for today," Quinn said when they were in bed, both exhausted.

"Thank you, Quinn."

"Tomorrow won't be like today, will it?"

"Let's not worry about that tonight, precious."

She nodded, rested her head on his chest, and fell asleep. As soon as he was certain she had, he slept too.

"Razor will be here with you today," he said to her the next morning.

"Okay." She squeezed his hand.

"You're safe with him."

She nodded. "I know. I just…"

He smiled, waiting for her to finish.

"I feel better when I'm with you."

"I feel better when you're with me too, but if it can't be me…"

"Think he'll want to give me another driving lesson?"

"I know he will. I also predict you'll be ready to quit before he is."

"You remember Burns," Paps said when Mercer arrived at the Harmony house.

"Of course he does, Gunner. We've had several conversations."

Mercer was glad to see him here. He planned to find a way to address the possibility of Burns joining Quinn's detail team.

The three men discussed the next winery Calder might target, and both Paps and Burns agreed Wolf Family Vintners made the most sense. In terms of production, theirs was quite low, which meant it wouldn't take much to compromise their financial stability. However, Jamison and August Wolf had paid off the land as well as recouped their capital investment several years ago, so forcing them to sell was unlikely.

"What else is there?" Mercer asked Burns.

"Inventory."

"Would that be worse in terms of loss?"

"Far worse. Every year of cellared inventory represents several years of income as a winery staggers its release."

"Did Razor tell you that Naughton saw Burns."

"He said he wasn't sure if it was something we needed to be concerned about. Is it?"

Burns nodded. "Naughton tends to speculate and subsequently investigate more than Maddox. I anticipate questions."

"Are you prepared to answer them?"

Burns didn't respond, but leveled his gaze at Mercer.

"I'd like to discuss Quinn as well," he continued. "Razor suggested you might consider assisting with her detail."

Burns nodded.

"Do you carry?"

"Always."

"Eighty-eight—" Paps interjected, but Burns raised his hand to silence him.

"I anticipated the interrogation, Gunner. Let him finish."

"You're retired," Mercer stated.

"In the same way you may be one day."

Retiring didn't end the lifestyle or the intuitive thinking that became more deeply ingrained the longer someone in their line of work stayed active.

"Make use of me as needed."

"Thank you, sir." Mercer nodded. "What do you think Calder is looking for?"

"His insurance policy," answered Paps.

Mercer agreed it made sense. Calder had something on the Russians that would ensure they wouldn't turn on him. Not being able to locate whatever it was, would cause him to become more and more desperate to find it.

"We've discussed the idea that Doc found it," added Laird.

The only reason Mercer doubted that theory, was the lack of anything from Doc indicating he had. The man had planned what would happen after his death down to the most minute detail, so why wouldn't he have left some clue about something that would allow them to neutralize Calder?

"Leech," Mercer spoke out loud. "Not Doc. Leech found it."

"And used it to locate Boiler," added Paps.

"Where would he have hidden it?"

That was the million dollar question. Had Calder captured Leech, and then interrogated him? If so, once he found what he'd hidden twenty-one years ago, Leech would be expendable.

There was a chance, too, that the Russians had both him and Doc, believing either of the men could lead them to whatever damaging information Calder had collected.

It was the first theory Mercer had come up with that gave him actual hope they'd find the two men alive. It meant that they either needed to find the "insurance policy" first, or prevent Calder from doing so.

Capturing him would do no good. Mercer suspected there was insufficient evidence to prosecute him for espionage or they would've arrested him years ago. The statute of limitations on rape crimes had recently been eliminated in the State of California, but putting him in jail for that crime would derail their search for Doc and Leech.

—:—

Quinn changed her mind a dozen times about whether she should tell Mercer about the only document she took from the cabin.

On one hand, she understood that he, Razor, and the rest of the people they worked with were protecting her. On the other hand, the letter she found was very specific about who she could talk to about it, and who she couldn't. Since she had a few minutes alone, she pulled it out of the pocket of her shorts and ran her fingers over the handwritten words.

Dear Quinn,

The circumstances of your reading this letter mean you are likely aware of other things that have happened in your life. I am sure you are confused, and even angry, about the secrets that have been kept from you.

I am also sure you have many questions about who I am to you, and why I'm writing this letter.

My guess is you will be frustrated by what little I have to say. However, it is important that you pay attention to what the rest of this letter says.

I have established a trust fund for you, separate from your mother's family's trust. You will be notified of your inheritance upon my confirmed death, and at the same time, your trustee will also be notified.

That trustee is my brother Naughton, who is unaware of both his involvement, and of your existence.

When you read this letter, establish contact with him, and let him know of its contents.

Other than my father, Laird Butler, no one else should be made aware of what I've told you. Please ensure Naughton understands the importance of this staying between the two of you. This includes other family members.

Regardless of what happens in your life, know this, Quinn Analise—your mother and I love you more than you could ever know.

The letter was unsigned, but she knew it was from Kade. She also knew that, somehow, she had to figure out how to establish contact with Naughton without anyone else knowing.

She tucked the letter inside the pocket of a pair of pants in her bag, glad she no longer had to carry it with her, and lay down on the bed, wishing Mercer was back. She knew better than to ask when he would be, and Razor had offered no clue.

When she opened her eyes again and looked at the time on her phone, she couldn't believe she'd slept three hours. Mercer must not have come back; otherwise, he'd probably be in bed next to her.

"Hey, there," said Razor when she came downstairs. "Good nap?"

"I guess I was more tired than I thought."

"Stress will do that."

She sat down at the table across from where Razor was working. "I wish you didn't have to babysit me."

"Me too," he grinned.

His smile quickly changed to a frown, and he stood. "Excuse me," he mumbled and went outside. Quinn watched while he talked on his phone. The look on his face was the same as it had been when he received word about the fire at Butler Ranch.

"What's wrong?" she asked when he came back inside and sat at the table. She really didn't expect that he'd answer, but he did.

"We suspect that the same person who was behind setting the fire, is about to act again." He scrubbed his face with his hand. "Both Eighty-eight and I are needed in the field, so we need to leave."

"We?"

"Yep. We'll hook up with Burns on Old Creek Road."

"Do I need to bring anything with me?"

"Nah. You're coming right back here. Burns needs you for access." Razor handed her a bracelet like the one Mercer had put on her wrist. "Give this to him."

Quinn did her best to blink away threatening tears, but not before Razor noticed.

"It's okay, Skipper. It's what we do."

"Be careful," she whispered.

He smiled. "Always. Be right back."

Razor came out of one of the downstairs bedrooms wearing a harness that held a gun. He sat down in the same chair he'd been sitting in before, and strapped a gun to his left leg too.

The more she saw and knew, the more Quinn found herself wishing she hadn't gotten on that plane, and was sitting in her apartment, bored out of her mind, and wondering when Mercer would be home.

19

Twenty minutes later, Quinn walked out of the woods where her grandfather used to live, and got into an old truck that Laird Butler was driving.

"Hello, Quinn. How are you holding up?" he asked.

"I'm fine, thank you," she murmured. "How are you?"

"I'm fine too, but hungry." He pointed to a container. "Sorcha sent soup, plus freshly baked bread, and a pie."

Neither spoke for the rest of the drive back, other than Quinn giving him the security bracelet and explaining what it was for.

"Are you Burns?" she asked after they were back at Happy Valley Ranch and had taken the food inside.

"I am."

Quinn found bowls and silverware while Laird looked for a pot to heat the soup. "Who is Sorcha?"

"My wife."

"I found a letter," she blurted.

Laird set the pot and spoon he'd been using on the counter, and faced her. "Go on."

"It's about a trust…"

"I see. Where is the letter now?"

"Upstairs."

"May I read it?"

Quinn nodded and went to get it. Considering the letter said Laird was the only person other than Naughton whom she could talk to about it, she saw no reason he shouldn't read it. When she took it out of the pocket where she'd hidden it, she removed it from the envelope and read it again, running her fingers over the dried ink. She folded it reverently and put it back in the envelope before going downstairs and handing it to him.

He took his time removing and then unfolding the paper. Before he started reading, he took a deep breath.

Quinn hadn't considered this may be hard for him. "I'm sorry," she murmured.

He shook his head and slowly read the front and back, and then the front again. He set the paper on the table and sat in one of the chairs. He sighed more heavily than he had before he started reading.

"Not yet," was all he said.

"The letter is specific," Quinn responded.

"It is, but it's too soon."

Quinn looked out the window, so tempted to ask if Kade was her father, but so afraid that Laird would confirm he wasn't. Why would he set up a trust for her if he wasn't, though? Why would he care what happened to her, or even tell her he loved her very much?

"I'm asking you to wait; however, the decision is yours, Quinn."

She nodded, unsure what to think. The letter said to establish contact with Naughton once she'd read it. There were no other stipulations other than the words "confirmed death."

"You don't think he's dead, do you?" she asked.

Laird sighed again and turned in his chair so he was facing her. "I don't know."

"Why do you want me to wait, then?"

"I'm asking because there are things at play presently that may compromise both your and Naughton's safety."

"Asking, not telling?"

"That's right. You're an adult, Quinn, and all I can do is ask you to consider my opinion."

"Who is Analise?"

Laird smiled. "My mother."

"And Quinn?"

"I don't know anyone other than you with that name."

She nodded. "I'll think about it."

"That's all I can ask."

"This smells really good, by the way." She was standing at the stove, stirring the soup.

"Have you had Cock-a-leekie soup?"

When Quinn told him she hadn't, he explained it was a Scottish recipe made of leeks, chicken, and rice. He added that, to be authentic, it would be garnished with prunes. However, neither he nor Sorcha liked them.

"Thank you," she murmured.

"I'll pass your appreciation on to Sorcha."

Quinn's eyes opened wide. "But—"

"Remember that she and I spent much time with you when you were little."

"Does she know I'm here now?" If she did, why wasn't she here? Why didn't the letter say she could talk to Sorcha as well as Laird? Didn't Sorcha want to see her? Her eyes filled with tears at the thought.

"She does, and she's anxious to see you again. However—"

"It isn't safe."

"For you, Quinn. It isn't safe *for you*."

"You're here."

Laird didn't respond, but she knew the difference.

—:—

Mercer volunteered to tail Maddox and Naughton Butler when they went wine tasting that afternoon.

Everyone had been taking his share of surveillance, which could be boring as hell.

He followed them to Pear Valley, went into the tasting room, and grabbed a seat near the back of the crowded bar. From there he could see outside, where Maddox and Naughton were sitting with Alex and Bradley. Moments later, Mercer received a text from one of K19's operatives at the same time the two brothers came inside.

Calder incoming, it said.

When Calder entered the tasting room shortly after, and walked straight over to Naughton, Mercer was poised to intervene if necessary.

Within seconds, it seemed, he heard Calder tell the Butlers they had a fox in their hen house, followed by Naughton taking a swing that landed hard. Mercer would've laughed, but he was in too big of a hurry to get between the two men before things escalated.

When he and a couple of other guys who had also been at the bar escorted Calder out, they came face to face with two sheriff's deputies. They immediately recognized Mercer, but didn't let on they had.

When another of the men explained what had happened, one of the deputies told Calder to leave the premises, or they'd arrest him.

"What are you doing here?" Mercer asked the other.

"Looking for Maddox and Naughton Butler. The arrest has been made official in the arson case. The family is meeting the sheriff at the house in an hour."

"You two follow Calder and make sure he's gone. I'll let the Butlers know."

Once Mercer was alone, the first call he placed was to Razor, asking him to get back to the house and cover Quinn. His second call was to Laird, alerting him that he'd need to return to the Butler Ranch, and also contact Maddox regarding the meeting with the sheriff.

—:—

"Why are you back?" Quinn asked when Razor walked into the house.

"Burns has a meeting."

"But I thought you were needed."

"I was, and I am, but this meeting is more important at the moment."

"Even though you think something bad is going to happen, you're still here with me."

Razor nodded.

"I hate this." Quinn stomped up the stairs and sat by the window. Had it been this way her whole life? Had Mercer, Razor, and the other guys been forced to live their lives around her? She wasn't more important than anyone else. Why did her safety come first when there was someone out there setting fires and God knows what else?

"Skipper?" she heard Razor say from the other side of the door. Her first inclination was to tell him to leave her alone, but *God,* the man had no life because of her, the least she could do was be nice to him.

"Come in," she called out. "I'm sorry," she added when he came through the door.

Razor sat in the other chair by the window and leaned forward, putting his elbows on his knees. "Talk to me," he said.

"I feel guilty."

"I get that, but once again, you're not looking at the big picture."

Quinn hated the way he knew exactly how to make her feel worse than she already did. "I'm not feeling sorry for myself. I'm feeling *guilty,*" she repeated.

"Because you're the princess in the tower, being guarded by all the king's men?"

"Essentially. And those men should be out protecting other people or fighting wars or maybe living their own lives. Do you have a life, Razor? That sounded worse than I meant it."

He smiled. "I know what you meant, and it hasn't always been this way."

"Why is it this way now?"

"Because Doc is missing."

Quinn hung her head. Once again she was making this all about her. "I'm sorry," she whispered. "I feel like I say that a lot to you."

"That's just because I tell it like it is."

"I appreciate it."

"Think about this for a minute. Let's say we believe Doc is still alive and so is Leech. Who do you think the two people are that they'd both give their lives for?"

"Oh, God," she groaned, tears spilling over her eyelids.

"That's right, Skipper. You and Barbie. As long as the two of you are safe, we don't have to worry about the bad guys using you to make things worse."

Quinn wiped at her tears. "You must think I'm a huge cry-baby."

Razor stood and messed her hair. "Nah, just a huge pain in the ass."

He walked to the bedroom door. "Get some rest," he told her.

Two hours later, Quinn went downstairs to find Razor was distracted by his phone.

"What now?" she asked.

"Burns is on his way back, and he has a surprise for you."

Quinn followed Razor to the kitchen and peeked through the window. Laird drove up, with someone in the passenger seat of his truck, and she looked at Razor.

"This is a huge gift, Skipper," he murmured.

"Oh, my sweet, beautiful bairn," Sorcha cried when she came inside. "Come 'ere 'n' let me hug ye."

"We can't stay long," Laird whispered, putting one hand on each of their backs.

"Na gabh dragh orm," she heard Sorcha say to him.

"Razor has to leave, sweetheart. We agreed."

Sorcha backed away far enough that she could look into Quinn's eyes. "Soon, child, this will all be over, and God will finally answer my prayers."

"We have to go," Razor repeated.

Sorcha held her shoulders. *"D'ye no ken* I love you, Quinn?"

She nodded. "I love you too," she said without even thinking about it.

20

"What happened earlier, with Calder and Naughton?" Paps asked when Mercer got back to the house in Harmony.

"It didn't turn into anything, but damn—the tension between those two is palpable."

"Just like Calder and Doc. It was immediate. Hated each other on sight, even though they both pretended for a while they didn't. You ready to roll?"

"Yep." They were on their way to Wolf Family Vintners, north of Butler Ranch, and they might be there for hours.

"Bored?" Mercer asked when Razor called an hour later. He'd been staked out south of Butler Ranch since Laird took back over with Quinn.

"Right? However, something interesting has just gone down. The new winemaker at Butler Ranch, who also appears to be Naughton's girlfriend, just left her uncle's place with Trey Deveux."

"Where are they headed?"

"Don't know, but I'm on their tail."

"Need backup?"

"I'll let you know if things go south. Otherwise, I think it's important to stay where you are. I have a strong feeling something sinister is about to happen."

Mercer felt the same way, and so did Paps.

"Have you talked to Skipper?" Razor asked.

"Briefly. She wasn't very talkative."

"Not like her, right?"

Mercer agreed. "What are you getting at?"

"She had a visitor."

"Who?"

"Sorcha Butler."

"Jesus," said Mercer. "Are you serious?"

"You know how Burns is."

Actually, he didn't.

"You are not going to believe this," Razor said when he called again thirty minutes later. "Calder showed up where Deveux and the winemaker are."

"What's happening?"

"I'm not certain, but whatever it is, we'll know soon enough. The bread basket has ears. Check transmission on your end. Right now the woman is leaving the table. I predict Deveux and Calder will connect while she's gone."

Paps hit a button on his phone and navigated to another button. Once he tapped it, both he and Mercer could hear the conversation as though they were sitting at the table near the two men.

"The land is worth it, always has been, particularly if we can add more along Adelaida Trail."

"Has she *forgiven* you?" they heard Calder's voice ask.

"I gotta tell you, Ror, the last four years have been a real struggle."

"Keep your eye on the prize, brother. And she ain't it."

"I hear ya."

"The stuff will go down at Jenson soon. Next week we'll go to plan B for Los Cab and Butler Ranch."

"You sure about this?"

"Why not? Are you backing out on me, Trey?"

"Hell, no, Ror. I'm just saying there's a lot of heat on us right now."

"Heat but no proof. Listen, if you're not in this one hundred percent, your father's gonna hear about it."

"*What the hell?*" they heard Trey gasp.

"What?"

"I think Bradley heard our conversation."

"*What the fuck? How?*"

The phone rustled.

"*Jesus,*" Calder seethed. "*You're such a fucking idiot. Where is she?*"

"I don't know."

"*Well, don't just sit here. Find her.*"

"Shit," groaned Mercer, sending a message to Razor. *Winemaker compromised. Needs back up.*

Already on it. She's secure.

Paps had started the truck, and they were on their way to Jenson. It hadn't even been on their radar, and it should've been, particularly given the connection between Calder, Deveux, and the winemaker.

They ran through the vineyards, hearing noise coming from the winery.

"I'll take the back," Mercer told Paps.

"Sheriff is on his way," Paps told him.

"Roger that."

Gun drawn, Mercer crept through the back door and saw wine flowing out of rows of vats. Just as he was about to start closing the spigots, there was more commotion coming from the front door.

"*Oh my God,*" he heard a male voice yell.

"*Who did this? Oh my God. It's all gone,*" cried a woman's voice.

"*The caves!*" A different voice yelled.

"*Go!*" answered the first male voice.

Mercer went back outside. It was too dark to see who the people running toward the caves were, but he followed. Just as they got to the caves' entrance, he saw two people run out and take off in different directions.

"What's happening?" he said to Paps through the radio.

"Authorities here. Your end?"

With the moon behind a thick layer of clouds, there wasn't enough light to see. Who would've guessed they'd need night vision devices here, in Paso Robles?

"Two suspects ran into the vineyards. It's too dark to identify or even track them unless you know the land well."

Mercer stomped his way back to the truck, furious with himself for letting this happen on his watch. They'd misjudged, and consequently, another winery had suffered tremendous loss.

At least now they had a slight advantage, knowing Calder was planning what he'd called "Plan B" at Los Caballeros and Butler Ranch. Whatever he had planned wouldn't be happening, even if they had to bring in an army of operatives to prevent it.

—:—

Quinn had been tossing and turning since she got into bed. Laird had told her to get some rest, but that was the last thing she could do. She hadn't asked if he'd heard anything from Mercer or Razor, knowing he wouldn't tell her either way.

She'd plumped her pillow and rolled from one side to the other when she heard voices downstairs. Before she could get up and grab a robe, the bedroom door opened.

"Hi, precious. I'm sorry I woke you." Mercer leaned down and kissed her forehead. "I'm gonna take a quick shower."

"Wait," she said, grabbing his arm. "Are you okay?"

He smiled and sat next to her on the bed. "I'm fine, I'm just dirty and sweaty, and want to shower before I get into bed with you."

"Okay," she murmured and watched him walk into the bathroom.

Quinn took off her clothes and followed.

"I would be very happy to get used to this," he said, holding the shower door open for her.

Quinn smiled, but that very thing was weighing heavily on her mind. She could get used to it too, this part. The rest concerned her. She'd been on edge all day, worrying about him. How could she possibly get used to that?

"What's wrong?" he asked, turning her under the water with his hands on her hips.

"I was worried."

Mercer kissed her forehead and wrapped his arms around her waist, hugging her tight to him. "I'm not sure what to say."

She nodded. "I told Razor to be careful, and he said, 'it's what we do.' I get that, but…"

"Go on, Quinn."

"Before I knew…all this…I worried when you were gone, but not in the same way. Then I worried that you wouldn't come back to me, because you'd decided you didn't want to, not because you couldn't."

"I understand."

"There isn't anything we can do to change it, right?"

"I'm not sure, to be honest with you." Mercer turned the shower off, grabbed a towel, and wrapped it around her before grabbing one for himself. "Let's talk," he added.

—:—

Mercer told himself he'd been prepared for this conversation, but now that it was happening, he was having trouble finding the right words to tell Quinn what had been on his mind for the last couple of months.

"I made a commitment," he began, but stopped when her eyes filled with tears. "Let me get through this, precious. I think what I'm going to tell you will make things easier for you."

She nodded and wiped at her tears. "I'm sorry, I feel like all I do is *cry*. Go ahead."

"We—Razor, Paps, and me—are in the middle of a mission. Doc is missing, Quinn, and we need to find him. It isn't just Doc; your grandfather is missing too."

"Leech?"

Mercer nodded, wondering how she knew his code name. "As I'm sure you understand, I can't walk away from this."

"I know."

"When it's over, there are several things I hope for. First, that we find Doc and your grandfather alive. Second, that the threat against you and your mother has been neutralized, so you both can live out the rest of your lives knowing you're no longer in danger." Mercer took a deep breath and blew it out slowly. "And lastly, my plan is to retire after I've made sure that happens."

"When do you think that will be?" she whispered.

"There is no way to know."

"I don't know if I can—"

Mercer silenced her with his lips. He knew, in the next few weeks or months, the stress Quinn would find herself operating under would seem unmanageable, but there wasn't an alternative. She knew too much, and even if she didn't, the threat in New York City would make it impossible for Mercer to allow her to return there.

Her arms wrapped around his neck, and she pulled him down on the bed with her.

"I need you, Mercer," she whispered.

"I need you too, precious."

He let her push his shoulders back, and guided her as she climbed on top of him. "Are you ready for me?" he murmured, and she nodded.

As she sank herself onto his hardness, Mercer's eyes never left hers. She hadn't said the words yet, but he knew she loved him as much as he loved her. No matter how difficult it was, she had no choice but to force her way through the rest of the mission.

Quinn slept, but Mercer had too much on his mind to sleep himself.

Before she drifted off, he asked how she knew her grandfather's code name, and she told him Razor had told her someone named Leech was missing along with Doc. From there she'd put two and two together when he told her about her grandfather.

That, along with the fact Laird had brought Sorcha to see Quinn, worried him.

It was time they had a meeting between Paps, Razor, Laird, and him, but that would be impossible without Quinn being there.

The other thing bothering him was something Trey had said to Calder. *"I gotta tell you, Ror, the last four years have been a real struggle."*

Four years? Had Calder been back that long? It didn't make sense. He would've shown up before Leech left to look for him. Was he somehow involved with his family's wine operation from a distance? Maybe he'd begun laying the groundwork four years earlier, convincing his family they needed to expand into the Central Coast, and thus giving him a cover story for being interested in buying property in the region.

As far as Deveux was concerned, it sounded as though he believed their goal was land, regardless of the manner in which they secured it. However, he also sounded uncertain about Calder's methodologies. He'd discuss the possibility of turning Deveux the next time he talked to Paps.

His phone vibrated on the side table, and Mercer picked it up.

Calder has ghosted, said the text from Paps. Three simple words and Mercer knew it might be days before he slept again.

21

Five minutes later, Mercer received another message from Paps.

Deveux is on his way to Butler Ranch.

On it, he answered.

He slid out of bed, making sure Quinn was still asleep, grabbed his clothes, gun, and phone, and as quietly as he could, slipped out of the bedroom and went downstairs.

"You get Paps' message?" he asked Razor who was standing in the kitchen, messing with the coffeemaker.

"Yep. He said you were going, but I can go."

"I'll do this. You stay with Skipper."

"Roger that." Razor set the coffee pot down on the counter, and padded back in the direction of the bedroom.

"If Quinn wakes up, tell her I'll be back as soon as I can."

Mercer thought he heard Razor grunt an affirmative response.

The location of Happy Valley Ranch was closer to Butler Ranch than the house in Harmony. In less than five minutes, he was there.

"Where's Deveux?" he asked Paps once he was positioned under cover of the nearest vineyard to the houses and turned on the radio.

"About to land."

Deveux pulled up in between the two smaller cottages at the same time Naughton and Bradley walked out the front door of one.

"You're trespassing," Mercer heard Naughton say.

"I need to talk to Bradley," Trey responded.

"Get off our land, or I'll call the sheriff."

"Hold on a minute—"

"The sheriff it is."

Mercer watched as Trey knocked the phone out of Naughton's hand. His hand went to his gun, ready if things escalated.

"What's going on here?" asked a voice in the darkness. It sounded so much like Doc that Mercer expected him to appear instead of Maddox.

The two Butler brothers argued with Deveux, who started in on Bradley, too, until Naughton asked her to go inside. With the sheriff on his way, Trey's parting shot of, "I'll leave, but this isn't over," didn't seem to phase anyone.

Mercer let out a sigh of relief when Deveux got in his car and left.

"He's headed your way," he said to Paps, who was waiting outside the ranch perimeter.

Bradley had come back out, and the three were talking about Deveux. Mercer didn't hear much until Naughton turned in his direction. "You don't have to be afraid of him, sweetheart. We have eyes and ears everywhere," he said.

He was more right about that than he knew.

"What's happening?" Mercer asked Paps.

"Deveux is covered by the Tablas Creek surveillance team."

"Any sign of Calder?"

"None. Once he left the restaurant last night, he was able to lose his tail. By the time I heard about it, his tracker had been off a full hour."

"Shit. He knows we're on to him."

"Roger that," agreed Paps.

"What now?"

"Regroup."

"Where?"

"Harmony."

Mercer sent a message to Laird and Razor, giving them an update. Laird said he'd be at the Happy Valley Ranch in fifteen minutes, and Razor confirmed he'd leave once Laird got there.

It was a little after four in the morning. With any luck, Mercer would be back at the ranch and in bed with Quinn before she woke up.

—:—

Quinn opened her eyes. It was still dark, but she knew Mercer wasn't next to her, and given the bed wasn't remotely warm, she guessed he'd been gone for quite some time.

She could go downstairs and ask where he was; Razor would more than likely be awake and at his perch in the kitchen, but she was sick of asking.

This was her life, her family, at least she thought it was her family. Even if Kade wasn't her father, her grandfather and her mother were her family, and she was sick of hearing part of the story instead of all of it.

When Mercer got back, they were going to have a talk, and this time, he'd listen to her instead of the other way around.

She closed her eyes, and slept off and on until she heard the bedroom door open.

"Where were you?" she asked when she felt Mercer getting into bed.

"I had to go out for a bit."

She still hadn't turned around to look at him. "That wasn't the question I asked."

"Quinn—"

Instead of turning around, she got out of bed. "I need some time to myself, Mercer," she said before she closed the bedroom door behind her.

—:—

Mercer knew Quinn was still at the ranch; he'd been watching her movements on the computer screen for over an hour.

"What's she doing?" Razor asked, looking over his shoulder.

"Driving."

"Huh."

"She woke up and I was gone."

"Right. And she's pissed."

Mercer scrubbed his hand over his face. "There's not a damn thing I can do about it. Especially now, with Calder MIA."

"She wants space, give her space." Razor was walking away when Mercer heard him mumble, "Sometimes she's just like Barbie."

He was right, and Mercer got it. For the last twenty-two years, Lena's life was similar to that of a convict who had been released from prison, but had to wear an ankle monitor. There wasn't a move she made that at least one of the K19 didn't know about. She had no real privacy, at least with her comings and goings. The only men she was around on a regular basis, she despised. It hadn't occurred to Mercer, until right this minute, that the woman couldn't have gotten into a relationship if she'd wanted to, which meant she was forty years old, and had been without love in her life for more years than Mercer wanted to think about. He had no idea how long things went on between her and Doc, but it had obviously ended before he'd gotten involved with Peyton Wolf.

Quinn had him, but not because she had a choice. What could she do other than what she was doing now? She was out driving in circles, with nowhere else to go.

Mercer knocked on Razor's door. "I'm heading out unless you want to," he said.

The door opened. "I'm good. Where you off to?"

"Giving her some space."

Razor nodded.

"If she asks—"

"I'll be honest with her."

"Right."

"Give it some thought."

Mercer turned around and walked out before he blasted Razor. He wasn't necessarily wrong, but he was in no mood for a lecture. He hadn't felt this kind of anxiety since he was in a war zone.

When he came back, several hours later, Quinn was in the library, reading.

"How was your day?" he asked, not knowing what else to say.

"Fine."

"Can I get you anything?"

"Nope."

"Quinn?"

"Leave me alone, Mercer."

"Got it."

He left her alone until midnight, when he found her sleeping in the library. "Come on, precious," he said. "Let's get you into bed."

She went along willingly, but Mercer got the impression it was only because she was half asleep. When he crawled into bed next to her, she turned her back to him.

—:—

When Quinn woke up, Mercer wasn't in bed with her—again. She went downstairs, and Razor was sitting at the table.

"Good morning, Skipper," he said, barely looking up from his laptop. "Eighty-eight said to tell you he'll be back as soon as he can."

She nodded and looked at the time. It was only a little after five. "When did he leave?"

Razor sat back and stretched, looking at his watch. "Let's see…around three I think."

Quinn knew better than to ask. "I'm going back to bed," she told him, even though she had no intention of doing so. They weren't the only ones with secrets, she had one of her own, and she planned to do something about it.

Yesterday, she'd spent all day thinking about her life. She was tired of feeling powerless. She was a grown woman who'd received a letter giving her very specific instructions, and she wasn't following them, because the men around her kept telling her she wasn't safe. Not that Mercer or Razor knew about the letter, but still. She couldn't do *anything* without one of them knowing where she was, who she was with, even what she was thinking. She pulled out her phone, not caring that the sun hadn't risen yet. Today was going to be different. Today she'd live her life on *her* terms.

"Hello? Quinn? Is everything okay?"

"You said to contact you if I need anything," she told Laird when he answered her call.

"Yes."

Quinn heard Sorcha in the background asking who he was talking to.

"What do you need?" Laird asked.

"Tell Razor you need to see me. Tell him to bring me to my grandfather's estate, and then meet me there."

"What is this about?" he asked.

"I think you know," she said before she hung up. She pulled her jeans out of her bag, checked to make sure her letter was still in the pocket, and then got dressed.

Kade, Doc, whoever he was, told her to contact Naughton when she received his letter, and that was what she was going to do. If he'd wanted her to ask permission first, he would've said so.

"What's going on?" Razor asked when she came downstairs. "Why do I have to take you to meet Burns?"

"He didn't tell you?" she said.

"No, Skipper. He didn't, and you know he didn't. Now tell me what's going on."

Quinn put her hands on her hips. "I can't tell you."

"Get serious."

"I am serious. Let's go."

Razor was pissed. She could feel the anger seeping off of him. If Laird hadn't been the one to call and ask him to bring her to meet him, none of this would be happening, Quinn knew that. And as far as him being pissed, so was she.

"This is bullshit," Razor said when she got out of the SUV.

She shrugged her shoulders and walked through the woods, just like she had the last time she'd met Laird here.

"Quinn," Laird said, getting out of the truck.

"I want to see Naughton. Now."

"Now? Yes, you can see Naughton, but not now."

"I need to see him."

"He's in the middle of a harvest, Quinn. There is no way I can take you to see him now."

"I don't care what he's in the middle of. The letter said to contact him after I read it, and that's what I'm going to do. That's what Kade told me to do, so, please, take me to see him."

Laird sighed, which to Quinn meant he knew at least part of what she'd said was right. Kade told her to make contact for a reason, even if she had no idea what that reason was. She could tell Laird was thinking the same thing.

"I understand, and I'll make arrangements for you to meet him, but not now. He cannot stop the harvest without raising suspicion. I promise I will make it happen, but it cannot be before the harvest has come in. Stop asking me to jeopardize your safety and my son's."

The tone of Laird's voice convinced her he wasn't making excuses. For now, she'd accept it, but if much more time passed, she'd figure it out on her own.

Laird pointed to the house, and she saw lights on inside. "Come on, let's go," he said. "It's too risky for us to meet here again."

"Where are we going?" she asked when they got to the highway and Laird turned left instead of right.

"Home."

"But it's the other way."

"My home—Butler Ranch."

"Why?" Had he changed his mind? Was he taking her to see Naughton after all?

"There's something I want you to see."

When they pulled through the gates of Butler Ranch a few minutes later, Quinn was overcome.

"It's so beautiful," she said.

The sun was up, and it looked as though a layer of mist hovered over the vineyards. She'd never seen vineyards heavy with fruit. The ones at her grandfather's estate had been dormant for years when she had last visited.

"Where is he?"

"Naughton?"

Quinn nodded.

"They're harvesting. That isn't why you're here."

"Why am I here?"

"You'll see."

—:—

Mercer was ready to rip the hair from his head. *"Where did you say she is?"*

"I don't know exactly. Burns called and ordered me to bring her to Old Creek Road. A few minutes later, she came downstairs, refusing to tell me a damn thing."

"Why didn't you say no?" Mercer was seething, and if Razor was in front of him instead of on the phone, he might consider killing him.

"Because Burns told me to bring her."

"Since when do we answer to Burns?"

"I don't know, man. I don't know. Maybe I'm... shit...I don't know."

First he got a message from Paps that Calder had been located, but by the time he arrived where he was supposed to be, there was no sign of him ever being there.

When he'd messaged Paps, saying he was on his way, he'd thought it was a damn good thing he'd asked Razor to stay at the house last night. He no longer thought so.

"I can't explain it, Eighty-eight. It's like...Burns and...Doc...and now, Quinn. I can't explain it, but I couldn't say no."

"I get it, but where are they now?"

"I don't know. I haven't been able to reach Burns since I left her there."

"Are you sure he met her?"

"Yes, Eighty-eight, I'm sure. A few minutes ago, you said we don't answer to Burns. I don't answer to you either."

Razor disconnected the call, but Mercer didn't care. He needed to find Quinn, and then get to the bottom of what she and Burns were up to.

—:—

"This was Kade's apartment," Laird told her, leading her up the narrow staircase. "To my knowledge, no one has been in here since he left."

They were standing at the threshold of the door. Laird had his hand on the nob.

"Are you okay?" Quinn asked, resting her hand on his arm. "We don't have to do this."

"I'm not doing anything," he responded. "You are."

Quinn laughed after she got over her shock at Laird opening the door of Kade's apartment and telling her to look around. "Call me when you're ready to leave," he told her.

The man was a neat-freak. There wasn't a single thing out of place, but it went further. Books were organized by fiction or non-fiction, and then subcategories of both. Each shelf went in height order too, and the books were pulled forward to the very edge of the shelf.

His kitchen was arranged in a similar manner. She opened a drawer and found wooden gadgets, while the drawer above it held metal. In another drawer, she found spices, in a rack, arranged in alphabetical order.

She opened the refrigerator, not surprised to find it and the freezer completely empty. Maybe someone had been in here and had at least gotten rid of food that might spoil.

His bedroom was equally neat and organized, but there was no sign of *him*. It could've been anyone's room. Just down the hallway, she found another door, but it was locked. She was about to call Laird and tell him she was finished looking around, but changed her mind. There was a reason that door was locked, and she wanted to know what it was. She wondered where a man like Kade would hide a spare key.

She searched in the places she thought were most obvious, at least to her, and then sat at the table when she ran out of ideas. Something she hadn't noticed before caught her eye on the bookshelves. A wooden tortoise held a partial row of books up, but its shape wasn't something she would've considered a bookend.

She walked over and picked it up, turning it in her hand. The base was solid wood, and as she studied the top and sides, she didn't see anything that appeared to open. She was about to set it back on the shelf, when her finger brushed against the tail, and it moved. Quinn grasped it with her thumb and index finger, and it moved more. She pulled it and out slid a tray that held a single key.

Padding back to the locked door, she said a silent plea that the key would open it, and it did. Nothing could have prepared her for what she found when she walked inside though.

Instead of computers or whatever she'd thought someone in Kade's line of work would have behind a locked door, there were photos. Everywhere. And they were photos of her. Some were with her mom. In some, she was alone, and in some she was with Kade. What every single photo of her with either of them together had in common, though, was they were taken before she was seven.

The others, the ones of her alone, were taken at every stage of her life, and most, with the exception of school photos, were candid—all taken without her knowledge.

There was a creepy factor, definitely, but she also felt a sense of security that was different than just hearing he'd arranged for her to be protected her whole life. Someone didn't keep photos of a person they were protecting, not like this. Every photo was framed and looked as though it had been placed deliberately.

There was one tucked behind another that she walked over to take a closer look at. This was the only one she'd seen where she was with Laird and Sorcha.

It had been taken at the house in Montecito. She might not have recognized it if she hadn't just visited. In it, she looked like a little girl surrounded by the love of her grandparents, but if that were the case, why wouldn't have anyone said so?

Quinn sat in Kade's desk chair and studied it and a couple of the other photos long enough that she lost track of time. Laird hadn't said anything specific about when they'd need to leave.

Something caught her eye from the window. It was Laird, heading in this direction. Instead of waiting for him, she decided to lock up behind her and meet him downstairs.

If anything had come of this discovery, it was that she was more determined than ever to talk to Naughton.

"I asked you to wait upstairs for me," Laird grumbled at her when she met him in the winery.

His tone of voice startled her. "No, you didn't. You didn't say anything of the kind."

"You don't belong in here."

There it was, the stab of pain that would wipe out all the good feelings she got when she found the photos, and replace them with feelings of being unwanted, unwelcome, unworthy of the Butler's love and affection.

Quinn folded her arms. "I'm done waiting, Laird."

"We've discussed this already, and you must wait until the harvest is complete."

"I don't care. He needs to know, and I refuse to leave until I see him."

"Not happening, precious," Mercer whispered in her ear. "Let's go."

Quinn nearly jumped. She hadn't heard him come in, or sneak up behind her. When she tried to jerk herself away from him, he wouldn't let her go.

"We're leaving, one way or another. I'll carry you out of here if I have to."

She glared at Laird as Mercer escorted her out a back door, adding betrayal to all the other things he'd made her feel in the last few minutes.

Mercer opened the passenger door of the SUV Razor typically drove, and told her to get in. Without another word, he closed it behind her, and didn't speak until they were almost back to Happy Valley Ranch.

"We're going to have a talk this afternoon," he began.

"Why bother? I can recite every word you'll say without needing to hear them."

"This isn't a joke, Quinn."

"You're right, Mercer. It's my life. *My life.* It isn't your life. You were hired to protect me. I'm sure Kade never expected that you'd take that to mean you should insinuate yourself into it."

The words hurt her to say as much as she knew they were hurting Mercer, but didn't any of them understand how much their words hurt her?

"I thought we were past this," he murmured.

"Past it? As in you've placated me with as little information as possible, expecting that, from then on, I'd simply toe the line, accept that I was nothing more than a pretty bird kept in someone's cage?"

"It isn't like that."

"No?"

"No." He shook his head. "Why were you at Butler Ranch?"

"None of your business."

"What did you mean when you said 'he needs to know, and I refuse to leave until I see him.'?"

"Like I said, it's none of your concern."

"Everything about you is my concern," he bellowed.

"Not anymore," she yelled back at him.

He didn't respond, but his grip on the steering wheel tightened.

"Let me ask you something, Eighty-eight. Were you the one who took all those photos of me? You know, the ones adorning your boss' office? Didn't you feel like a stalker, or maybe even a pedophile, taking photos of an innocent little girl?"

When Mercer turned and looked into her eyes, she immediately regretted her words, but she couldn't take them back, and she wouldn't apologize, because she wasn't sorry for the majority of what she'd said. Only the last thing she said.

Mercer didn't slow down to take the turn into Happy Valley Ranch.

"Where are you taking me?"

He didn't respond, so she asked again, this time raising her voice. He still didn't respond. It was like he didn't hear her.

"I hate you," she spat at him. "I hate all of you."

"You sound just like Barbie."

—:—

"Wait here," he told her when he pulled into the garage of the Harmony house.

"You're just going to leave me here?"

He slammed the door behind him and stomped into the house.

"Talk," said Paps, meeting him just inside the door with his arms folded.

"She hates me. Hates all of us, but mainly me."

"Where is she?"

"In the SUV."

"Take the bike and go. I'll handle this."

Mercer hadn't realized the bike was in the garage. The last time he'd seen it, it was at the house in Montecito. He nodded his head and walked out.

Someone she didn't recognize approached her door as Mercer sped off on a motorcycle.

"Hello, Quinn," he said in a voice that reminded her of the way Hannibal Lecter spoke to Clarice Starling. "Please, come inside."

"Who are you?"

"My name is Gunner Gadot, but everyone calls me Paps."

She followed him inside, and he motioned to a chair in the kitchen. "Sit," he told her, and then left the room.

"We're going to have a little chat," he said when he came back, "whether you want to or not."

22

As right as he knew Paps was, staying away from Quinn was going to be the hardest thing Mercer had ever done. It was necessary though.

The words Paps had said to him back in June haunted him. *There won't be any coming back if she's dead. Let her be mad at you. Hell, let her hate you if it's gonna keep her safe.*

That was the life he had to live, with Quinn hating him, until Calder and his cronies no longer walked freely on the face of the earth, and until he knew, one way or another, if Doc and Leech were alive or dead.

"What was that about with you and Quinn?" he'd called Laird and asked.

When he told him it was nothing he needed to know for the time being, Mercer put his fist through the wall of the Harmony house garage. Fortunately, Paps and Razor were both staying at Happy Valley Ranch with Quinn, so he could repair it without them knowing what had happened.

Being completely off Quinn's detail for the time being meant he was the first responder for anything that came up. On deck for him tonight was an emergency meeting of the Westside Winery Collaborative that Alex Avila had called. He'd have backup tonight from Razor, who told him he had a bad feeling.

"If Calder is going to act, it would be tonight," Razor had said.

Mercer agreed and paced while he waited for him to arrive at the designated time. Razor wanted to pick up some of his extra gear that was stored at the house, and suggested Mercer bring his along too. Instead, Mercer wore it. It had been a long time since he was in full tactical gear, especially in the end of summer heat.

It immediately took him back to Afghanistan and the oppressive hell it always felt like. That's why he never got cold, like he'd told Quinn. After being out for over twenty-four hours straight on a run, Mercer vowed he'd never complain about being cold again, no matter how long he lived.

"Where you at?" he heard Razor call out.

"In here." Mercer grabbed the only gun he wasn't already wearing and met him in the kitchen.

"Guess we don't have to flip a coin to determine who's inside and who's out."

"Figured I'd save time," he mumbled.

Mercer stood outside, near the back entrance of the winery, while Razor was inside, near the front. He was there as a "guest" of Laird Butler's, so no one would question his presence. Each of them wore a mic and earpiece tonight, so he could hear when Alex called the meeting to order.

"I'm sure you're all aware of what took place at Jenson Vineyards Monday night," Mercer heard her say. She went on to say that the authorities believed it was connected to the arson at Butler Ranch, as well as what had happened with the ATB at Los Cab.

"We also believe there is further imminent threat to Los Cab, Butler Ranch, and the other vineyards and wineries on the westside, and that is my reason for calling tonight's meeting," she added.

Alex explained that a collaborative member had overheard a conversation between Rory Calder and Trey Deveux, and the specific things that were said.

"Why haven't they been arrested? If someone overheard them mention Jenson, isn't that proof enough?" Mercer heard someone ask.

"You know it isn't, Bob. As much as we wish it were."

"Who was that?" Mercer asked Razor.

"Maddox."

The discussion continued, but Mercer had stopped listening. Instead, he surveyed the perimeter of the building, not seeing anything that looked suspicious.

When he heard someone say, "The Deveux family and the Calders are more than connected. They're related. By marriage," he started paying attention again.

"Some say it was an arranged marriage. One of Rory's brothers married one of the Deveux daughters."

In and of itself, that news wasn't something that needed to be kept under wraps, but he hoped the group refrained from further speculation.

"Something's happening," Razor said a few minutes later.

"Be right there," Mercer told him. He was about to step out into the light when he saw a black SUV pulling away from the curb.

"What's your twenty?" Mercer said into the mic and waited to move until he received Razor's response.

"Raz, give me your twenty," he said again, watching as Maddox pulled up in another vehicle and yelled for Naughton to get in.

Moments later, Razor pulled up alongside Mercer with the passenger door already open.

"What the hell happened to you?" asked Mercer noticing blood on Razor's forehead.

"Bastard got me good enough that I saw stars for a minute."

"Who?"

"The man who just abducted Bradley St. John."

"Was it Calder? Deveux? What the hell happened?" Mercer asked as Razor did his best to tail Maddox.

"It wasn't either, but whoever it was looked enough like Calder that he caught my attention. Unfortunately, I caught his too, and that's when he pistol-whipped me."

"What was he carrying? Could you tell?"

"Beretta Bobcat," answered Razor, trying to keep his focus on the road while blood streamed from the gash on his head.

Mercer knew better than to ask if he could drive. There was nothing they could do if he couldn't. Other than the blood, Razor appeared to be functioning okay.

When Maddox looked like he planned to go east on the highway, Mercer made a call. "Don't follow him. Head to Tablas Creek," he told Razor.

"You're readin' my bleedin' mind," he said, making the turn on what felt like two wheels.

When Razor got close, the number of vehicles out front told them they'd guessed right. "Let me out," Mercer asked, and jumped when Razor came close to a stop.

He stayed low, making his way through the trees, trying to get a fix on what was happening. He only needed to hear the words, "He's got a gun," to make his move.

Razor's voice came through the earpiece. "Sheriff and SWAT incoming."

"Roger." Mercer went around the back of the winery and froze.

"She recognized me. What the fuck was I supposed to do?" he heard someone yell. *"Get your ass over here and help me straighten this mess out."*

Without a second thought, Mercer slammed open the back door of the winery building, leveling his gun at the man on the phone who spun around and did the same to him.

"Drop it or I'll shoot you, and I don't miss," he warned.

It was a split-second flinch, but Mercer saw it and fired first, shooting the man in the chest and arm.

"Get out. Get out!" Came Razor's voice through the earpiece.

"Roger," answered Mercer, exiting the way he'd came in and running through the woods toward the coordinates Razor sent to his phone.

He jumped in the SUV the same way he'd gotten out. Razor hadn't needed to come to a full stop before he was inside and they were speeding away.

"He's dead," Mercer told him, checking his gun. "I think he was on the phone with Calder when I shot him."

"Affirmative. He was Calder's brother."

"You got ears?"

"Yep. On Naughton."

"Shit."

Razor continued listening until they were back at the Harmony house and certain the situation was secure for the time being.

"He was gonna kill her," Mercer told him.

Razor nodded. "I heard, and if it had been me in there instead of you, I wouldn't have bothered warning him before I took him out."

Mercer called Paps.

"You're goin' under for a while, Eighty-eight."

Exactly what he expected Paps to say. He'd killed their primary target's brother. He had to ghost before Calder figured out a connection and put a million dollar bounty on Mercer's head.

23

Things had changed drastically for Quinn since the day Paps had sat her down and told her what was what. If she'd felt like a bird in a cage before, now she felt like one whose wings had been clipped. Even if she escaped, she wouldn't be able to fly.

Most days she saw only Razor and Paps. Occasionally Laird would be at the house, but he never spoke to her. He hadn't since the day in the winery when he told her she didn't belong there.

It had been almost two months since the last time she heard anyone mention Mercer, and she hadn't asked about him. In fact, she rarely spoke to anyone. Paps had taken her phone away, telling her that her friends had been informed that she was safe, but unreachable for the next few weeks, just like her mother had told her. Otherwise, they both knew no one else would be looking for her.

She ventured into the kitchen, one morning, when she thought she heard someone leave, hoping to find Razor alone. Instead, Laird was at the table.

"Good morning, Quinn," he said.

"Good morning," she murmured, and turned to go back up the stairs.

"Wait," he said and stood to follow her.

She had her hand on the banister, waiting for him to continue, but she refused to turn around.

"I made you a promise, and I intend to keep it."

"What's that?" she asked, still refusing to look at him.

"It's time for you to talk to Naughton."

She turned slowly, almost afraid to look in his eyes. The last time she had, he hurt her as badly with his words as he would've if he'd slapped her.

"I'm sorry, Quinn."

"What for?"

"I didn't mean the things I said in the way you took them."

"Yes, I can see how someone could misinterpret the words 'you don't belong here.'"

"There's no point arguing. I apologized, and now I am honoring my promise to you."

Quinn folded her arms. "How is this going to work?"

"You're going to go upstairs, get dressed, and find the letter you received from my son."

"I don't have the birth certificate."

"I do."

"Wait in there," Laird told her, pointing to the entrance to the tasting room where he'd said those awful words to her.

When she hesitated, he said, "Go, lass. It's time."

"Where will you be?"

"I'll wait near the back entrance, where you left from before."

"You don't want to come with me."

"This is between you and Naughton. No one else."

"Who are you?" the man asked a few minutes later. "We aren't open yet."

"You must be Naughton," she said.

"I didn't ask who I am; I asked who you are."

She stepped forward and held out her hand. "I'm Quinn."

Naughton folded his arms. "Quinn who?"

"My last name's Hess although, recently, I've discovered that on my birth certificate it's listed as Butler."

"Who the hell are you?"

Quinn hated his words almost as much as his tone of voice. "I'm your oldest brother's secret, and I have a lot to tell you, *Uncle* Naughton," she spat at him.

He didn't think she belonged here either? Well, maybe finding out she was his niece would change his mind. Not that she was certain she was.

"Have a seat," he said, motioning to a stool at the tasting bar.

"You haven't been easy to get an audience with."

"You're here now. Start talking, Quinn."

"I'm not sure where to begin…"

Quinn heard someone walking through the winery. Naughton noticed it too. Should she say that no one else could know what she was about to tell him?

"Before you get started, I have to make a phone call."

Quinn nodded and waited, hoping Laird had intercepted whoever had been about to come in.

Quinn looked up when she heard another door open. She turned around, and a man and woman came in. *Shit, shit, shit,* she swore silently. *What now?*

"Who's this?" the man asked, walking over to meet her.

"I'm Quinn."

"What's your last name, Quinn?"

"As I was just telling your brother—"

"Hess," Naughton said before she could continue.

"Interesting." Maddox studied her. "Any relation to the Hess family we know?"

"Lena Hess is my mother."

"I'm Bradley. I'm Naughton's fiancée."

Quinn shook the woman's hand but kept her eyes on Naughton, hoping he'd ask them to leave so they could talk.

"It's nice to meet you, Quinn," said Maddox. "We don't know your mother that well and had no idea she had a daughter."

She hadn't prepared for this. She'd only planned what she was going to say to Naughton, and even that hadn't gone as she'd planned. "I've been away...until recently. First, boarding school, and then college."

"Fall break?" Mad asked.

"Something like that."

"We haven't seen your mother since...when was the last time we saw Lena, Naught?"

"Late June, early July, from what I remember."

"That's actually why I'm here...about my mother." It seemed as good of an excuse as any other, since they'd brought her up. "But I can see this isn't a good time."

"It isn't, actually. Bradley and I have an appointment this afternoon," said Naughton.

"Maybe I can help you," Maddox offered.

"Thanks, but...I'll, uh...be in touch." Quinn picked her purse up from where it sat on the bar and turned to leave.

"Wait," Maddox said. "How do we get in touch with you?"

Quinn looked at Naughton. "You don't. I'll get in touch with you."

When she walked out the back door, Laird was waiting where he'd said he would be.

"Total disaster," she mumbled.

"I'm sorry. They were on their way in before I could stop them. What did you tell them?"

"Nothing. I told Naughton who I was and that was it." Quinn looked out the window as Laird drove through the back vineyards. "He wasn't very nice."

Maybe she didn't want anything more to do with this family than they wanted to do with her. So far, Sorcha had been nice to her, but she'd only been with her for a couple of minutes. Laird had been at first, but now he was as mean as Paps and Razor were being. Since Naughton wasn't any more welcoming, maybe she should rethink her plan to get to know him. Why bother? She didn't need Kade's money; she'd be fine on her own. If they tried to contact her about the trust, she'd hire a lawyer to tell them she didn't want it.

"There will be another time," Laird said.

"There won't. I'm not interested in talking to him again."

"I see."

When he pulled up to the house at Happy Valley Ranch, Quinn got out, went inside, and straight upstairs. If Razor thought she was feeling sorry for herself again, he was right. If anyone should be entitled to, it was her. Her life fucking sucked.

Three weeks later, Quinn was sitting in her bedroom, where she spent all day, every day, looking out the window. She'd just finished another book, the only thing she could do in her confinement, but hadn't picked the next one in the pile up to start yet.

Razor rapped on her door. "Dinner is ready."

"I'm not hungry." She was never hungry. The only time she ate was when she crept down at night, and grabbed enough fruit and bread to get her through the next day. Sometimes Razor would bring food and leave it outside her door. She'd always eat what he brought. She wasn't stupid enough to starve herself, only stubborn enough not to be willing to spend time with them.

"It's Thanksgiving, Skipper."

Her eyes filled with tears. "Thanks for the reminder," she managed to say before she was full-on crying. The last time she spoke to her mother, she'd said she hoped to be back by Thanksgiving.

"Please let me in," Razor pleaded.

She kept the door locked, not that it would bar any of them from coming in if they'd wanted to. It was one of those simple locks that a hairpin could open.

"I need to talk to you."

She got up and walked to the door, opening it and then walking back to where she'd been sitting, keeping her back to him. She heard him approaching and closed her eyes tight.

"I thought you should have this," he said, handing over her phone when she opened her eyes.

"Why?"

"Because there isn't any reason you shouldn't."

"Is the warden just going to take it away from me later?"

"Stop it. You're not a prisoner, Quinn. You're the one who has chosen to behave like one."

"I didn't hand my phone over to him willingly. He took it."

"Paps did what he thought was best at the time. I would've given it back to you weeks ago if you'd told me what happened."

She shrugged. "You say that now."

"Look at me.

When she didn't, Razor grabbed the arms of her chair and turned it so she was facing him. "Ask me anything you want to know, and I'll tell you. Talk to us. Stop hiding out upstairs, only coming out at night, like a bat. Hey, that would be a better name for you than Skipper. I'm gonna start calling you Batgirl."

Quinn refused to smile even though she knew he was trying to break through the barricade she'd erected around herself. She powered her phone on, thankful to see he'd charged it.

"No word from my mother, right?" she said before sobs overcame her and she couldn't say anything else.

Razor picked her up like some kind of doll, sat in the chair, and held her on his lap. "Let it out, Skipper. Cry all you need to."

He held her there, stroking her hair, until she'd finally cried herself out.

"I'm sorry," she said, wiggling off his lap.

"Don't be. It's way overdue."

"She said she hoped she'd be back by now."

Razor nodded. "I know she wanted to be. We wanted that too."

"Nothing's changed?"

"No, in fact, it's worse."

"Why?"

"Sure you want to know?"

Quinn nodded.

"Eighty-eight killed Calder's brother."

Her hand flew to her mouth, and she felt as though she was about to be sick. "Oh my God, is Mercer..." Sobs overtook her again, and she threw herself on the bed, burying her head in the pillow.

Razor pulled at her arm. "He's fine. He's just had to go underground for a while. I would've told you that too, if you'd ask."

At least she knew why he hadn't been there, besides the fact that she told him she hated him. "Do you talk to him?"

"Yep."

"Can you tell him I don't hate him."

"Sure, I could do that, or you could tell him yourself."

Quinn looked at her phone. Maybe that's why Razor gave it back to her, so she could call him. "Thank you."

"You're welcome. Now, let's go eat."

"I'm sorry, but I'm really not—"

"How are you going to tell him yourself if you won't even come downstairs to see him?"

Quinn flew off the bed and ran downstairs where Mercer was waiting with his arms open.

"I'm sorry. I'm sorry. I'm sorry," she repeated, wrapping her arms around his neck.

"I'm the one who's sorry, precious."

"I don't hate you. Not at all."

He looked into her eyes and smiled. "I know that."

"I was mad at you, and then..."

"I'm sorry I disappeared on you. It couldn't have been prevented."

"I know. Razor told me what happened."

"He did?" Mercer looked around her and glared at him.

"Somebody had to tell her," he said, holding his arms up in the air.

"Actually, no one did," added Paps, but he was smiling too. "Let's eat. I'm starving."

Mercer had his hands on the sides of her waist. "They told me you weren't eating."

Quinn looked at the floor, but Mercer tilted her chin so he could see her eyes. "We'll talk later. For now, let's eat."

She nodded and sat in the chair he held for her. It had been so long since she'd sat at a table and eaten a meal, she wasn't sure her stomach could handle it, especially with Mercer so close.

After he'd cleaned his plate and had seconds, he turned to her. "Take a walk with me?" he asked.

"Sure." Quinn stood.

"She'll need a jacket. It's cold out there," said Razor.

She couldn't help but smile at him. "Thank you. I'll get one."

"Shoes would be a good idea too," he shouted behind her.

She came back downstairs and followed Mercer outside, and gasped when he spun around, put his hands under her bottom, and lifted her off her feet.

"Wrap your legs around me," he said, carrying her until her back was up against the house. He covered her mouth with his and kissed her so deeply it hurt, but she didn't care, and pushed back at him just as hard.

He held her with one hand while he gripped the side of her face with the other. "I couldn't stand not having you in my arms another minute," he breathed. "I missed you so much."

Quinn kissed him again, not wanting her lips anywhere but on his, and her body wrapped around him. I missed you too," she said, running her tongue down his neck.

"Don't mind us," she heard Razor say, and looked to see him and Paps getting in the SUV they kept parked by the house. "See ya tomorrow, Batgirl," he shouted.

"Batgirl?" Mercer asked.

"His new name for me."

"Let's go inside," he said, setting her on her feet.

"I don't want to talk, Mercer."

"Neither do I, precious."

24

The past three weeks had been a slice of heaven. He had Quinn in his arms twenty-one days, during which the only thing Paps or Razor would contact him about was Calder, Doc, or Leech reappearing.

Mercer took her body every way he'd imagined in the time he was away from her. Some days they never went outside, some days they didn't bother getting dressed, because they knew it wouldn't be long before their bodies were joined together again.

The tea kettle started to whistle, and Mercer went to the stove to turn off the burner. When he turned around, Quinn stood before him, bare, the way he preferred her to be.

"I don't want you to leave our bed without telling me," she pouted. "I hate waking up and finding you aren't there."

Mercer walked over and wrapped his arm around her waist. "Come here, precious." With one arm, he swept everything off the dining room table, not caring if it clattered to the floor, and then lifted her. "Lie back," he told her.

"Mercer," she groaned, weaving her fingers in his hair.

He ran his tongue from the inside of her knee, up her thigh, until he got close enough to her sex that he could breathe in the scent of her. "Stay still for me," he murmured.

Every day had been this way, since Thanksgiving. Quinn was his, body and soul, and he proved it to her. Again and again, he'd take her body soaring to the pinnacle of pleasure, let her fall back into his arms, and then begin again. He craved her moans of ecstasy as much as her mewls of bliss.

"Tell me what you want, precious," he demanded from her, needing to hear her say the words.

"I want you inside of me."

"My tongue is inside of you already."

"I want more," she pleaded. "You know what I want, Mercer."

He brought her to the brink and then backed off over and over until she finally screamed the words he wanted to hear.

"I love the way you beg," he answered, thrusting inside of her, giving her what she asked for.

Sometimes, like now, her pleasure would be so intense, he'd swear her eyes rolled back in her head. Other times, she'd be moved to tears.

Later today, he'd have to tell her that their time at Happy Valley Ranch was coming to an end. The family who owned it had graciously allowed them to stay an extra week, but they would be arriving for the Christmas holiday tomorrow.

He'd made arrangements for them to stay at a house on the beach instead, but it wouldn't be the same.

"What are you thinking about?" she asked, sitting up so her legs were wrapped around his waist. "Whatever it is, you don't look happy." She scooted forward so her wetness rubbed against him. "And right now you should be very happy."

"I am happy."

She squeezed her legs tighter. "Tell me now, or I'll torture it out of you."

"We're moving to the beach this afternoon."

"That isn't so bad." She unwrapped her legs, climbed off the table, and sat in the chair next to him. "It's back to reality though, isn't it?"

"I'm afraid so."

"When are we leaving?" she asked.

"Whenever you're ready."

"Can we go now? I mean after we pack and then clean up?"

"Sure. Why the rush?"

"There's something I want to do on the way."

"Are you going to tell me what?"

"I want to get a Christmas tree."

Mercer smiled. "I'd like that too."

There was a lot, on the west end of Cambria, where the farmers' market was held in the summer, that had trees for sale. It took Quinn half an hour to decide which one she wanted, but he didn't care. This was as close to normal as he could imagine life being, and he never wanted it to end.

—:—

The call came in from Paps on December 23, and Quinn knew by the look on Mercer's face that he had to leave. She wanted to beg him not to, ask if he could wait until after Christmas, but it didn't work that way in his world. And if it was news about her grandfather or Kade, she wanted him to go, even if it meant he had to leave tonight.

"It's okay," she said before he spoke. "I understand. Just tell me when."

"Tomorrow."

Christmas Eve. Quinn tightened her fists, determined not to let herself cry. For the last six months, she'd cried more than she had in her whole life, and that was saying something given she was sent to boarding school when she was seven.

"Is there anything you can tell me?"

Mercer shook his head. "I'm sorry."

She plastered the best smile she could on her face. "We'll celebrate Christmas tonight, then."

"I made dinner arrangements."

Mercer took her back to the Sea Chest, where they dined in the private room for the second time. There'd been a Christmas party the night before, so when they walked in, the room was filled with decorations and hundreds of twinkling white lights.

"Did you do this?" she asked.

"I wish I could take credit for it, but no." He explained about the party.

As much as Mercer tried to focus on Quinn, everything he had to do before he left ran through his mind. There was one more package to be delivered on Kade's behalf before Christmas, and he'd already asked Laird to take care of it.

They'd tried to find another operative Mercer felt confident in, to aid Laird with Quinn's detail while he,

Paps, and Razor were gone, but there were none he trusted.

"Max is active," Paps had suggested.

"Max-the-idiot? Are you serious?"

"Just to cover Laird," he'd pressed.

Mercer relented. At least Max was a known entity. What choice did he have?

The news they'd received from an operative in Moscow gave them good reason to believe either Doc or Leech, or both, were still alive.

The source was someone they'd been working with for over two years, someone Doc himself had found. When the call from Paps came earlier, saying the man had finally been successful in infiltrating the organization they suspected Calder was connected to, and that he believed they had at least one prisoner in captivity, they knew they had to act immediately.

Paps and Razor were already on their way, but Mercer's transport had been scheduled for tomorrow anyway since he had to make arrangements with Laird and now Max.

"You're distracted," Quinn said, holding her wine glass up.

He refilled it. "I'm sorry, precious."

"You know what? I've had your undivided attention for an entire month. Do you realize that? It's a month today. So I'm not going to complain or worry. I'm just going to enjoy every minute with you that I can."

"Do you know how much I love you?" He'd only said those words to her once before, but it was important that he say them again tonight. For so long, things had been tentative with them, as though their love for each other was somehow on hold until the mission was over.

"I love you, too, Mercer."

He stood and pulled her into his arms. "Dance with me."

Christmas music played through the room's speakers as Mercer held her close to him.

"Say it again," he whispered.

"I love you, Mercer."

More than anything, he wanted to get down on one knee and beg her to marry him, but he couldn't, not until he could also tell her he was retiring, and he'd never have to leave on another mission again.

Quinn held him tight, the next morning, when Laird came to the house, and Mercer knew he had to say goodbye.

"I'll be back as soon as I can be. While I'm gone, please do as Laird asks you to, precious."

"I will, Mercer. I promise."

"Good girl."

He walked away then and got in the waiting SUV. As it pulled away, he turned to look at her one more time, but she and Laird had gone inside. A feeling came over him that he'd never felt before. It was a fear that chilled his whole body. In that moment, Mercer wondered if he'd ever see her again.

25

New Year's Eve had always been one of Quinn's favorite nights of the year. Not this year, though, since she was on the wrong side of the country, and alone— just like she had been for Christmas.

The energy she'd put into hoping she'd hear something from her mother had proved to be as much of a waste of time as it had been every other year of her life.

Razor and Mercer had both told her that her mother knew she could contact Quinn, and yet the countless messages, texts, and emails she'd sent had gone unanswered.

She stood in the kitchen of the rental house, staring out at the dark, dreary and frigid-looking ocean, wishing more than anything that Mercer was here with her, even though she understood why he couldn't be.

Since that was as big a waste of energy as hoping she'd hear from her mother, she decided to go for a run. Maybe she'd feel better. And if not better, at least less pathetic.

Quinn changed her clothes and went outside.

She stretched and took it slow until her muscles warmed up and she got into a rhythm. Normally she'd stop at the park, but today she felt like going farther.

The beach was more crowded than she'd expected it to be, considering it was cold as hell. She took the wooden steps down from the boardwalk to the sand and continued her run.

When she got to the cliffs at the far end of the beach, she stopped and checked her phone, not really expecting a message, but that didn't mean she could keep herself from looking.

Quinn turned around to start on her way back and ran into a woman who'd just come around one of the big rocks.

"Shit. I'm so sorry. I wasn't watching where I was going," Quinn stammered.

"It's okay, probably my fault. I wasn't looking either," the woman answered.

There was something about her, like they'd met before.

"You look familiar," the woman said and Quinn laughed.

"I was just thinking the same thing."

"Really? How funny. Do you live in Cambria?"

"Nope. Just visiting."

"I'm Ainsley Butler. It's nice to meet you…"

What were the odds that she'd run into a Butler today of all days?

"And you are…"

"Oh, um, sorry…I'm Quinn. Quinn Hess."

Ainsley took her hand, but didn't let go.

"Hey, Ains. What's up?" asked a staggeringly attractive man. "Who's this?" he asked, noticing Ainsley still held Quinn's hand in hers.

"Cris, this is…"

"I'm Quinn," she answered.

"Cris Avila, nice to meet you…wait a minute. Quinn?" He looked at Ainsley, who linked their arms.

"Quinn, this may sound crazy, but there's a family I want you to meet."

Grabbing the arm of a person she'd just met probably wasn't the most polite thing Quinn had ever done, but it had been a reflex. She'd grown so accustomed to being kept a secret, that someone knowing who she was, stunned her enough that she felt light-headed.

"Sorry, I didn't mean to put fingernail marks on your arm." Quinn dropped her hand, shook her head, and looked out at the ocean. "How'd you know?"

"My brother Naughton told me you paid him a visit."

"Did he tell you anything else?"

"That you're my older brother Kade's daughter."

"Daughter—that's an interesting word choice," she said, and then apologized for being so bitchy.

"It's okay. Tell me what you know about Kade."

"Other than his name is on my birth certificate, not much."

"What are you doing right now?"

"Running back to the house, and then not much of anything."

"There's a letter I want to show you."

"Is it from Kade?"

"I think so. I mean, he sent me one, but I have another one that I think belongs to you. I got it on Christmas."

Now Quinn was confused. "Um, I'd need to shower." *And to check in with your father to figure out how I can arrange to spend time with you when he's my current bodyguard.* "What did you have in mind?"

Ainsley wrote an address on a piece of paper. "We aren't far from here. We're staying at Cris' sister's house, about a block up from the beach."

Quinn looked back at Cris who was sitting on a rock, patiently waiting for Ainsley to finish her conversation.

It made her think of Mercer, who she missed more than she could bear, but now even more than that.

"You can walk if you want, or drive, depending on how far the place is where you're staying."

"It's just on the other side of the park," Quinn said, wondering if she should tell her she'd walk when, more than likely, Laird would figure out a way to drop her off.

"Give me an hour?" Quinn said. "Unless you want to get together later."

"An hour is perfect," Ainsley said as she walked away with her boyfriend. "See you soon!"

Quinn looked around the beach, but didn't see Laird anywhere. He was probably waiting until Ainsley was gone before he approached her.

They'd made an agreement that he wouldn't hover when she went for a run, but would stay close enough to see her if she needed him. She guessed it didn't work the other way around, because she needed him now, and she had no idea where he was hiding.

She ran back to the house, looking over her shoulder every few feet, but there was still no sign of him. She unlocked the door, went inside, and found a note from him on the counter.

Max is on your detail today. Let him know if you need anything. —L

That was odd. He hadn't said anything to her about it before she left on her run. Maybe he'd seen her talking with Ainsley, called Max, and then came back to the house to leave the note. It was the only logical explanation she could come up with.

She showered, changed, and was getting ready to leave when she remembered she hadn't checked in with Max, and Laird's note didn't tell her how to go about doing so.

She went outside and saw the black SUV parked across the road, and waved.

"Hi, Max," she said, trying to remember if she'd met him before. He looked vaguely familiar.

"Miss Sullivan, where would you like to go?"

"Um, it's Hess. I haven't gone by Sullivan since... anyway, it's Hess. And I'm going here." She handed him the piece of paper.

Max got out and opened the back passenger door for her.

"Oh, that's okay. I get car sick. I'll just sit up front. It isn't very far."

"Mr. Sharp left explicit instructions as to how you should be transported. In the back, on the floor."

"Surely this isn't necessary. That was when I—"

Quinn saw his hand come up and the white cloth that was about to cover her nose and mouth, and then everything went black.

—:—

The flight from Moscow to Los Angeles had taken close to thirteen hours, and Mercer still had another hour to go before he even landed in San Luis Obispo, followed by an hour to get to the house in Cambria.

He'd been trying to reach either Quinn or Laird since the plane landed, but both phones were going straight to voicemail. If he hadn't been on a commercial flight, he'd pull out his laptop and track them. That would have to wait until he was off the plane and seated somewhere private.

His excitement over seeing Quinn in just a couple of hours was tempered by the devastating disappointment he, along with Paps and Razor, had felt when they arrived at the location where their source said the Russians held captives, only to find their contact dead in a pool of blood, and no other sign of anyone in the building.

They all agreed Mercer should head back while Paps and Razor stayed on and continued to search for clues about Doc and Leech.

Now, twenty-four hours later, he was so close he could practically feel Quinn next to him, yet at the same time, he still felt six thousand miles away.

He tried again to reach Laird and her, and when he couldn't, called Max. When his phone went to voicemail too, Mercer started to panic.

Something was wrong. Very wrong.

"Sorcha, this is Eighty-eight," he said when she answered.

"Oh, Mercer. Yes, what can I do for you?"

"I need your help."

"What?" she asked, in her usual matter-of-fact tone of voice.

"I need you to ask Maddox or Naughton to contact their father. If they are unable to reach him, tell them that he was going down to the beach to look at a house he was thinking of investing in."

"Tell me the address."

Mercer rattled off the house number and name of the street, hoping Sorcha could handle this.

"Goodbye, Mercer," she said.

"Wait."

"What?"

"Call me as soon as you hear something." He heard her mumble something he didn't understand, but somehow knew meant "stupid." He didn't care. She could call him any name she wanted to as long as she sent her sons looking for their father.

Five minutes later she called back. "They're on their way, but you have other operatives on the ground here, Mercer. Did you not know this? I've engaged them to look not only there but the house in Harmony as well as Happy Valley. Where else should I send them?"

In the time she took to do all of that, Mercer had only begun putting the same plan together. He could only attribute his sluggish reaction time to his extreme worry and lack of sleep.

"Is it my Quinn?" she said quietly, her accent more pronounced and her demeanor so drastically different from the take-charge woman who'd been barking at him moments ago.

"I can't locate either of them. Or Max."

The sound she made could only be described as complete anguish.

"You *dinnae* find my Kade either."

"No, Sorcha, but Paps and Razor are still looking."

He heard the announcement that his flight was boarding. "I'll call you back as soon as I land in San Luis Obispo."

"Aye," she said and disconnected the call.

An hour later, he powered on his phone as the plane taxied in. There was one message from Sorcha, telling him to call back as soon as he landed.

"We tracked both Laird and Max to Tablas Creek," she told him. "I've told the boys to hold off until you give the word."

"Which boys, Sorcha?" God, were Maddox and Naughton involved in this now?

"Your boys, I *canna* keep track of all the names. Never mind that. What do you want them *to do?*"

Mercer thought for less than a second when he heard the phone jostle.

"Eighty-eight, this is Monk. I'm here with Sorcha, and waiting for your orders."

He raced the bike over the back roads from the airfield to Tablas Creek. He knew the layout of the place from going in when Calder's brother had abducted Bradley St. John.

He pulled off the road where he'd arranged to meet Monk. Seconds later he arrived, and gave him the rundown of what the team had found.

"From what we've been able to piece together, Max brought Skipper here, but once he arrived, his tracking terminated."

"He wanted us to know he was here," mumbled Mercer. "Just in case." Maybe Max-the-idiot wasn't as clueless as they'd assumed he was.

"Affirmative, sir."

"What else?" he asked while he changed into the tactical gear Monk had brought for him.

"We have a portable ZBV that detected four people inside the building. Only one is active."

"Can you tell if the other three are alive."

"Affirmative on two of the three."

Which meant one of the three was dead.

"Radio, sir," Monk said, handing him the earpiece.

It would take him approximately four minutes to get from where he was to the building where Quinn was being held. This wouldn't go down like it had with Calder's brother. This time the person holding her, Laird, and Max, knew he was coming—and one of those three was already dead.

Mercer crept closer to the building and decided to go in one of the side doors. " Monk, wait at the back until I give the word."

"Roger, sir."

He'd entered the building on the side he knew was filled with barrels, and made his way through them.

"*Eighty-eight,* I know you're here," he heard a voice call out. "I have your *precious* with me."

"You won't hurt her, Calder. You know who she is."

"She's nothing to me," he yelled.

"You knew the minute you saw her." Mercer kept his voice steady, making his way around the walls the barrels formed until he could see both Calder and Quinn.

She was gagged, her hands bound behind her. From where he was, he couldn't get a clean shot without risking her life, so he circled back and went in a different way.

From there he could see Laird, about ten feet from where Calder held Quinn. He was slumped over in the chair he was tied to, but breathing. Another body, which Mercer assumed was Max, was just inside the front door of the building; he'd been shot in the back several times.

"You have until the count of five to come out, or I'll kill her before I kill Burns. You come out, and I'll change the order."

"She's your daughter, your own flesh and blood, Rory. You can't kill her."

"She's nothing to me," he yelled again.

"What do you want, Calder?"

"Don't play games. You know what I want."

Mercer had a clear line of vision and a clean shot. Right before he pulled the trigger, Calder turned in his direction. The gun he held in his right hand was aimed directly at him, while the barrel of the one he held in his left was against Quinn's temple.

"I want the files, and I know you have them."

"I don't have them. We couldn't find them." Mercer changed his angle and fixed his sight on Calder.

"Give me the fucking files, or I'll kill her."

"I don't have them. We couldn't find them, just like you couldn't."

Mercer leveled his gun and aimed, not sure whether the shot was clean enough. Who would get the shot off first? It was too close. She was too close.

In the split second it took him to decide, another shot rang out.

"No!" he screamed. He flew from between the barrels, watching in disbelief as Calder fell to the floor instead of Quinn.

He cut through the rope binding her hands and called out to Monk. "Get your ass out here and help me." He'd think about why the man hadn't waited for his word later, but right now he could only thank God he hadn't.

"Oh my God, Mercer," Quinn cried when he removed the gag from her mouth.

"I'm here, precious," he said, holding her trembling body close to his while he shouted out again for Monk.

He kissed her lips, her cheeks, her eyes, her nose. "I was so scared," he whispered. "I love you so much."

"I love you, Mercer."

Quinn turned her gaze from him to the man walking toward them.

"Let's get one thing straight, Eighty-eight," he heard a familiar voice say as the man in full tactical gear approached. "She never was his daughter. She's always been mine."

Doc cupped her cheek with the palm of his hand. "Hello, Quinn," he said, as Mercer let her go, and her father took her in his arms.

Keep reading for a sneak peek at the next heart-poundingly sexy novel in

Heather Slade's

Butler Ranch Series,

available now.

Kade

1

He'd been waiting over twenty years to be close enough to kill the man who had ripped the life of a woman Kade had loved, to shreds. Finally, he was able to avenge the horrors she'd faced the day Rory Calder raped and left her for dead. He'd almost killed him then, but Leech Hess, the woman's father, had stopped him. He wondered now if Leech also regretted that Kade didn't get the shot off.

As he walked out from the shadows, he came face to face with a different woman. The last time he'd talked to her in person, she'd been a little girl. Between then and now, he'd only watched her from afar, although there hadn't been a single day he didn't think about her, worry about her, or pray he did right by her.

"Let's get one thing straight, Eighty-eight," Kade said to the man with whom he'd entrusted her safety, Mercer Bryant. "She never was his daughter. She's always been mine."

Kade walked over and cupped her cheek with the palm of his hand. "Hello, Quinn," he said.

Mercer let her go, and Kade held her in his arms for the first time in fourteen years.

"Hi," she murmured, burying her face in his shoulder. "I remember you," she whispered.

"I'm so happy you do."

"Are you really my father?"

He understood why she asked. When he'd crept in the back door of the building where she was being held with a gun to her head, Kade had overheard Mercer tell Calder, the man threatening to kill her, that he wouldn't do it, because Quinn was his flesh and blood. Moments later, Kade had contradicted that by saying she was his daughter.

"Welcome home, son," said his father, who Mercer had untied and helped to his feet.

Kade let go of Quinn and walked over to embrace his da, whose eyes filled with tears.

He took a step back and looked him over. "What did Calder do to you?" Kade asked.

"Knocked me out with something. I don't remember much," his father answered.

Laird Butler, retired CIA agent, code name Burns, had always been his oldest son's hero—today more than ever. At seventy years old, he was still as fit and strong as men half his age.

Showing emotion was something trained out of people in their line of work, but Kade couldn't deny the feelings seeing his father invoked anymore than Laird was able to.

"We should get Burns and Quinn checked out," suggested Mercer.

"Good idea, Eighty-eight." Kade looked over to the other side of the building, where a man lay face down in a pool of blood. "Who's that?"

"Max Lista," Mercer answered. "Our hire, but evidently working with Calder in some capacity."

Later, Kade would discuss the breach with him and their two other partners in K19 Security Solutions, Paps and Razor. He looked at Quinn, who stood with Mercer's arm around her shoulders. She was studying him, curiosity etching lines in her face.

"You're safe now," he said, walking closer to her. Kade knew she was waiting for an answer to her question about whether he was her father or not, and soon he'd give it to her. But not here, not surrounded by death and evil. "Let's get you out of here," he said instead. "I'll have Mercer take you to see my ma," he added. "Da, you go with them."

While Kade was a trained physician's assistant, he had fallout to deal with here and wouldn't feel comfortable examining either Quinn or his father in this setting.

The operatives the K19 team had lined up as backup were making their way into the building and removing all traces of evidence of what had gone down in the last hour. They'd need a sweep and clean crew in here as soon as possible too.

"Should we take that one, Doc?" the man who had introduced himself as Monk asked, pointing at Max Lista's body.

Kade nodded.

"I'll gather the family," said Laird.

"Not today, Da." Kade motioned in Quinn's direction. "I need some time."

"Sorcha will meet us at the Harmony house," Mercer told them.

As far as his siblings were concerned, tomorrow would be soon enough for Kade to see his brothers. The following day, he'd see his two sisters, Skye and Ainsley.

He rubbed his chest, knowing the hurt he'd rained down on them would be difficult to overcome. While his siblings had been kept in the dark, believing, for the past two years, that he was dead, his parents had been uncertain. They knew to wait until they received final confirmation from the K19 team before giving up hope.

The four partners, including himself, were former agents who'd worked for the CIA's Special Activities Division of the agency's National Clandestine Service, or NCS. Three years ago, they'd all left government employment and founded the private security and intelligence firm they called K19 Security Solutions. Ironically, almost one hundred percent of their assignments came from the NCS. However, they made a lot more money carrying them out than they did before.

"Welcome back, Doc," Mercer said, embracing him before he walked Quinn out to the vehicle that had just arrived to transport them.

"Good to be back."

"How's Leech?"

"We flew him to Ramstein. He'll be ready for transport home in a few days."

"Anything I can do?"

"Paps and Razor are still over there. Get 'em out as soon as possible."

Mercer nodded and held up his phone. "They're already out, sir. Someone named Fatale is arranging transport now."

Kade nodded. He would've gotten them out himself if Merrigan, code name Fatale, hadn't briefed him on Calder's return to the United States.

Once Mercer was gone, Kade surveyed the building one last time.

"Moving out, sir," Monk reported.

"I'll ride along." Kade intended to transport the two dead bodies to Camp Roberts personally.

He and Leech had taken out the rest of the Maskhadov faction when they'd mounted their escape after two years of captivity. Calder had been the only surviving member of the organization responsible for killing countless US agents and operatives in the mid-nineties, and that was only because he'd returned to the States shortly after the Maskhadovs captured Leech.

In order to leave the country and exact his revenge, Kade had been forced to make a deal with the most unlikely of allies—United Russia, the only organization who wanted the Maskhadovs dead more than the CIA did. As part of the deal, Kade had agreed to turn Calder over to UR, dead or alive.

He had no intention of leaving Calder's body until he was absolutely certain it was in UR's possession. Only then would he know that the nightmare that began over twenty years ago was finally over.

The hand off of Calder's body had happened quickly and covertly, and for that, he was thankful, particularly since that meant he got to the Harmony house quickly.

"Quinn's asleep," Mercer told Kade when he walked in the back door.

"Where's Ma?" he asked right as she came around the corner, almost knocking him over.

She held him tight as her body shook with cries of happiness, and she murmured what Kade could only assume was a prayer of thankfulness. At the same time, his father rested his hand on Kade's shoulder.

Out of the corner of his eye, he saw Quinn come around the same corner his mother had. Her bewildered gaze traveled back and forth between him and Mercer.

"How are you feeling?" he asked.

"Okay," she murmured in response.

"Would you like to talk?"

"Now?" she asked, once again looking at Mercer.

"It doesn't have to be," Kade answered. "But we can if you want to. I'm sure you have questions."

It was only when Mercer reached his hand out to her that Quinn came all the way into the room.

"There isn't any rush, precious," Kade heard him say to her.

"My head hurts," she said, turning to Sorcha, who rushed to the sink to get Quinn a glass of water.

"Drink this, precious," she said, which elicited a smile from both Quinn and Mercer. "And take these," she added, handing her what looked like aspirin.

"How about you, Da?" Kade asked, wondering if they should consider taking him and Quinn to the hospital.

Before his father could answer, his mother pointed to a bag sitting on the table. "Have someone run this to the hospital and ask Susan in the lab to analyze it."

Of course his father had made sure to collect the cloth used to knock him out, or maybe it had been the one used on Quinn. Regardless, having tests run to determine whether simple ether or something more powerful had been used should be done immediately. Kade wished they'd let him know earlier; he would've taken it to Camp Roberts with him. He looked over at Mercer, who was studying something on his phone.

"What's up?" Kade asked.

"It was chloroform. Someone beat you to it," he reported.

"Who?"

" Monk. Evidently, he picked up a second cloth at the scene."

"Who uses chloroform these days?" his mother said, more than asked.

That was a valid question, although, with the Russians, it depended more on what they could get their hands on. What Kade wanted to know was why Monk hadn't informed him of what he was doing.

"Who is Monk? Who brought him in?" Kade snapped at no one in particular.

"I did," said his father.

"Sorry, Da." Kade rolled his shoulders. He needed to decompress—something he'd always made arrangements to do in the past—but this time, his return was nothing like any other. He'd been gone over two years. First, deep undercover, and then the majority of it held in captivity. Not to mention, reported dead.

"I need a minute." Kade walked out the back door.

"Want one?" Mercer came out later and offered him a beer.

"Ten would be better."

Kade twisted off the cap and downed half the bottle. "Been a damn long time."

"Do what you need to do, Doc."

"Yeah?"

"Yeah. Everyone is going to understand, and if they don't, screw 'em."

"Even if what I need to do is escape to a deserted island somewhere?"

Mercer laughed and nodded.

As tempting as it was, this time, for the first time, Kade had to put his family before himself, something he'd never been able to do before. Quinn needed him now, if only to explain the last twenty-one years of her life.

He leaned forward and rested his forearms on his knees. "I don't know where to start," he said. "How is she?"

"Quinn? She's okay. She has questions, but she knows more than you think she does."

Mercer told him about the time they'd spent at Casa Carrizo, the house in Montecito where she grew up, and how Laird had also given her access to Kade's apartment above the winery.

"She remembers me."

"She does. Bits and pieces at least. She remembers you teaching her how to ride a bike."

Kade smiled. He remembered that day well for its normalcy. He, Lena, and Quinn had spent the morning in town. When they came back to the house, he'd asked if she was ready for him to take the training wheels off her bike. She'd told him she was scared, and he'd promised her that he wouldn't let go until he was sure she was ready. Quinn hadn't pedaled twenty feet before she wanted to try on her own. She'd ridden around and around the circular drive, making him dizzy. He could still hear the sound of her giggling.

Two days later, before the crack of dawn, he'd left on another mission. Lena had begged him not to go, even though she knew damn well he had no choice. The joy he'd felt with Quinn was replaced by guilt and remorse. His guilt, though, wasn't because he was sorry he had to leave. Instead, it was because he couldn't wait to get out of there.

"I'm a selfish bastard," he muttered. "Always have been." He looked up at Mercer. "Right now, all I want to do is leave. That's about as honest as I've ever been, Eighty-eight."

Mercer took a swig of his beer. "Talk to Quinn first, and then leave. However much time you need, take it. I know, without you saying a word, that you've been to hell and back. You look like it too."

Kade laughed. He knew he did. His body was soft, and he probably weighed fifty pounds less than he had when he left.

"I can't, not until I've seen everyone. By the way, how's Lena?"

"No different."

Kade laughed. "She can come back now."

Mercer shook his head and looked away.

"What?"

"If it weren't for Quinn, I'd say we should let her stay gone."

Kade knew exactly what Mercer meant. "She wasn't always this bad."

"Paps told me."

"Paps? Interesting."

Mercer laughed. "I've never seen two people hate each other more than Paps and Lena."

"You know what they say about love and hate."

"Not this time." Mercer shook his head. "So, who's Fatale?"

"MI6."

"How'd he get involved in your mission in Moscow."

"She."

"Huh?"

"Fatale is a woman, and to answer your question, she infiltrated the Maskhadovs about six months ago."

"What was she after?"

"Same thing they were." Same thing Calder was. Same thing he was. MI6, CIA, UR—everybody was after what Calder had hidden over twenty years ago.

"Must be important, considering Calder was willing to kill me to get it."

He hadn't heard Quinn come out the back door. Kade stood. "Have a seat."

"No, thanks. I just came out to see if you were hungry. Sorcha made cock-a-leekie soup."

"She did? Huh." Kade scratched his chin.

"It's my favorite."

"You used to…well, that was a long time ago."

"No, tell me. Please." Quinn sat in one of the other empty chairs and motioned for Kade to sit back down.

He told her about her mother insisting she wouldn't like it, but she had, even when she was little enough to still be in a high chair.

"You used to call it—"

"Kukie-lukie." Quinn laughed. "I remember now."

"Excuse me." Mercer stood and went inside.

"I, uh, guess I better get used to this. There's a lot I need to tell you, not just stories about soup, but stories about your life, Quinn."

"Not today," she murmured, her eyes filling with tears.

"You asked me a question—"

Quinn stood. "Don't answer. Not yet."

About the Author

I write stories set in places I love with characters I'd be happy to call friends. The women in my books are self-confident, successful, and strong, with wills of their own, and hearts as big as the Colorado sky. And the men are sublimely sexy, seductive alphas who rise to the challenge of capturing the sweet soul of a woman whose heart they'll hold in the palm of their hand forever.

I'm an Amazon best-selling author, and a PAN member of Romance Writers of America. I speak, teach, blog, am an executive sommelier, and all-around entrepreneur.

I grew up an East Coast girl, and then spent half my life on the West Coast. Now my husband, our two boys, and I happily call Colorado home.

I would love to hear from my readers, you can contact me at: heather@heatherslade.com

To keep up with my latest news and releases, please visit my website at: www.heatherslade.com to sign up for my newsletter.

MORE FROM HEATHER SLADE

Made in the USA
Middletown, DE
03 September 2020